your SOUFFLÉ *must* DIE

DEANNA KNIPPLING

WONDERLAND PRESS

FREE EBOOK

Get a free ebook and sign up for the Wonderland Press-Herald at https://wonderlandpress.com/free-ebook/.

Contents

CHAPTER 1

Sam stared at the screen in disbelief. She couldn't hear a sound, and someone had sucked all the air out of the room while simultaneously replacing it with ice.

YOUR SOUFFLE MUST DIE, DEC 3 LOL.

Someone, some horrible internet troll, had left a comment on her latest post on her website, FoodSlutOnline.com. Horrible internet trolls had happened to her before, but she'd always had Harry to deal with them.

But her problems were no longer Harry's problems, and she had no intention of calling him to ask what to do about a rude comment on her website.

Someone was making death threats on her cooking. And *LOL.* Honestly. It wasn't funny.

She wished the comment would just go away, then suddenly realized that it could, if she wanted it to. Her mouse pointer hovered over the Trash button for a second. What if she needed it later? What if the troll sent another comment, just like it? What if they murdered her soufflé and she needed evidence for the police?

Okay. Time to stop going off the deep end, Sam. That's exactly the kind of comment from you that would start a fight with Harry. Keep thinking things like that, and you're going to prove him right: You're a spaz. Six months without him, and your bank accounts are going to be a shambles, your site will close down, and your new catering business will fail!

Sam sighed, leaned back in her computer chair, and rubbed her eyes. Clearly, this was not a night to be alone. She turned off her computer monitor and the banker's lamp over Granny's roll-top desk, then padded downstairs in her sweatpants to call Kaley.

The house phone was downstairs on the far side of the kitchen, where she could pretend she couldn't hear it ringing if she didn't feel like answering. She picked up the handset, dialed Kaley's number from memory, and waited. First ring, second ring...

Kaley's mom answered. "Hello? Lugano residence. Marilyn speaking."

"Hi, Marilyn," Sam said, dancing from foot to foot on the cold tile. "Is Kaley home?" She felt like she was twelve again, instead of thirty-three.

"She is, dear. Would you like to speak to her?"

"If you please." Sam giggled as Marilyn dropped the phone on the counter and yelled her daughter's name at the top of her voice.

Kaley shouted back, "Got it!" and picked up the upstairs phone. Sam never called Kaley on her cell phone at home. The sheer drama and politics of family members answering each others' calls was just too funny.

"Yeah?" she said.

"Aren't you going to ask who it is?"

"I already know who it is," Kaley said. "What do you want?"

"If you ask your mom if you can have a sleepover at my house, do you think she'll be mad?"

Kaley snorted like a pig over the phone. "God, you're such a twit."

Sam laughed. "I promise I won't get you drunk and fat."

Kaley blew air across the phone, and it hissed in Sam's ear. "Nervous about tomorrow?"

"No, I mean yes, some douchebag left a comment on Food Slut threatening my soufflés tomorrow."

"How did they know that?"

"What?"

"That the soufflé class was tomorrow? You didn't announce the date change."

"Oh, that's true. I just sent out an email to the class." Sam paced back and forth through the kitchen, running one hand across her countertops and her new marble slab for chocolate and a butcher's block in the center island. "Hm...I don't know."

"Did you ask Harry about it?"

"When you get divorced, that means that the other person doesn't want you to come running to them with all your problems anymore, Kaley."

"Yeah, but death threats on your desserts."

Sam wanted to laugh it off, but she couldn't. "So come over? We can watch something out of Jack Malpeque's *oeuvre* and try out the winter aphrodisiac nibbles for next month's class."

Kaley squealed. "The truffles came in?"

"No, sorry. We're just going to have to use the frozen truffles."

"When are they coming in?"

"Monday. Supposedly." Three days away; an eternity, as far as she was concerned. "I'll throw in some chai vodka."

"Deal." The phone beeped off, and Sam went back upstairs, turned on her monitor, and looked at the comment again.

She had no idea how to tell who it was from. She pasted the email address into a search engine; all that came back was that the address belonged to a remailer, which was (she looked it up) a service that took off your real address and replaced it with another one. It sounded like something that even Harry would have trouble with. Weird. One, why bother making empty threats on her soufflés? Two, why bother going through all the secrecy? Usually trolls didn't bother hiding their identity too hard. They usually just wanted to yell at her for trying to make cooking funny and sexy instead of too complex and boring to bother with.

She usually got comments that boiled down to *What's the point of making delicious food if it isn't hard?* And *Why do you have to make so many jokes about sex?* Which always struck her as pretty stupid.

She turned off the monitor again, went into the back pantry and started pulling down ingredients. Raw avocado-chocolate pudding: avocados, cocoa powder, agave, sea salt, vanilla...Figs and chorizo: dried figs, Spanish sausage, pimentón, cinnamon, Manzanilla sherry, olive oil...Truffled ravioli: fontina, dried truffles, honey, pears, and walnuts... She stopped. She couldn't remember what the last dish was.

Ah. Shrimp bisque. Harry's favorite.

When the doorbell rang, she dumped everything on the counter, sniffed back tears, and opened the door for Kaley.

"Cutting onions?" Kaley asked.

She shook her head. "Shrimp bisque."

Kaley dumped her bag on the floor and hugged her, then stepped in out of the cold. "Poor thing. You should take it off the menu."

"No...it's perfect," she hiccupped. "I can't tell you the number of times he dragged me to bed after I made him shrimp bisque. It works. I have to move on."

Kaley shook her head at her. "Now you know why I never married."

"You just haven't met the right man yet."

Kaley rolled her eyes. "I have met the right man. He's just married and a professional hockey player. Oh, yeah. And I've never actually met him."

"He signed your jersey." But Sam was feeling better, wiping her face on a tissue, leading Kaley back into the kitchen.

"He signs everyone's jerseys. Ooh, we're going with the pudding? I don't know about that. Raw food. It just sounds like it's for a bunch of weirdos. I don't know if anyone will try it."

"We'll give them some first and then explain how to make it. They won't know what hit them." Sam checked the avocadoes, which were hefty, full, and with just a little give under her fingers. "So rich...so delicious." She stroked the avocado suggestively. "So...*ahuacate*."

But she had already shocked Kaley with her explanation of the Aztec word for avocado (testicle), and Kaley, whose eyes must be in a perpetual state of dizziness from rolling at Sam's bad jokes all the time, ignored her and went straight for the freezer. "I believe I was promised chai vodka."

They worked on the appetizers for half an hour before Sam remembered the reason she'd asked Kaley to come over. "Oh! I almost forgot. That stupid threat on the soufflés. Would you help me check the kitchen? I want to make sure there aren't any booby traps or anything like that."

"Paranoid much?"

"You know me."

They searched the kitchen, checking the eggs and the other ingredients, looking over the guest list for any possible saboteurs, and discussing the possibility of whether a truck with a super-loud stereo parked on the street could knock over a soufflé: Sam for, Kaley against. Colorado Springs seemed to have become a haven for giant trucks over the last decade.

"Anyone who had to park on the street would be blocked by the house, Sam. He might rattle windows on the west side in the living room, but there's no way the sound could make it all the way back here, not loud enough to knock over a soufflé."

Sam shook her head, waving her short blonde pigtails back and forth. "This is our first class, Kaley. I'm so nervous I could almost puke. I just know this is going to be a failure. Like Harry always said—"

"—Nobody trusts a skinny cook," Kaley finished for her. "Honestly. Could you just have a little faith in me for a while, even if you don't trust yourself? If the company falls flat, it's as much my fault as it is yours."

"Sorry."

"And don't give me that puppy-dog look, either. Save it for your gentlemen callers."

Sam snorted. "And who might those be?"

"You're doing better than me. The only man under the age of sixty-five who's been in my house for the last six weeks is Dale."

Sam laughed, then said, "How are things going with him?" Dale was Kaley's older brother, an electrical engineer at a computer hardware company.

"He's…"

"Do you think you can still work with him, if we need to hire him to help with catering? He's been asking. But if you don't want him to be around, I'll tell him no. I won't explain why or anything. Or I could lie."

"You shouldn't lie to people anymore. You say the craziest shit. No wonder nobody believes you. No, I can work with him, I just can't talk to him about mom and dad and the garage."

"Neither one of you knows anything about cars. You should just sell it and split the profits. After your parents pass on."

"He still thinks he should inherit the whole thing. So he can run it into the ground, I guess. He thinks it's his ticket out of a desk job. After all, if *you* can run a business, why can't he?"

Sam sighed. "He shouldn't take me as an example. It just kind of fell into my lap."

"Don't be silly. All right, I think we've checked everything we can check."

Sam took off the lid of the pot where the shrimp stock was simmering. "I think we're good, here." She reached out for her fine-mesh strainer from its hook overhead and swiped her hand through nothing but air. "Oh, I forgot. It's out in the garage. Harry took it with him by mistake and brought it back a few days ago. I'll be right back."

She went into the garage, swinging her arm around through the dark for the cord overhead. She hit it so hard that the cord popped away from her hand and she had to wait a moment for it to come back to her.

She pulled the cord. For a second, the light flashed brightly, casting shadows all over the garage, and she thought she saw something moving around behind her SUV.

Just then, Kaley screamed and something that sounded as loud as a gunshot cracked out from the kitchen.

CHAPTER 2

Sam ran back toward the kitchen, grabbing a chef's knife from the magnetic strip and raising it over her head as she whipped around the corner.

Kaley was running cold water over her hand, shaking her fingers back and forth, trying to pull something invisible away with her other hand. One of the dining-room chairs lay flat on the floor, its seat pointing away from the oven.

Sam laughed and put the knife back on its spot on the magnetic strip. "You checked behind the oven and got a handful of spider webs, didn't you?"

"No but I felt *something*. Check my back," Kaley said. Sam carefully inspected the back of her shirt, first the outside, then peeked down the inside, then rubbed her hands all over it. Better a squashed spider on Kaley's back than a rapidly crawling one.

"You're fine," Sam said.

"Ugh!"

"Well, are the spiders planning to sabotage us tomorrow?"

"Shouldn't the heat kill them back there?"

"Apparently not. Oh! The light went out in the garage, and I thought I saw something. I'm probably freaking out over nothing." Sam pulled open her odds-and-ends drawer at the end of the counter, which included a screwdriver, a handful of fuses, and a flashlight, after she'd shorted out the electricity in the kitchen a number of times by running every appliance she owned at the same time. She clicked the flashlight on and off and on again, shook it. It seemed reliable, like it wouldn't fuzz out on her, anyway.

"You can't go out there by yourself," Kaley said.

"Why not?"

"What if there's someone out there?"

Sam pulled the knife back off the magnetic strip. "There. Feel better? You know I can chop an onion at ten paces."

"I'm coming with you."

Sam handed her the flashlight and unlocked the door to the garage, kicked it open, and screamed out a *hiyaaa!* that her self-defense coach had made her practice in class.

The door almost bounced back in their faces, and Sam pushed it open with her foot, more gently this time.

Kaley shone the flashlight around the garage, even covering the ceiling.

"Check under the SUV," Sam suggested. "If I were going to try to rape and murder two women in a garage, I'd want to grab them by their ankles first."

"Don't you have a gun?"

"Somewhere, if Harry didn't take it," Sam admitted. "But I'm much better with this big, gigantic knife. *Chop chop chop*, little burglar. I'm coming to get you…"

Kaley squatted down and shone the flashlight under the SUV. "Nothing."

Sam grabbed the strainer off the top of a box of Harry's things that she'd found in the basement, cans of malt of all things. He hadn't used canned malt for years. She had mostly kept them in case she needed an excuse to call him. *Oh, by the way, I have a box of your old cans of malt that you need to pick up and please come back I can't do this alone!* He'd hang up on her in a heartbeat.

"Okay, if there are any burglars or soufflé saboteurs in this garage, we're leaving now," Sam announced. "It was probably just me being spooked when you screamed."

She and Kaley went back out of the garage, and she shut and deliberately locked the door behind her. "There. All better."

But Kaley kept the flashlight next to her for the rest of the night.

· · · · • · · • · · ·

They contentedly cooked together, chatting about this and that, and finally sat down to stuff themselves, drink chai vodkas with cream and honey, and watch *Pirate Moon III*, Jack Malpeque's new movie on DVD.

"I can't believe you turned down that job for Danielle," Kaley said.

"I promised we would start a catering business together, and that's that," Sam said.

"But you'd be working under Robert again. Didn't you have the hots for him?"

Robert Langoustine had been one of Sam's first chef crushes, back when she was just starting out cooking. She would go to the Rose Hotel to eat dinner with Harry as often as they could afford it (which wasn't often) for years, trying to figure out how everything that came out of his kitchen could taste so good.

And then she'd decided to make the switch over to full-time cooking, and he'd hired her. Ugh. It had killed the romance in a heartbeat, the abuse and insanity of that kitchen. It was good training, but bad on the stars in her eyes.

She'd quit at the end of a screaming match, threatening to upend Robert's ludicrously lame ideas about food by starting her own business...and that's how Sweet Granadilla Catering had started.

Oh, the food was good at the Rose.

But it was boring. Large, expensive slabs of meat with potatoes and roasted asparagus. Beet and goat cheese salad still on the menu a year after it had stopped being interesting at merely average restaurants. Truffles, truffles, and more truffles. Not that she had a problem with truffles, per se, but you shouldn't be able to order a meal with nothing but truffle this and truffle that, from beginning to end. Unsurprising truffles. Expected truffles. It was a waste of truffles, that's what it was. And the chocolate volcano cake with raspberry sauce that had been on the menu for what, a decade?

Sam didn't know if she would succeed as a dot-com businesswoman with an inventive catering company on the side (or was it vice versa?), but she knew she would fail as a sous-chef under Robert Langoustine. She'd make a mild suggestion of adding vanilla to a lobster bisque; he'd take offense; it would be knife-throwing across the dining room before she knew it.

"Robert hates me," Sam said.

"He does not. He's just loud and authoritative."

"Exactly. It's like being kicked in the gut." She popped another spoonful of pudding in her mouth. Creamy, buttery, yummy. And easy on the heart, too.

Kaley leaned back, sighed, and put the bowl of shrimp bisque on the side table. "That's really good. I still think you should put the roasted red peppers in there. And use the same sherry that's in the figs and chorizo. The Marvolio? Manzanilla? Madeira? Too many chai vodkas."

"You had it. Manzanilla. Look! Shirt off!"

They had a long-running game of raising a toast whenever Jack Malpeque took his shirt off in a movie. They clinked glasses and took a drink of vodka.

"I have to go to bed," Kaley groaned. "No more drinking."

"No more drinking. Look at those abs. It's like looking at corn on the cob."

But neither of them moved. Finally, Sam noticed that Kaley was asleep with her head on the back of the couch, braced between a couple of quilts. Sam laughed, put a pillow from the spare bedroom on the couch beside Kaley, and went up the stairs to bed.

Suddenly, there was a thump from the front door. Sam rushed back down to make sure the front door hadn't blown open, but she'd locked up hours ago without realizing it. She looked outside through a couple of different windows, but didn't see what had happened.

As she passed the oven, she found that it was still hot. She'd forgotten to turn it off after they'd agreed they had to have some broiled sourdough croutons to go with the bisque. *Idiot*, she thought. Could have burned the house down.

With Kaley in it. She had to be twice as careful now that she had a business partner.

Chapter 3

"The first thing you need to know about soufflés is that they are *not* difficult. They are horribly, horribly simple," Sam said. "Soufflés are the same as meringues are the same as angel food cake are the same as marshmallows are the same as a bubble bath. That's all they are. Bubbles. If you make the bubble wall stronger than the air pressure inside it and you heat the bubbles, then the bubbles expand without popping.

"One good way to strengthen the bubbles is by using protein. Protein, whether you get it from wheat, as gluten, or from eggs, as albumen, is strong and stretchy. For example, gluten, the protein in wheat that we use in bread, comes from the same word as glue. And, if you think about it, you can notice many similarities between bread and a soufflé. They both have bubbles, right?"

Her twelve students around the room nodded.

"One of the main differences between gluten and albumen, for our purposes, is that gluten will hold its shape rigidly after being baked, while albumen will not. That's why, if you're making something with egg whites, you will generally add something to the egg whites to strengthen their structure after cooling. In the case of meringues, it's sugar. The more sugar, the stiffer the meringue. In the case of angel food cake, it's flour. In the case of a marshmallow, it's not even eggs at all. Even though a homemade marshmallow looks like a meringue, it contains no eggs. Instead, it has gelatin, which is—you guessed it—a protein. Although in this case, gelatin gets less stable as it gets warmer, rather than more stable.

"In the case of a soufflé, what makes it so divinely light and angelic is that it doesn't use gluten, that very gluey protein, to make it stand up. It doesn't use a whole heck of a lot of sugar to stiffen it by creating a network of crystals, either. You might add some protein in your ingredients, like cheese, sugar, or a little flour, but that's not going to be the main reason that a soufflé stands or falls."

Kaley passed around a plate of marshmallows, angel food cake, and soft and hard meringues for people to compare (and eat). Danielle, who considered herself a terrible, hopeless cook, was one of their first customers; she'd paid them sixty dollars to learn how to make a dish she was never going to make again. Ever. Unless Sam and Kaley talked her into it, of course. But if they could teach Danielle, who considered herself way out of her league (Sam had to laugh at that; the general manager of the Rose Hotel? Out of her league? She talked to movie stars, five-star generals, and politicians on a daily and familiar basis), they could teach anyone.

"First, the eggs themselves. For the best, strongest protein, you're going to want to take into consideration two things, the grade of the egg and the age. Double-A eggs are best, because they have the thickest, best proteins. If you've ever made a sunny side up egg and seen a plateau halfway along the white of the egg, that's because it has thick proteins that stay together, rather than spreading out perfectly flat. However, albumen degrades over time, so the longer you leave your double-A eggs in the fridge, the more like A or even B eggs they will be. So buy fresh, best-quality eggs for any cooking project where you need to have a lot of structure coming from your egg whites, like angel food cake or meringues.

"A trick for determining whether the protein in your eggs has degraded is by measuring how much water has evaporated out of the shell. Eggshells are slightly porous and lose water every day. So more air in the shell means older eggs means less strength in your egg whites. I have two bowls of eggs here. One of these bowls is full of eggs that we're going to use in class today. Can anyone tell me which bowl it is?"

Sam loved finding out tricks like this, because she couldn't rely on her memory for anything (like shutting off the oven last night).

One of the women shyly raised her hand. "Yes?" Sam asked. She *knew* what the woman's name was. She *knew* it. She just couldn't remember it to save her life. She was the shorter of the two retired ladies who had come to the class together, determined to finally, once and for all, learn how to be the kinds of cooks that their grandchildren worshiped. She'd promised them a cookie class in time for Easter, if everything went well. She *should* have had a cookie class today, so people could go home with a couple dozen cookies to give away as presents. But she just couldn't resist the challenge of a soufflé, after Kaley had begged her.

"Add water?"

Sam grinned at her. "Perfect!" She pulled out one of the two pitchers of water behind the bowls and slid it toward the woman. "You pour in one bowl, and I'll take the other. Slowly."

Sam tried to time it so both bowls were filled at about the same rate.

The eggs in her bowl turned on end, the top of the egg straining to get out of the water.

"Wow!" the woman said.

"That's right. We're using the eggs in *your* bowl, not mine. I'll be making mine into devilled eggs in a few days for a party, but that's a trick for a different day. *Your* eggs were laid four days ago at a farm nearby. If you want to buy eggs from them, their contact information will be in your handout and recipe packet that I'll send home with you."

Sam had everyone start separating their eggs, and she and Kaley went around the kitchen, making sure that they were doing it properly. A few old hands who had been making angel food cakes for years had no problems, but a few of the others were almost in tears.

Danielle scowled at her bowl. "I broke one."

"That's okay," Sam said.

"In the wrong bowl."

Sam looked down. Danielle had accidentally dumped the yolk into her larger bowl of egg whites. Sam clicked her tongue. "I'll use those in something else." She pushed the bowl away and took down another from a cupboard.

Kaley said, "Remember, if you end up with any yolk in your egg whites, you need to start over with new egg whites. It's okay. Eggs are cheap. Just use the yolky eggs within two days and keep them in the fridge."

Then they started them on their bases. The first one was the cheese base; the second was the orange-chocolate. Their students doubled up on portable burners lining the room. Sam breathed a sigh of relief as they all turned on and stayed on: this time, she hadn't blown a fuse. They thickened the bases slightly, one after the other, and set them aside to cool.

After Sam talked for a while about the importance of beating the eggs to stiff but still wet-looking peaks, she let them rev up their beaters.

A few splats of egg white landed here and there around the kitchen, but it was really no more of a mess than Sam was used to making herself. Soon enough, they were done, except for one guy who overbeat his whites and ended up breaking them; Sam patiently started him over.

"Soufflés are one of most versatile dishes you will ever find. Well, except for other dishes based on eggs, like quiche or custard. You can do anything with a custard.

"I thought you couldn't have fat and egg whites together," said one of the old hands at angel food cake.

"You can't," Sam agreed. "When you're beating the egg whites, fats will chemically bind with the albumin proteins in the whites—instead of the albumin proteins binding to each other. You end up with broken chains of proteins, and broken chains means less structure. However, when you have the whites beaten properly, then you can mix in whatever you want, as long as you do it gently, so as not to knock the air out of the egg whites, because they've already firmed up and bound together."

"What's this stuff?" Danielle poked the little dish of cream of tartar.

"Cream of tartar. It's acidic."

"What good does that do?"

"I'm glad you asked, because I was just about to blather on about it anyway," Sam said. "You'll notice how our egg whites are pretty stiff, right? Through the action of beating them, we stiffen up and tangle their proteins together. If we're not careful, we can tangle those proteins so tightly together that the squish out all their water, or break. If you mix an acid with the eggs, however, you keep certain chemical bonds from forming quite so often, which has the side effect of making it harder to overbeat your eggs. You're still building structure, but the structure ends up being more elastic."

"Tom, stop overbeating. It makes you leak," one of the women joked, and they all laughed.

Then it was time to fold. She had them do the cheese soufflé first, folding slowly with wide, curved spatulas, leaving streaks.

"Streaks are totally acceptable. They add character." Sam lightly touched the arm of a woman who was stirring the top of her mixture rapidly, trying to get rid of her streaks. "The more you stir, the flatter your soufflé. The perfect soufflé lies in accepting the imperfection of the swirls. It's all right."

Soon enough, all the cheese soufflés were in their buttered ramekins, resting in a pan of hot water that came halfway up their sides.

"As with any egg dish, you have to be careful of uneven heat. With soufflés, steam can get trapped in pockets and explode in your oven. This is especially a problem with high-altitude soufflés, because of the low air pressure up here, which really does have an incredibly strong effect on anything you cook or especially bake.

"We're lowering the temperature from 375 to 360, to slow the cooking. Because there's less air pressure, everything rises—and falls—more for us than people at sea level. A higher temperature means a faster rise and a faster fall."

Then the soufflés were in the oven.

"All right, rather than stand here, stamping around and shaking the oven, let's go into the living room and...drink some wine!"

Everyone cheered and filed out of the kitchen, picking up big glasses of Chablis from the dining room table that would pair well with their first soufflés.

"This is so wonderful!" one of the men said, a gambler who was learning how to cook after losing a bet to his partner. "I mean, you really make me feel like I might possibly be able to learn a logical way to approach this. I'm not an artist. I'm not creative. But what you're saying is that cooking isn't creative. I can learn it!"

Sam laughed. "Cooking *is* creative. I'm just babbling on about why it works."

"I guess what I mean is that it isn't magic. You don't have to be just born knowing how to cook."

"Oh gosh, no."

There was a knock from the front door, and Kaley went to see who it was. Nobody. Sam relaxed and kept on talking to people, asking them how it was going so far, that kind of thing.

Then Kaley went into the kitchen.

A second later, she screamed, and Sam's first thought was *shhh, you'll wake the soufflés.*

Chapter 4

Sam followed the sound of the shriek, which cut off suddenly, into the kitchen. Kaley was squatting in front of the paired ovens and looking inside.

"What's wrong?" Sam asked, mentally going, *don't say the soufflés are flat, don't say the soufflés are flat...*

"The soufflés are flat." Kaley's voice was steady and calm, as though the scream had been all in Sam's imagination. The class was filing back into the room, holding their wineglasses, looking either relaxed or only slightly interested. Clearly, whatever was happening in the kitchen wasn't going to be a big deal, as far as they were concerned.

But her soufflés had fallen. She peered through the glass on the other oven and saw them, all nestled sleepily in their dishes. The water in the pan was rippling, and the oven appeared to be full of steam.

Well, to be honest, she had to admit that *everyone's* soufflés had fallen. But it was her class, her idea, her responsibility, *her recipe*. She felt like she'd betrayed everyone in that room, Kaley especially. She was already trying to figure out how to make it up to her. It would probably involve a lot of chocolate.

She stood up and faced her class, feeling dizzy. "I'm so sorry. The soufflés...have fallen. I don't know why, but they have. They all seem to have received a terrible shock and collapsed from popped bubbles. If it had happened earlier in the cooking process, we could have let them sit in the oven for a little bit longer to try to regain some volume as the liquids inside them evaporated and turned into steam, but the eggs have already set. You can tell because the tops of the soufflés are browning. If you'd like to come and see...?"

Well, if her first set of soufflés was going to fail, she was going to make sure that her class learned something from it. That was the thing about cooking. Sometimes you failed. Sometimes you failed and there wasn't anything you could do about it. She sighed. The story of her marriage, too. She wasn't sure what she'd learned from *that* debacle.

Kaley was still standing there, looking calm as anything. Sam recognized the look from back when they worked together at the office. The more stressed Kaley got (she'd been the secretary), the more calm and soothing her face appeared. Which was probably a good trait for a secretary to have, really. No sense in a) letting anyone else know that there was something to panic about or b) letting anyone else know that the most competent person in the building was going batshit.

But it was hard to see, knowing that her friend was probably feeling even worse about the collapse than she was. Sam slid behind the members of the class, who were taking turns cooing at the soufflés, and hugged Kaley.

"We still have one more set. It's fine. It had nothing to do with the way we made them. That knock at the door—well, it must have been some loud noise outside that just knocked them all flat." Sam was stretching the truth a little bit; she suspected that her recipe had something to do with it; she should have added more flour in with the cheese...

"I don't know," Kaley said softly. "I feel like it's all my fault."

Sam blinked. How could Kaley possibly think it was her fault? When it was clearly Sam's own fault? Good grief, Kaley must be feeling paranoid today. She gave Kaley another hug, and then the two of them pulled the soufflés out of the oven before they overcooked.

Everyone claimed their soufflés (identified by the different colors of ramekins she'd passed out), using potholders.

"Even if it's flat, it will be delicious," Sam said, crossing her fingers mentally as she dipped her fork into the dish.

Her students did the same, scooping out bits of cheese soufflé, flat. Blowing delicately on the hot mixture. The sound of it was all wrong. Scooping out a bit of proper soufflé should sound like the world's smallest bubble wrap being squashed; this sounded more like quiche.

Finally, Danielle chomped down on her forkful, even though it was clearly too hot. She opened her mouth quickly, then shut it again, chewed (although you didn't really need to chew, with a soufflé), and swallowed.

"Delicious." She grabbed her wineglass, took a sip, and smiled. "Ah! *Molto bene*. Makes me want to stare deeply into my lover's eyes and speak Italian to him with a loving mouth."

Sam laughed. "Soufflés are French."

"I refuse to believe that."

The rest of the students followed, some sucking cold air over their tongues as they rushed it just a little too quickly, some smiling, and one of the retired women's faces turning bright red and crumpling into tears. She sniffed loudly. "I made that. I made it. Can you believe that I made that?"

Sam knew that cooking could be emotional, but she hadn't anticipated anything or anyone bursting into tears of joy. "Are you all right?"

"My husband won't be able to make fun of my cooking anymore. I made a soufflé."

Sam didn't know what to say (the soufflé had been flat, after all), so she put her free arm around the woman and hugged. At least Harry had never made fun of her cooking. Well, unless it was really bad and deserved it. But not as a matter of course. She let the woman go and took a bite of the soufflé.

She'd kept it simple on purpose, so she could talk about all the different things you could do to it, and people wouldn't get hung up on whatever particular set of ingredients she'd used.

But it was, she had to admit, good. Flat, but good. Good parmesan. She smiled. From Italy.

It didn't take long for the soufflés to disappear out of their ramekins or the rest of the wine to disappear from their glasses.

Sam sent them back to their stations and passed out the other set of ingredients, including their separated eggs.

"Now, for the chocolate orange soufflés. Hopefully, we won't have as difficult a time with these."

It was going to be all right. It was going to be all right.

They cheerfully made ganache, dropped in pinches of orange peel, and stole sips of Cointreau, whipped up peaks of foamy whites ("I'm peaking! I'm peaking!" Danielle yelled, and Sam wasn't sure whether she was trying to be funny or not), and folded, gently folded everything together.

It was going to be all right.

They arranged the ramekins on trays and slid them into the oven.

Sam crossed her fingers, and saw Kaley doing it, too. She sidled over to Kaley. "Do you want to guard the oven or pour the beer?"

"Oven," Kaley said. Her eyes never left the glass.

"Okay. Back in a bit." Sam led the class out of the kitchen, chattering away. "You'll notice that we don't have wine glasses for you poured already. That's because we're not having wine."

"Awww," several people said.

"Instead, we will have beer."

A shocked silence. Upscale cooking? And beer? Beer and souf-flés were *not* supposed to go together. Several women frowned at her, not angry frowns but thoughtful ones. Sam felt her lungs start to go tight, but closed her eyes for a second and let herself relax. It was one of the last things that she and Harry had agreed on, that beer could be just as appropriate with different types of food as wine.

"This is double chocolate stout." Aha. People's eyes lit up at the word *chocolate*. "The first chocolate in the malt isn't chocolate at all, but chocolate malt. That means the malt, or the sprouted barley grains that are used to make beer, has been toast-ed until it's a deep chocolate color. This gives the beer a slightly toasted taste. Not burned or bitter, but very dark and almost caramelized. Whenever you toast something, what you're doing is caramelizing the sugars. This works even when the sugars are currently formed into starches.

"The second type of chocolate in the double chocolate stout are nibs, or crushed pieces of cacao beans that have been roasted and prepped to be turned into chocolate bars, but haven't been processed into bars yet. That means, if you're feeling just a little bit health-conscious, that this beer is *very* good for you, because it contains all the complex compounds in dark chocolate, the flavenoids, that help, uh, what's the word, antioxidants. They act as antioxidants in your body."

"What does that mean?" one of the retirees asked.

"I have no idea," Sam said. "I haven't researched it yet, but it seems like everyone's interested in it right now, so I thought I'd mention it in case anybody cares. I'll dig more into it later." While she was talking, she was also opening bottles and handing out oversized wine glasses.

"What's this for?" the gambler asked. "Aren't we drinking beer?"

"It's a fancy beer-drinking glass," Sam said. "All the beer snobs have them now. Go ahead and pour your beer into your glass. This is not going to be the kind of beer that has an amazing head on it, so it's not absolutely vital whether you pour down the side of the glass or straight into the glass." Harry had lectured her on this, but she couldn't remember, and, honestly, it was beer. If you fussed with it too much while you were drinking it, you killed all the fun. Some things taste better when you fuss over them; some things don't, and she just wasn't prepared to fuss over it as much as Harry would have.

She had to stop herself from outright laughing at a room full of people drinking beer and discussing it just as seriously as if it were a century-old wine, swirling it in their glasses, sniffing at it. It was as though she'd completely transformed the stuff by having them put it into the glasses. She didn't even have to put the beer in the glasses for them. They could do it themselves, and it was still a magical transformation.

She was just starting to flit comfortably from guest to guest, finding out how they liked the class so far, pretending that she knew their names but chose not to say them, and blathering away, answering questions about cooking so automatically she suspected half her brain had left the building. Danielle squeezed her hand as they talked. *Good job.*

"Did you hear something?" the gambler said, and she froze.

She had? She hadn't? She skimmed through the last few seconds of her memory and realized she'd heard something, a thump. Her chest clenched at her heart, which beat so hard it almost crushed her throat.

"Someone at the door?" a woman asked.

"Excuse me." Sam pushed her way through the students, ignoring her hope that it was just something at the door, and went into the kitchen.

Kaley had no color. Sam knew she had to hold it together, but she just couldn't. She gasped for breath like a goldfish tossed out of a bowl by the flick of a cat's wrist. Her teeth started to hurt, her forehead to burn. She leaned on the edge of the counter, trying to catch her breath, but it was too fast for her. No. This couldn't be happening.

Maybe both of them were panicking unnecessarily. Sam bent over, glanced into the oven, and ripped her eyes away. No. This couldn't be happening. It was all a dream, a terrible nightmare that she was having the night before her real class.

She had almost convinced herself when she burped, and tasted the chocolate stout trying to come back up. While she had occasionally tasted things in her dreams, she'd never burped in one before.

Harry was right. She was never going to be able to make it on her own.

The next thing she knew, Kaley was hugging her and patting her on the back. "There, there. It'll be all right," and similar nonsense. It wasn't going to be all right. It was going to be *terrible*. The thing was, she knew she shouldn't be having a meltdown, not now, not in front of all of her paying students. Over a stupid soufflé. But she couldn't seem to help it, and the more she tried to stop, the worse it got. Finally, she dropped out of Kaley's arms and ran off to the bathroom to blow her nose and wash her face. She might have to cry in front of her students, but she surely didn't have to drip boogers in front of them.

She blew her nose, washed and dried her face, and went back into the kitchen.

"All better?" Danielle asked.

Sam nodded, feeling like a complete idiot. And *not* all better. In fact, she had a little niggle of a flame building up in her. She didn't know how, she didn't know why—no, she knew why, if not *how*—but all of this? It was Harry's fault.

She smiled and nodded. The soufflés, of course, had turned out delicious, and they paired perfectly with the beer. She hadn't had any doubts about *that*. The only thing that could possibly go wrong, well, other than a flood down the side of the mountain, earthquake, attack from random terrorists, the gas line exploding...her normal list of things to worry about could go on and on and on. However, the only *reasonable* thing that could go wrong was the soufflés falling.

And they had. Twice.

That was more than coincidence. That was sabotage.

CHAPTER 5

After the guests had left, Sam cornered Kaley, who took one look at Sam's face and backed up against the counter, holding her dish towel between the two of them like it was her only defense.

"What happened?" Sam growled.

"I didn't do it," Kaley squeaked.

"I'm sorry. I'm not trying to be scary. But twice in a row? Twice in a row after I just got divorced? Harry is involved in this, Kaley."

Kaley opened her mouth to talk, and Sam interrupted her. "No, don't try to defend him. I've been trying to find a way to forgive him and move on with my life. But I can see now that that isn't going to work. Living my life isn't going to be good enough. I have to get revenge. And the first step in getting revenge, in making it *perfect*, is to find out exactly what he did. So I can ruin him in the same way that he's ruined me."

A small part—a very small part—of her brain knew that she wasn't being rational. However, that part was overwhelmed by all the emotions that had been running around in her brain since their divorce or even earlier. The kind of anger that you can build up at your ex is not a force to be denied or rationalized away. Rationalized, sure. But that anger had opened up in a way it hadn't since she'd finished signing paperwork, and it ripped up her sanity like a sudden spring thaw rolling down the mountains.

"A loud thump," Kaley said. "Almost a snap. I was watching the oven when it happened. I don't think I blinked more than once or twice while it was baking. A crack. A pop. The water in the pans shook so hard that it splashed out of the trays and all over the oven floor. It steamed over the windows, but I could already see the soufflés collapsing."

"I will kill him," Sam announced. "But first I will destroy his beer."

She had heard about parents who became violent when their kids were in harm, throwing people out of their way, turning over semi-trucks, ripping fire hydrants out of the ground to throw at possible kidnappers who were looking funny at their kids. She knew exactly what that felt like, at the moment. In her anger, she had the strength of ten men. She could rip the stove out of the wall and throw it all the way to Harry's apartment on top of The Shandy, his brewery. She would have, too, if she hadn't wanted to take her revenge against his beer first.

Kaley said, "I don't know what direction it came from. It echoed all over the kitchen. Knocked over your basil on the windowsill."

Sam hadn't noticed. She backed away from Kaley and looked at the sink. Sure enough, the basil had dropped off the window over the sink. The cracked pot had scattered potting soil throughout the sink. Sam took a lowball glass, scooped up some of the soil, and gently repotted the basil, which she was hoping would help keep her sane until the farmers' markets opened back up in late spring, six months away. A lot of hope to be hanging on a little basil plant, she knew.

She scraped the rest of the mess out of the sink and into the trash while Kaley pulled one of the leftover bottles of stout out of the fridge and started drinking. "I don't know, Sam. Harry just doesn't hate you."

"Hah," Sam said. "You weren't here for most of our fights."

"I heard about most of them later."

"I can't think of anyone else. Who could possibly be that spiteful. That petty. That...well, smart. Harry's smart enough to figure out how to sabotage my soufflés. He could have set this up before he left."

Kaley shook her head. "It just feels wrong. But I think you should find out the truth before you...do anything to his brewery. What if it isn't him? You don't want to get tangled up with him again."

Sam blushed, hiding it with anger. Hadn't she been thinking about it just the previous night? But she was dead set on it being Harry. "All right. But I say he's guilty."

"At least go talk to him before you do anything." Kaley took the top off the beer with one of the three church keys magnetized to the fridge, dropped the cap on the counter, and drank.

"Weren't you telling me not to get tangled up with him not two seconds ago?"

Kaley finished the beer with a gasp. "Better that than go to jail as a crazy woman."

Sam growled in the back of her throat. Crazy woman. She'd show him a crazy woman.

· · · ● · ● · · ·

She didn't bother to call Harry first before she went over. He'd be home, that was, at his brewery. He never went anywhere but to brew festivals. No brew festivals this week; therefore, he was home. At the bar, watching a TV show about a) beer brewing, b) bowling, or c) reality TV. For every time she had to agree with him that the differences between high-class and low-class entertainment had been artificially established, she wanted to strangle him about ten times for being in such a low-class rut! What about the finer things in life, like escargot?

Well, maybe not escargot. You could only be so invested in escargot. She considered the short, ironic lives of snails (*Garden pest to haute cuisine! Film at eleven!*) on her drive over, then parked in the customer parking lot.

She walked past the front window to alert his early-warning system of regulars on the lookout for The Crazy Ex, then circled around the building to the back door and let the air out of his tires. The SUV's doors were unlocked, so she climbed in the back seat and waited.

Within a minute or two (she didn't bother to check the time on her cell phone), Harry was fleeing toward her, putting his coat on as he walked quickly to the SUV. He jumped inside and started the engine, only seeing her when he turned around to make sure that he wasn't backing into anything.

"I wouldn't do that if I were you," she said.

"Jesus!"

"I let all the air out of your tires. You shouldn't drive on your rims."

"Sam, what the hell. What the hell?"

"Like you don't know."

"I *don't* know."

"You sabotaged my soufflé class. One soufflé? I could understand it. But two? Two, Harry? I would think one would be enough to humiliate me." She was going over the deep end. She had gone off the deep end. She had jumped the shark. She had, literally, gone insane. She was going to chop up somebody's bunny and boil it. A complete loon.

He sighed. "Is that all?"

"Is *that* all? How would you feel if someone were to happen to sabotage your beer, Harry. Because you're taught me enough to do that."

"I could be recording you."

"Hah." She doubted it, although she kept an eye on his hands. One was on the steering wheel, the other on the other front bucket seat as he braced himself to turn around in his seat. "You're so arrogant."

"I'm arrogant when I'm not guilty."

"You're always arrogant."

"I'm never guilty."

"Hah. So why do you always run?"

"All right. Sometimes I'm guilty. Also, you scare me."

"What did you do this time, if it wasn't to sabotage my soufflés? Not that I believe you."

"I plead the fifth."

"I'll find out." She would, too. "So what did you do to my soufflés?"

"Nothing."

"Sounds suspicious." Funny. If she didn't know better, she could almost suspect that they were flirting, not fighting.

"Are you sure you didn't screw up the recipe? Adjust for altitude? Did you account for the humidity in the air?"

"Harry."

Harry stopped. "No, of course you did. And Kaley was there, I presume. Checking that you didn't make some kind of airheaded mistake."

"Harry."

"Right, right. You never know. It's always good to have someone double-check your work."

She'd probably deserved Harry. Really. If he was this much of a mental case all the time, and she was this much of a mental case (as she well knew), then she probably deserved him. Harry, the ever-worrying, ever-double-checking, ever-undermining Harry, was what she was destined for. She may as well give in now and jump him in the car. She'd move back in with him, done forever with this silly attempt to prove that she was her own person. Hah! Failed. Now, to let Harry take care of her for the rest of her life.

In her gut, she knew she'd failed. No matter what Harry had done to sabotage her soufflés, she should have been able to anticipate and prevent it. The fact that she hadn't—failure. Once again, she'd come running back to him to let him tear her down, which proved it a) was her own fault and b) that she wasn't fit to be on her own.

Nevertheless, she was too proud to give in.

"Where were you last night?" she demanded.

"Vancouver. Just got back."

"What?" She looked around the car. It was scrupulously clean, except for the large, wheeled suitcase in the trunk.

Harry took his arm off the seat, raised the cover of the center console, and pulled out a wrinkled printout of his ticket info and a parking slip. Of course, he could have prepared for such a thing, if he was guilty of sabotaging her. He had to have known that she would be coming after him, sooner rather than later.

"What were you doing in Canada?" she asked, as she slid over the back of the seat and into the trunk area. She squatted on the floor and unzipped the bag. Ugh.

The clothes inside stank of beer and cigarette smoke, maybe even cheap cigars. "Did you start smoking again? Ugh. Is this...lipstick?"

She looked over the divider at him. Harry's face was bright red. "She didn't mean anything to me."

"You slept with someone?" Well, they were divorced; she really couldn't expect otherwise. Nevertheless, it distressed her, and she felt the clutch at her lungs. But maybe it was just from the smoke. She zipped the suitcase shut again and slithered back into the back seat.

"Well, no," he admitted, as though *not* sleeping with the woman was his guilty secret, rather than the other way around. "She was disgusting. All over me." He twitched, like a cat that didn't want to be touched. "And her perfume made me sneeze and swell up."

Sam sighed. "You know you're going to have to get over that eventually, Harry. People like to be touched. You twitching at them is bound to throw anyone off."

Harry stuck his tongue out like he was trying to push something bad-tasting out of his mouth. "And later I found out that she was the wife of one of the other poker players, too."

"Poker?" she asked. "You? When did you start playing poker?" That was almost as bad as the thought of him sleeping (or not sleeping) with someone else.

"A buddy of mine invited me."

"Who?"

"I plead the fifth."

Okay, fine. Sam rolled her eyes to check her halo, as Danielle would say. "So if you didn't sabotage my soufflés, who did?"

"Honestly, Sam."

"Two, Harry. When have you *ever* known me to lose two batches of soufflés? There was a loud thump before they went, both times."

"Hm..." he looked thoughtful for once, as though he was prepared, maybe, to consider the fact that Sam's failures in life weren't solely due to his lack of supervision. "Maybe there's something wrong with your oven."

"I can't imagine what."

"You should have someone come out to inspect it. It should still be under warranty, right?"

Sam shrugged. It probably was, but she'd no doubt tossed the paperwork after Harry had moved out; she'd thrown out a lot of things she probably should have kept.

She *deserved* him. She *deserved* to be told "I told you so" for the rest of her life.

"I just can't think straight. If it's not you, who could possibly have done something to my oven? Or who would even want to?"

"It's just out of whack. Have it checked."

"Are you listening?"

"Are you?"

Sam sighed. No, not really. Not either one of them. She opened the door and started to slide out.

"Or talk to Dale," Harry said. "He's pretty good at that stuff."

"Just because he's an electrical engineer doesn't mean he knows how to fix ovens. He does computer chips."

"Call him."

"Fine." She slid out of the SUV and slammed the door behind her. "If you would stop running away, I would stop letting the air out of your tires."

"It's not like I'm going anywhere," he said.

"Hah." She walked around the side of the building, deliberately not looking back, very conscious of the fact that she was wobbling a little in her boots, which she had picked specifically because the heels were so high that they made her feel taller, if somewhat more wobbly. She'd also made sure she had her tightest blue jeans on, because she'd known that at some point, she was going to have to walk away, and she wanted to make sure that Harry got an eyeful of what he was missing.

She missed him. Couldn't live with him. But missed him.

Chapter 6

The phone rang three times and Dale picked up. "Hello? Dale speaking. Please leave a message at the tone. Beep." That was Dale; the kind of guy who would answer the phone pretending to be a voicemail message. But people *did* keep trying to leave messages.

"Dale," she said. "It's me, Sam. I need your help."

"What's up?"

"I don't know if Kaley told you, but we had problems with the oven during the soufflé class. It collapsed both sets of soufflés."

"Dang," he said. "Isn't that a bitch?"

"Would you come over and check the oven for me?" Sam watched some people coming out of the brewery carrying growlers full of beer. Harry didn't want food at the brewery. On the one hand, she could understand; she had been the logical person to run his food operations, and he hadn't wanted to get into *that* mess at the time. On the other hand, beer was meant for food. If *she* couldn't do the food, he should at least hire someone else to do it. A cute blonde who couldn't cook for shit but who would remind him of *her*...painfully.

Dale brought her back out of her own little world. "Shit, Sam. I don't know anything about ovens. Why don't you get someone who knows what they're doing to come out and look at it?"

"Because I probably threw away the warranty, that's why," she said. "And I don't want to have to pay for a service call if I don't have to."

"But Harry registered the warranty for you," Dale pointed out. "All you have to do is call the company, and they have to give you another copy of the warranty. It's not like it's a magic piece of paper or something. They have you on file."

"Pleeeease?" she whined. "Just take a look at it. I trust you a lot more than I trust some repairman. Just to tell me if there's something obvious." She really didn't want to have to have repairmen in her house, to have to wait hours and hours for them to show up on a service call, with a four-hour window, then showing up the following day. She didn't like to be toyed with.

He surrendered. "Fine. I'll come after work."

"When is that?"

As though he were reading her mind in order to find the worst possible thing to say, he said, "I'll give you a four-hour window. Or maybe tomorrow."

She groaned. "If you show up right after work tomorrow, I'll let you help design a flaming cake."

He stopped breathing. "A flaming cake?"

She tried to think of some occasion that would require an actual, flaming cake, and came up with nothing. Wait. "I want to do it for someone's eightieth birthday."

"Whose?"

Crap. She wished he hadn't asked her that. "Nobody in particular. I just want to do it. The thing is, I want to figure out how to hide the flaming mechanism in the cake, yet still leave the cake edible. Maybe even better tasting for the fire, kind of like grilling it, you know?"

"You got it. I'll be there at five. When are we doing the cake?"

"I want to show it off in April, at the cooking class. For *my* birthday."

He hung up on her without saying goodbye. Well, she had her oven inspection. And something interesting to serve at the April cooking class, although she had to wonder if she'd just signed up to have the house burned down. Oh, well.

· · · • · • · · ·

Sam spent a few hours working on FoodSlutOnline, typing up a rant about the soufflé failure, castigating herself. She had to stop typing when she realized she was literally punching herself on the side of her head with both of her fists in frustration. But she posted the rant and recipes anyway, knowing that some soul out there would try out the recipes for her and tell her whether they worked in a non-thumping oven. She'd have to talk more about beer pairings later, she knew, but that could wait.

She fixed herself a curried-chicken salad out of leftovers and scooped it up with crackers and brie. Comfort food.

The phone rang while she had her mouth full. She picked up the handset without thinking. "Arrah?" She swallowed. "Hello, Sweet Granadilla Catering. Sam speaking."

"Good news," Danielle said. "You got the job."

Sam frowned. Job? "What job?"

"The chocolate festival."

Sam's eyes grew wide. "What?"

"The chocolate festival. You beat out Robert."

"Robert?" For a moment, she had no idea who Danielle was talking about.

"Robert Langoustine? Remember? My chef at the restaurant at the *hotel*? Remember? I run a *hotel*?"

She just couldn't grasp it. Hotel? What hotel? It was like there was a hole in her memory. She was amnesiac, when it came to things like— "I got the chocolate festival job!" Sam screamed into the phone, holding it at arm's length and shaking it back and forth. When she sucked in air, she heard Danielle laughing at her from the phone. She screamed again, dancing around the kitchen, completely losing it.

It was the catering job of a lifetime.

A chocolate festival came through town twice a year, passing out samples and selling all kinds of food and luxuries: handcrafted soaps, chair massages, wine tastings, and celebrity meet-and-greets.

This year's star was Jack Malpeque, he of bare-chested piratical sexiness. His new movie, *Pirate Moon IV* would be out early next year; it was bound to be fun. And maybe even bare-chested. He had a cabin somewhere up in the mountains near Vail and spent some time up there every year so he could ski.

And Danielle had talked him into appearing at the chocolate festival.

There was no question of whether the staff of Sweet Granadilla Catering would attend the event. They would. They would be standing in line trying to get autographs. Sam had already signed up for a booth, was planning to bring the weirdest chocolate truffles she could get away with, or couldn't get away with but was going to bring anyway, like lemon/potato chip/thyme and one with a filling based on her shrimp bisque. She was still trying to figure out the one based on the Moroccan red-pepper dip muhammara. She'd been obsessing about savory chocolate flavors lately.

But now.

Oh, but now.

She could throw those out the window. She'd enter the truffle contest with them, sure, but most of her time would be taken up with something else. They were going to recreate the pirate ship from one of Jack's earlier movies, *Murder Most Pirate*. In chocolate.

"I don't have time!" Sam shouted into the phone. "Oh my God I never thought I was going to get this so I didn't finish the planning and I have to run, Danielle!" She hung up the phone and ran to the other side of the kitchen, remembered something else, and ran back across the kitchen, grabbed the phone, and called Danielle back, hung up before the poor woman could pick up, and called Kaley instead. She took some deep breaths while she waited for Kaley to answer the phone, trying to calm herself down to the point where she could tell her what had happened rather than just screaming.

She thought of roasting blueberries. Thyme, lemon, blueberries, cream…

Kaley: "What's up, Sam?"

"We got it."

Kaley paused. Paused just a beat longer. The phone hit the floor with a loud clatter. "Sorry. What did we get? The truffles?"

Sam giggled. There was Kaley, sounding like a rock. Her hands must be shaking for her to sound that calm. "We got the *boat*!"

"The ship," Kaley corrected automatically.

Sam held her breath, crushing her eyes closed, pinching the phone with her neck, and balling her hands into fists. What was she going to do? Scream? Hang up? Cheer?

Kaley sniffed. "We got the ship." Her voice slid up, filling with tears, getting squeaky. Sam's eyes watered in sympathy. "We got—" She swallowed audibly. "—the ship!"

Sam squealed. "Oh my God we are so screwed we have no time!" The doorbell rang. "Shit. That's Dale. I'm having him look at the oven. Call you back." She hung up, ran through the kitchen, threw open the door.

"Dale we got the chocolate ship job!" She grabbed him in a hug and dragged him inside.

"Excellent," he said. "I worked on some plans for the cake at work today, but that'll have to go on hold."

"We'll have plenty of time before April to work on it."

He nodded, chewing on his bottom lip.

"Chocolate fountain for the ocean?"

"Of course," he said.

Talking to Dale was kind of strange. He jumped from idea to idea so fast you could barely follow him. But when Sam was in the kind of mood where ideas were running through her head so fast that she could barely keep up with them, he could keep up with her. She never had to explain anything to him.

He was tall and handsome and always smiling, but...he was like a brother to her. Trying to imagine him in a relationship with someone was like trying to imagine your parents having sex. Ew. She wished that he would settle down with someone and get it over with, so she could stop trying to imagine if he would be suitable with anyone she met. Kaley was always trying to set him up with someone (to get rid of him more than anything else), and the habit had rubbed off on her.

"Won't melted chocolate get too cold too fast? And if it's hot, won't it melt the ship?"

"We've discussed this before," he said patiently. He had a red tin box of tools with him, with grease on the outside.

Sam ran into her utility room and pulled out a big rag, an old bath towel that she used for messy tasks, and laid it on the counter next to the oven. He put the tools next to it, stood back, and looked at the oven.

"If it's too creamy…"

"Blue," he said.

"White chocolate!" she exclaimed. "The water out of white chocolate. High fat anyway. I knew there was something I could do with those roast blueberries. I'll roast blueberries and break them down in the Vitamix. They won't know what hit them. Then we can use all the cream in the world. It won't matter!"

"No royal icing."

"Agreed. That's cheating; it's not chocolate."

"I'll have to step down the heater."

"Would you?"

He opened the oven door. "Molds."

A cold hand grasped her heart. "There's mold in the oven?"

"No. Molds for the ship."

"I don't think we'll need them."

"For the *characters*," he said.

"Don't talk to *me* like I'm an idiot. You *said* the ship." She couldn't always follow him, and it irritated her. "Besides, how am I going to get molds?"

"Action figures." He closed the oven door, climbed up on the counter, pulled a flashlight out of his toolbox, and peered behind the oven.

"Ohhh…" she said. "I'm not sure how to set those, but I see what you mean. I'll have to…"

"Silicone. Food-grade silicone."

"Really?"

"Yep." He climbed off the oven, then turned it on.

"Did you fix it?" Sam peered through the window, watched the element turn on.

"No," Dale said. "I'm just looking at it. I have to figure out how it works before I can fix it. How hot does it get for soufflés?"

"I had it set to 360."

He set the oven for a similar amount of time. "Let's let it get hot and see if we can find out where the thump is coming from."

They stood back and leaned against the opposite counter. Sam could feel the heat coming from the oven, not much, just enough to tell her that she needed to clean it again. One of the chocolate soufflés must have spattered when it fell; the smell was of burnt sugar.

"The sails?" she asked.

"Do you *really* want chocolate sails? They're bound to weigh a ton."

"I was thinking about silk, actually."

"What, paint them with chocolate? It'd just crack and fall off."

The same thing she'd been thinking. "How about food dyes?"

He shook his head. "It's just not satisfying."

"I know."

She made a pot of coffee (he did like coffee over wine or tea or even beer) and they waited.

"How long?" he asked.

"Just before we were supposed to take them out, eighteen minutes? Nineteen?"

He checked his watch. "Should be any minute now."

They waited.

He looked down at her, one eye raised, then back at the oven. Nothing.

More time passed. Two minutes. Three. Five. She paced back and forth. "I tell you..."

"I didn't say I didn't believe you," he said testily. "I'm just saying it's not doing it now."

She growled at the oven, feeling like it had betrayed her. "Just like a car, you know? Take it to the mechanic, and it stops making the knocking sound."

"Exactly," Dale agreed, sounding relieved that he hadn't had to make the explanation to her, painfully, slowly. "I'm sure it'll be fine now."

"You're just saying that because you have no idea what was wrong with it."

"How could I? We can't reproduce the problem."

Sam threw her hands up in the air. "Fine. Just fine. I'm going to make a soufflé in it tomorrow and find out, though."

"Let me know how that goes."

"Let me know if you come up with anything on the sails," she said.

"This is in what, two weeks?"

Sam nodded. "I just hope I don't screw it up."

He patted her on the shoulder, then pulled his hand back. He was worse than Harry, honestly, for being awkward around people. Why didn't she know more men who were charming? Probably because they weren't nuts enough to keep up with her, that's why. She sighed.

"It's just bad luck," he said. "The universe working against you."

She snorted. "You're just saying that. You don't believe a word of it."

He shrugged, closed his toolbox, and said, "My work here is done."

"You didn't do any work."

"That doesn't mean I'm not done."

"What are you doing for dinner?" she asked. "Want me to make you something? I owe you."

He made a grimace. "I still have half a pizza left in the fridge, and I have a lot of work to finish tonight, and I'm sure you want to spend time with Kaley. I'd rather not, if it's all the same."

"I have all kinds of things in the freezer. It's no problem...really..."

But he was already halfway out the door. Which, she had to admit, was kind of relief. He and Kaley weren't getting along, and she did want to spend the evening enthusing with Kaley, who might have better ideas of what to do with the sails. And rigging! She'd forgotten the rigging!

"Thank you," she called. He waved over his shoulder without turning back to look at her. She stood at the door until he'd driven off in his huge, bright-red truck.

Two weeks to pull it off: A six-foot chocolate pirate ship, complete with a shirtless Jack Malpeque standing on top of a pile of corpses of rival pirates with his sword in one hand and a wench in the other. Complete with a blue, white-chocolate ocean.

She was going to kill herself.

Chapter 7

That night, she dreamed of the chocolate ship floating in a (mostly) cream sea. Except it was a stormy sea. She could see it, blueberry waves tossing at the side of the ship, frothing like a blue cappuccino.

The little chocolate people fought as their ship tossed on the waves. One of them fell, screaming, into the waves, and was eaten by a marzipan shark.

She was just a jinx, that's what it was. Just a jinx. When someone else was there, nothing was wrong. It was all her fault.

No! It wasn't her fault. It was her stupid oven. Except she liked her oven. Not as much as some people liked their ovens; she'd never named it or anything. But she liked her double oven, with its rows of gas burners and two wide, friendly doors...

She tossed and turned and was glad that Harry wasn't there, or she'd wake him, and she'd have to tell him her dream, and they'd fight...

No, the ship, the ship...

She finally woke all the way up, climbed out of bed with a quilt wrapped around her, and went over to the computer. She'd find a bunch of dumb pictures of cats or zombies cooking and amuse herself until her dreams had cleared out of her head and she could start over.

Danielle still believed in her, and she'd been at the cooking class. She knew what magnificent heights of scatterbrained behavior Sam was capable of. And she still thought that Sam was the best person for the job.

She wondered what Robert had submitted. Probably a cake covered in chocolate roses or something. No, that wasn't fair. Robert had imagination, he was just afraid to push it to the limit. He had so much reputation that he was afraid to smear it with something ooky. He was afraid to fail.

That was it, she decided. She had gotten the job because she could, temporarily, convince people that she was *not* afraid to fail. That's why they believed in her. That's why everyone had taken the class: because they knew that no matter what, they were going to try. She was going to make them try to make those damned soufflés, which was a sight more than most of them had done in their lives. They didn't go to the class in order to make the perfect soufflés. They had gone to the class to get over their fears of trying.

So that's what she owed Danielle. She would try to make this completely improbable creation, and she would fail, because none of her ideas lived up to what she wanted from them, and it would be good enough. Because she wasn't just going to fail, she was going to fail spectacularly, yet nobody would notice, because they wouldn't see what she had intended in her head.

They would only see what was right in front of them, damn it, and it would be wonderful.

Now, if only she could hang onto that kind of attitude in the morning, instead of feeling like it was all a dream.

Sam yawned and checked her email, running on autopilot. She was going to have to email the whole crew in the morning. She checked the clock. It *was* morning. Close enough.

She brought up her list of people who used to come to her cooking parties, before she started the catering business. It felt like calling up the gang to pull off one more heist, the big one, in a caper movie. However, instead of having car chases all over the European countryside, they were going to build a chocolate ship.

She typed up the email, exhorting her friends to let her know whether they were available beforehand, and insisting that she was paying them. They weren't just her friends anymore, they were contractors. She was going to have to go over things afterward with her accountant, but she wasn't going to let it stop her. She was ready.

She had almost clicked "send" when she noticed Harry's name on the list. She'd always kept him on the list, whether he was cooking or not, so he could stay on top of things for her.

Her mouse hovered over his name for a long time as she tried to decide whether to delete his name off the list or not. To notify or not notify. Did she really want him to show up? It would be awkward. But could he bring anything to the table that she couldn't get anywhere else? Was he essential?

She thought about it. No.

He wasn't. She could, if she had to, do this all by herself. Even Dale wasn't essential.

She deleted Harry's name from the list of recipients and clicked "send."

If Harry wasn't essential, why did she feel like she'd done irreparable damage by taking him off the list?

The list of messages she was supposed to take care of—without Harry—in her inbox was fairly large. She felt tired, but not tired enough to avoid nightmares, so she started clicking through them, hoping the mindless tedium would ease her back into sleep.

Then she saw the comment, just *waiting* to be moderated.

SO YOU THINK YOU CAN SALE THE SEES, SINK AGAIN, DEC 20 LOL.

Damn it!

She picked up a cooking magazine that she'd left on her desk and threw it against the wall. It slid down and flopped on the floor. The photograph of a white-frosted cake with strawberry garnish looked up at her, its feelings clearly hurt.

"Serves you right," she told it. "Hah. Serves."

Once again, she considered deleting the message but didn't.

If it wasn't Harry—and Harry didn't know that she'd been offered the job yet—then the only person coming to mind as having a possible grief against her was Robert Langoustine.

She'd shown him up.

Younger than him, and a woman. Less experienced, and a friend of the management. That had to have pissed him off.

He was the one. She didn't know how, but he definitely had the motivation.

Now, Sam, she told herself. *Don't make up your mind about his guilt before you get any proof.* But it was already too late. She was already flamingly angry at him, ready for filleting knives at ten paces.

She would confront him, and he would admit everything.

Yeah. That was realistic.

She would just have to trick him into admitting everything. How, she wasn't sure. How did you trick someone into admitting something in real life? Maybe she should go begging him for help and advice and equipment and staff.

"Ha ha ha," he would say. "I knew you could never do it, not without my help. That's why I sabotaged your soufflés. Because I knew that otherwise, you would be too arrogant to ask for assistance."

"How did you do it?" she asked.

He gave her an answer that made perfect sense. It was beautiful in its simplicity, really. Unfortunately, her computer pinged at her, jerking her awake, and the answer vanished. Her computer screen was full of the letter "d." She crawled back to bed. Anger had done what sheer boredom couldn't: made her fall asleep.

· · · · **·** · **·** · · ·

The games and hobbies store had a ship that was almost close enough. The model was only three feet long, but that was all right. They weren't going to build the ship using the model; the balsa wood wasn't going to be strong enough. She'd only wanted it as a guideline for how the larger pieces were going to fit together.

Luckily, her friend Ralph Mooli had signed up to help with the project, and he could build the frame out of metal plates in less time than it would take most people to assemble a flat-pack office desk and chair. Well, in less time than it would take *her*.

The sides of the ship were going to be supported by metal mesh. She'd already called Dale to rule out the ship riding up and down on the waves; he was just going to have to settle for making realistic waves. Dale sounded disappointed, and she apologized.

"There's only two weeks, and I can't risk doing anything that will destroy the ship, because the prototype has to be the final product. We just don't have time."

"I understand," he said sulkily.

"Do you have any other ideas? Something we can add to the ship to add more interest? Movement?"

"I'll think about it." He hung up.

She tried to brainstorm how they could possibly do the sails with Kaley. They were no further along at the end of the day than they were at the beginning, and Sam was starting to think that she was just going to have to go with cloth sails, no matter how unsatisfying a solution it was.

She ordered twice as much chocolate as she could possibly need, then ordered that much again. One hundred fifty kilograms of chocolate, over three hundred pounds, and another ten pounds of white that was meant for the thin ganache that was going to be their blueberry ocean. She bought the lining for the ocean's container. All the action-figure molds for the characters.

And then...she ran out of things that she could do. If she had too much time, she was going to start thinking up things she could add, like tentacles and mermaids. She obsessed about whether using fondant would be cheating, or if she had to do the whole thing in chocolate. Except the sails and the rigging. Maybe she could make them out of candied orange slices, hooked together...or rolled-out cotton candy with spun-sugar rigging. She experimented. The spun sugar wouldn't last the entire festival; it was just too thin. And the cotton candy wouldn't hold together, if she used enough oil on her silicon mat to keep it from sticking; the threads blobbed up. She bought heavy black thread and tan silk, just in case, then had a flash of inspiration in the checkout lane: marshmallows. She'd make flat marshmallows, squish them, and cut them to size. After a day or two of drying, they'd be the perfect leathery texture.

Which left her brain all the time it needed to start on Harry and Robert.

She still wasn't entirely sure how she was going to trick Robert into admitting that he'd sabotaged her soufflés. And she wanted to yell at Harry, but she hadn't come up with an excuse to do it. Really, she should relax. Instead of getting herself worked up about it.

She found herself pacing around and around, trying to figure it out.

Robert. It had to be Robert. If not Harry, there was nobody else who was angry at her. Who could possibly care. But how had Robert gotten into her house? Had he broken in?

She imagined Robert climbing in through the window over the sink. Surely, he would have knocked over the basil plant; it had tipped off the ledge easily enough when the oven had thumped.

Or maybe she'd left the back door unlocked. Maybe that had been him that she'd seen out of the corner of her eye in the garage and not just a figure of her imagination.

It was terrible being such a space case and trying to be a detective at the same time. She was always fouling up her evidence (or lack thereof), giving the bad guys all kinds of opportunities to slip one past her. If it wasn't Robert sneaking into her house, it was stupid salesmen ripping her off, or being late paying her taxes.

No. She would go with her original plan after all, go running to Robert and claim that there was a problem, she couldn't handle making the ship all by herself. What should she go to him with? Oh, God. She was going to have to make her problem simple enough for Robert to solve, and that would give her away in a second. He already knew that she thought she was God's gift to creative problem solving; he'd lambasted her for it before. She'd never be able to fool him into thinking that she had run against a problem that she thought *she* couldn't solve that *he* could...

The rigging. Well? It was something she honestly had no idea how to do, without resorting to real thread. So what if he couldn't come up with a solution? Maybe he'd be just as forthcoming if it was something neither one of them could solve.

That was it. She'd made up her mind. She grabbed her purse and headed out to the Rose Hotel.

Robert was working.

Of course he was working.

He was always working.

Even when he shouldn't be working, he was working.

He had no family and no friends. He had the restaurant. As far as Sam knew, he literally lived at the hotel, never taking more than a few steps outside it, and then only to argue with fleeing delivery drivers about the inferior quality of supplies that had been delivered.

At two in the afternoon, the front of the house would have emptied and the staff would be cleaning and prepping for dinner. Which meant that Robert would have as much free time as he ever did, and that the entire rest of the staff would know she was there. And possibly overhear them.

Sam knew she couldn't have stayed at the restaurant, but she still felt bad about leaving.

The real reason she'd turned Danielle down wasn't because she thought for sure that the catering business would support her and keep her in house payments for the next twenty years, but because the thought of managing a restaurant gave her hives. All the little details that had to be perfect—and exactly the same—day after day, year after year. Just the linen management alone would destroy her, let alone making the sacrifices demanded by maintaining a consistent food cost.

Robert did what he had to do. Which was sacrifice his creativity, apparently.

The front of the restaurant had its own valet service, but she decided to park herself in the hotel garage. Always better to have a known escape route than to stand around waiting for a high-school student in a suit to get off his butt and bring back her SUV. She leaned out of the door and took her ticket from the machine, then drove downwards into the dark.

The parking garage across the street from the restaurant was clean and so new she could still smell the paint, but it was still dark, unpleasant, and disorienting. She wrote her parking space number on her hand and stuck the ticket in her purse. Now that she was here, it was almost too creepy for words, what she was thinking about doing. It wasn't like it was Harry, who would forgive her (more or less) for being a complete idiot. No, this was Robert, who had been one of her heroes, once.

She found the elevator up—the transition from the paint-and-cement world of the parking garage to the cream-colored velvet walls, brass, and mirrors of the elevator was abrupt—and let herself out at ground level.

She walked across the street, her boot heels clicking on the asphalt of the crosswalk. She wished she'd changed; she had a streak of chocolate down one pant leg. No, it was all right. It was totally believable. Young caterer, distressed at her failure to solve a fundamental problem, consults amazing, inspiring chef for solution without bothering to change into clean pants first. *Robert-wan, you're my only hope...*

She giggled at herself. How she was going to keep a serious face in front of Robert, she didn't know. But she had to try. *Focus. Remember, you're not here to make smartass comments and mock his food. You're here to a) get a solution for your rigging and even more importantly, b), to find out how he got inside your house to sabotage the oven, so be nice.*

Even though Dale thought there was nothing wrong with the oven. But maybe Robert had set it up so that whatever it was would self-destruct, or at least stop working, after the two times that were necessary, with the soufflés. He wouldn't want to get caught, of course.

And then she was at the front door of the restaurant. And then she opened the door (the doorman must be taking a smoke break). And then she was inside, the sound of her boots drunk up by the thickness of the carpet. Chandeliers overhead, silver candlesticks, the grand piano. The place intimidated her, to be honest.

She waved as she passed the hostess at the front entrance. The woman looked familiar, sort of. She pushed her way through the double doors to the kitchen (one of the doors was damp for some reason) and went inside.

Men in white coats with only their toques to distinguish them from doctors stood around a range, where something delicious was simmering. It smelled familiar, but she couldn't place quite where. Even if her brain didn't recognize it, her mouth did and started to water.

"Hello?" Sam said.

One of the cooks looked up, reached into the mass of white coats, and poked someone.

Robert's head popped out of the mass of cooks. "Aha. Just the person I wanted to see."

Sam actually took a step back, her heel tap-tapping on the tile as her legs shook. "Me?"

He crooked his finger at her, and the cooks stepped out of the way. She walked over to the range, stepped close, and, out of habit rather than thinking it was what he wanted her to do, stuck her face in the steam coming from the pot. She closed her eyes. Delicious. Some kind...of...shrimp...bisque.

"Are you trying to make my bisque?" she asked.

He nodded, trying to keep a serious look on his face.

"Why?"

"Just taste it."

She took a spoon from him, dipped the tip in the pot, swirled it back and forth a second to check the thickness and texture. The thickness was right. It was smoother than she liked, but he'd probably run it through a chinoise out of habit. "Like silk on the tongue," she murmured, which was something that he'd said to her time and again. "But it shouldn't be like silk."

"I'll add more chunks of shrimp later."

She shook her head but didn't say any more. He'd never understand the importance of a lack of perfection. She lifted the spoon to her lips, tasted. Ah, no. It was fine enough, but it wasn't *hers*.

Robert, who had been watching her face, frowned. "What? Isn't it good?"

"It's fine," she said.

"What?" he demanded.

"It's not mine," she said. "If you were trying to make my bisque, that's not it."

He grunted. "What did you want?"

"I'm stuck. I need help."

His thick eyebrows went up. "My? Help? The *wunderkind* of Colorado Springs cooking? *My* help?"

She nodded. She hadn't planned to blush, but it seemed to be working perfectly. She looked at Robert's feet. His pant legs were wet toward the bottoms, but only in the front.

"With what? Not that damned ship, is it?"

She nodded. *I wouldn't help you if it damned me to hell.* She waited for him to say it, but it didn't come.

"The sails?"

She shook her head. "Figured that out. The rigging."

"Really?" he said. "I thought the rigging would be easy. What are you doing with the sails?"

"Marshmallow," she said. "Have to time it right so it's leathery rather than rigid. I'm sure the floor is going to shake, with that many people. But what about the rigging?"

"Licorice," he said. "Reinforce it with wire on a few pieces to help it support the weight."

Sam pounded both fists on a counter. "Ah, hell! Why didn't I think of that?"

Robert chuckled under his breath. "Because you don't think of licorice when you think of chocolate? I don't know. I used to tie all my licorice whips together before I could eat them, as a kid."

"I can't—"

"Oh, just buy some. Nobody expects you to reinvent the wheel. Except for you, of course." He put his arm around her shoulder. Why don't you come with me? You all," he waved at his cooks. "Eat that. I'll see if I can seduce her recipe out of her. A little liquor, a few sweet words like ganache in her ear, she'll tell me anything."

Sam couldn't understand it. The last time she'd seen him, working in the kitchen under him last summer, they'd been at each other's throats, screaming at the top of their lungs during service. The maitre d'hôtel had had to literally push them out the back door to keep the guests from hearing them.

"So. What is it? Have you decided to get out of the catering business and come work for me?"

She went stiff and tried to get untangled from his arm, but he wouldn't let go. She hissed at him; couldn't help it. He laughed as he took her back into his office, which was stacked with papers, cookbooks, newspaper articles on the wall, an old computer in the corner for recording inventory, making schedules, etc. The office of a man who hated to be in it. A place to shove things and forget them.

"Forgive the mess," he said, and closed the door. "But I find this is the only place in the kitchen to get any privacy. Now, dear, tell me what's really going on."

She couldn't believe it. He was being so nice to her. How was she supposed to trick him when he was being so nice?

"Someone sabotaged my soufflé class," she blurted out. They were both still standing, neither one of them willing to take the chair. She leaned against one wall and heard newspaper crunching behind her. "I had two sets of soufflés fall. The oven made this enormous thumping sound, almost like someone pounding on the door, when I was out in the living room with the students, at exactly the worst imaginable time, right before we were supposed to take everything out of the oven."

"I'm sure they were delicious," Robert murmured, but it sounded like he wasn't listening to himself talk. "Go on…"

"At first, I thought it was Harry. But he was out of town."

"I see, I see."

"And then I thought of you. And how angry you were at me when I left."

"And so I sabotaged your soufflé class. To undermine you as a caterer. Yes, that makes sense why you would think that, after the way we got on while you were working for me. Any idea of how it was done?"

"None."

"Had the oven checked."

"By a friend."

"And he has nothing against you? Forgive me, but I have been working in kitchens too long to entirely trust anyone. Enough stress, and anyone will break."

"No."

"Hm. And you're sure it was not your partner, I cannot remember her name, the secretary?"

"Kaley? Good God, no." His concern was touching, but she didn't entirely trust him either, not after some of the things he'd said the last time he'd seen her, like *I hope you burn in hell* and *If you were the last woman on the planet I would stab you with this knife, right through your heart, for the way you have betrayed me.* Which seemed pretty definitive of his ill-will at the time. But, she supposed, if you disagreed with your chef, the best time to get into a shouting match with him was probably not during service at the height of the summer tourist season. Irrational things were bound to be said. "But this isn't about her. It's about you."

"I realize some extremely painful things have been said," he said, echoing her thought. "However, I have put that all behind me. It disappoints me that you, perhaps, have not done the same. I know that you are an intensely emotional woman. I, too, am an intensely emotional man, and you had said some things that, at the time, I found unforgiveable."

Oh, she remembered them. *It wouldn't occur to you to add milk to a béchamel if it weren't in Escoffier* and *Would it kill you to experiment with a recipe that you hadn't stolen from someone else once in a while?* and *You should at least have better taste in your thefts.* She could feel her face turning red.

"However," he continued, "with time, I found that I have forgiven them. They were, if not entirely correct, at least a call to adventure. I have been trying to copy some of the recipes that you inadvertently left behind, and I find that some of them have turned out so satisfactorily that I have added them to the menu."

"What?" Suddenly, it occurred to her, without her really believing him, that if he wanted her to work for him again, the best plan would be for him to destroy her catering business, then offer her a job.

"The mushroom loaf. Breaded in panko, fried, on Japanese greens." He handed her a printout; it looked like the draft for a menu. *Asian fusion salad. Mushroom paté, mizuna, mustard spinach, white miso, sesame, daikon, yuzu vinaigrette.*

"That?" she said. "I just brought that for lunch out of leftovers. *That?*"

"Apparently, 'yuzu' is the magic word this season."

"Pfft. Throw a couple of different types of enoki or something on it, and you can call it three-mushroom salad. Asian fusion salad. What kind of name is that?"

Robert coughed into his hand. "The best I could come up with, apparently."

"Sorry. How's it selling?"

"Well enough. The foodies eat it. It's hard to build up a fan base, you know, with all the people going in and out. And the ones that do show up here, they don't come often enough for me to train their palates easily. But I've sent it out, complimentary, a few nights, and it's gone over well."

"That was just my *lunch.*"

He shrugged. "I'm trying, Sam. I'm an old man, and it's hard to teach me new tricks, but I'm trying."

She couldn't believe it. Just couldn't. "You were so—"

He raised a hand. "Please don't remind me." Then took her hand in his, kissed it. "You could do me the favor of telling me that I'm not too old."

"Too old for what?"

He kissed her hand again, raising his eyes to hers. She pulled in part of a breath.

He was attracted to her?

She was going to faint. She was just going to faint.

At first, when she'd started working for him, she followed him around like a puppy, acting like the words that dropped from his lips were divine texts. Then, as she'd started to question his creativity—even after she'd learned about food costs and the demands of tourists, even high-class tourists, for comfort food—she'd started to see him as a person, flawed, but still sexy for all that. The gray hairs at his temples seemed devilish, rather than old. Besides, he was what, maybe nine or ten years older than her? Hardly old. And very young for a chef. He'd been, in his own way, a *wunderkind.* It was a perfectionist's way, a way that ensured no recipe reached the menu unless it had been tested and tested until there was no more way to squeeze another penny out of it, no way it could be improved upon and still remain the same recipe. A perfection of technique. She'd learned a lot from him.

"Of course you're not old," she muttered. "But I'm—"

She'd forgotten for a moment that she wasn't married. And, apparently, the chef she'd had the hots for, before she'd screamed her head off at him, had the hots for her, too. She wasn't sure what to do about it, but she was...flattered?

She still didn't trust him. "I'm not going to tell you the recipe for the shrimp bisque just because you kiss my hand a couple of times."

"I'll have to try harder," he said.

Chapter 8

Robert stepped close to her, grabbed her arms, and stuck his face toward her with his lips puckered. Part of her couldn't help but find the face he was making incredibly ridiculous; part of her raised her face toward him, her heart skipping beats and her body turning hot, with attraction or embarrassment or both.

Robert touched his lips to hers, with the lightest of touches, a caress of his skin across hers. She opened her lips, leaned forward, and kissed him back. Suddenly, she seemed to have not a whit of sense in her body, or rather, in her brain. She wanted to rip off all her clothes, straddle Robert right here in his office, and make love to him as fast as she could, just so she could do it a second time, sooner rather than later. One kiss, and she was all to pieces. She smiled and shook her head, and he leaned back a little, in order to see her face. Well, whatever he saw there didn't stop him from kissing her again, this time pulling her closer. She'd lost all sense of where the space between them was supposed to stop.

But she shouldn't have to worry about it. She was a free woman now; she could do whatever she wanted. She reached around behind Robert, starting with her fingers in the small of his back, finding her way under his jacket, then his shirt, then his undershirt. His back was hairy, furry really, rather than smooth like Harry's, and she rubbed her hands back and forth, trying to decide whether she liked it or not. It wasn't bad, she decided, just a different flavor. A different taste sensation.

She spread her hands out and pulled his hips toward hers. Like it or not, her body seemed to know what to do. She leaned into him, shifting her hips until all their bumps and grooves were lined up properly.

He's taller than Harry, she thought. This might be tricky.

Good grief, a few months of drought and she was turning into a slut. But it was Robert. She'd had fantasies about him...oh, for years. Hadn't told Harry a word of it. Couldn't. But she was sure he'd known, the way she'd turned beet red every time she talked about him.

Robert lowered his hands to her chest and ran his thumbs up her ribs from her waist, under her breasts, rubbing back and forth at her bra line for a second, then onto her nipples. Even through her shirt and bra she could feel them moving back and forth under his thumbs. She pushed closer to him, her hips rocking hard with her heartbeat.

His thumbs moved past her nipples, up her chest, to her neck. He tipped her head to the side, then lowered his teeth onto her neck. His teeth scraped her nerves; his tongue tasted her. Her earlobe, soft. She could hear his breath panting across her neck.

He turned with her, backing toward his desk, until she had to move her hands or have them crushed underneath him. He half-sat, and she spread her legs, straddling him, still grinding into him helplessly, getting hornier and hungrier by the second. She was going to have to do something about that in a second, before she starved to death.

She pulled out the front of his shirt from underneath his jacket, feeling the thick coat of fur under there, too, and worked her hands up under his shirt, finding his nipples. She shoved his shirt upwards, then licked a bare spot right over his breastbone, to see if she liked the taste.

Salty, yes, but she expected that.

Musky. More of a smell than a flavor. Full of hormones. The way it creeped up her nose burned her from the inside out. Buttery undertones.

She moved to his nipple and ran it through her teeth lightly. He groaned, grabbed her, lifted her head up to his...

And stuck his tongue in her ear.

She flinched.

"What?" he said.

A sound came out her mouth that was halfway between an "ugh" and a "ew" but undoubtedly signaled that he'd done something wrong. He looked at her, worried.

"Don't do that," she said.

"I thought women liked that."

"I don't."

He bent toward her again, but it was too late.

"I'm sorry," she said. "I shouldn't be doing this..." She looked down at herself. Her shirt was mussed. She pulled it straight. "I, I don't know, it's too soon..."

She grabbed her purse, which had somehow ended up on the floor by the door, and fled. Just fled. She was a coward, and had taken the first excuse she could find to run out of that office faster than...

The cooks were looking at her.

She frowned, snorted, and looked like she was offended. Maybe it would work. Even though her legs were shaking, she let them pound across the tile in the kitchen with firm snaps, as though she were angry. There was a language to the sound of a woman's heels across kitchen tile, and if there was a language for something, you could lie in it, if you had to.

She wondered what Robert would tell the others. It didn't matter. She shoved one of the kitchen doors out of the way. The sound of her heels disappeared as she hit the carpet.

She snorted again as she passed the hostess. And then she was in the lobby. And then she was out the door.

She kept it up until she was in the elevator, thank goodness, by herself. And then her knees sagged. Why on earth had she run? She could still feel the taste of him on her tongue and on her lips. She was still panting.

Maybe she'd sabotaged the oven herself, somehow. She was certainly good at sabotaging every other potentially good thing in her life.

·········

He called and left a message on her phone, but she deleted it without even listening.

Coward.

·········

Danielle called and left a message while she was on her way home. Sam didn't dare delete it the way she had Robert's. She could just pretend the whole thing hadn't happened as far as Robert was concerned, but if it had spilled over enough to make Danielle's life harder, she wouldn't forgive herself: she owed Danielle enough favors that, even if Danielle was calling to make fun of her for running out after getting hot and heavy with Robert, she would have to sit there and take it.

But she didn't have to listen to the message first. She pulled off to the side of the road and dialed Danielle's number.

"Hey babe," Danielle said.

"What's up?" She tried to sound calm, but it was incredibly difficult.

Danielle paused for a second. "Did...Robert piss you off?"

Sam sighed. It was going to all come out, anyway. "Oh, Danielle. I think I...I don't know, insulted him?"

"Are you in a fight with my chef again? You don't even work for him anymore."

Sam squished her eyes shut. "Danielle...I came by to confront him about the soufflés."

"What about the soufflés?"

"There's no way that two sets of my soufflés could have fallen. Kaley was in the kitchen when it happened. She said there was a loud thump just before the soufflés were due to come out of the oven."

Danielle didn't say anything. Sam's SUV shook as a semi passed it.

After it had gone by, Sam said, "I checked Harry out first. It doesn't look like he could have done it. He was out of town last weekend."

"Harry? Out of town? Was there a festival somewhere, or was he meeting with a potential buyer?"

"Poker. And a woman."

Danielle clicked her tongue. "Oh, Sam. I'm sorry."

"He says he didn't sleep with her. She panicked him."

Danielle laughed under her breath.

"Oh, it gets better. But you can't say anything about this, all right?"

"Okay," Danielle chirped.

"I mean it. It's so embarrassing I just want to die."

Danielle's voice dropped conspiratorially. "Do tell."

Sam sighed again. She was probably going to sigh a lot more before all of this was over, actually. What on earth had possessed her? Other than being desperate for…she thought back…something like nine months now? She'd heard about women who had gone without sex for years, and they hadn't gone as boy crazy as she had at the first scent of temptation. She breathed in, sighed again at the memory of the way Robert had smelled and tasted. Damn it, she was doing it again.

"So, after ruling Harry out, the next, erm, person on my list of people who might hate my soufflés and know about the date change for the class—"

"What?"

"Oh, wait, I didn't tell you. Before the class, I got a death threat on my soufflés." She knew she was reaching out for anything, anything, that would give her a few seconds' reprieve of having to tell Danielle about Robert.

"A what?"

"A nasty comment on my blog saying that my soufflés must die, the correct date of the class, which, mind you, I hadn't announced online or anything, except to the class members, and LOL."

"LOL."

"Netspeak for 'laugh out loud.'"

"I know that," Danielle said irritably. "I'm just trying to think who might use LOL in a message. It's so lame."

"I know, right? Especially in conjunction with a death threat on a dessert."

"Yeah." Danielle paused, and Sam could just see her shaking her head. "But you were telling me about your suspects."

Here we go, Sam thought. "The next person on my list of people who might wish me ill was Robert."

"Robert. I can see that. Well, at least from your perspective. You do know that he got over that a lot faster than you did. I think he admires you for it. He likes women who can stand up to him." She laughed to herself. "Too bad they can stand up to him enough to tell him no. Eventually," she added, then literally purred: "Rowr."

Sam gasped back whatever she'd been about to say. "Did you sleep with him?"

"We didn't sleep."

This just got better and better, didn't it?

It all came out in a rush. "Danielle, this afternoon I went over there to confront him and he dragged me back to his office to try to convince me to give him the recipe for my shrimp bisque and oh my God I almost screwed him right then and there after he kissed me."

"Good for you," Danielle announced. "Almost. Why didn't you?"

"He stuck his tongue in my ear. It felt like a snail." She opened her mouth and stuck her tongue out, as though it could push the memory of the feeling of it right out of her ear. Harry had never done that to her. Ugh. She stuck her finger in her ear. It was still wet in there. Suddenly, she wanted to hang up on Danielle, race home, and clean her ear out.

"What's wrong with that?"

"I don't like it."

"Did he keep doing it after you asked him to stop?"

"No."

"Then I fail to see the problem. You have to get over Harry eventually, you know. Robert should be fine for taking him off your mind for a while, as long as you don't think that he's going to stay faithful to you or anything."

"I don't know, Danielle. When he stuck his tongue in my ear, it was like a spell broke or something, and I knew I had to get out of there before I fell under it again. I just don't know. So. I'm sorry I upset him. I'm sure he's just furious with me."

Danielle paused. "Well, more embarrassed than anything else, I think. He was a bit red in the face when I saw him, but I think that was more to do with the way his cooks were trying not to laugh than anything else."

"Oh God," Sam said. "I can never go back in there again."

Danielle laughed. "You'll have to come back to the hotel at least, to set up your ship. You simply must stay to watch everyone's reactions. How's it going, by the way?"

"Ironically, I came up here with the excuse that I couldn't figure out how to make one last thing, the rigging, out of chocolate. I have everything else down, but I'd given up on that; we were just going to use string."

She could hear the smile in Danielle's voice. "So you came begging, the humble ex-student returning to her teacher for advice."

"Well, I thought I could get him to storm and thunder and brag about how he knew I'd never succeed, and he'd brought me low in my soufflé class, oops, I shouldn't have said that, that kind of thing."

"Except he seduced you instead."

Sam muttered, "I wouldn't say it like that. Makes it sound like I wasn't crawling all over him."

"You're desperate, dear. We understand. He was probably planning on it, actually."

"Really?"

"You don't know him like I do," Danielle said. "Always good in a pinch. Knows just what to say."

"Except around me, apparently."

"I think he likes you. Throws him off his game."

Sam closed her eyes again. "Anyway, as soon as I told him the problem, he came up with the solution. Just like that. I've been wracking my head for days. And he just tossed it off." Her eyes filled with tears. Oh, she was so angry at herself, for all kinds of things. "Licorice. All I have to do is use whip licorice." She sniffed.

Danielle said, "It's all right, Sam. You don't have to do this all alone, you know. We all trade favors. That's part of the business, no matter what business you're in. And you know that if things don't go your way, you will always have a job with me, even if you have to eat crow to work under Robert to do it."

"Not ready to give up."

"I know, dear," Danielle said. "Now, drive home, wipe your face, and get to work on my boat! I told Jack about it already."

Sam's skin turned to ice. "Jack? You know Jack *Malpeque*?"

"Of course I know Jack," she said. "I know everyone. Didn't I tell you that?"

As a matter of fact, she had at some point, but Sam hadn't believed her.

"What did he say?" she squeaked.

"He said, and I quote, 'Well, I certainly hope she gives me a bigger package than I'm showing on those action figures. It's a crime, that's what it is.' End quote."

Sam burst into a cackle of laughter, too startled to make it sound like anything other than mad glee, snorting when she inhaled. "He did not! You made that up."

"If you say so, dear. Gotta go."

"Talk to you later," she said, still laughing.

CHAPTER 9

The people who were going to be working on the setup crew now included Sam, Kaley, Dale, Ralph Mooli (who was doing the metal work), and Donia Pantmar, another friend of hers from her cooking club.

The cooking club had kept her sane during everything that had gone wrong with Harry. They would get together and cook something that would be unimaginable to try to accomplish alone by anyone lacking a team of ancient grandmothers to assist them. An edible graveyard they'd seen in a book. A medieval feast with an entire roast pig stuffed with baby pigeons and eels (what a pain in the ass getting baby pigeons had been, too, and the thought of all those dead baby pigeons had finally made her break down and cry). Their pig-roasting pit was still in the back yard, on the off chance that they might want to do a luau at some point. A dim sum spread with thirty different dishes, from pork buns to fried chicken feet. She had begged off doing another one while she was starting up the catering company, just until she got a little better on her feet.

Although sometimes it looked like that was never going to happen.

Donia was a divorced retired Army captain who liked to cook. If anyone should be running a restaurant or a catering company, she was the one that Sam would have picked as the logical choice—over herself, anyway. But it seemed like Donia liked working at her desk job better than she liked making food for people. In fact, she ate out most of the time, really only getting involved in big cooking projects during their cooking club.

It puzzled Sam sometimes. Donia had the ability; Sam had the desire. Funny old world.

They met at eight a.m. in a conference room at the Rose Hotel. Sam had been nervous about going into the hotel, but Robert had been nowhere to be found as she slunk through the halls. She didn't, by any stretch of the imagination, think she was safe, but at least she'd made it into the building without humiliating herself.

Danielle had seen to it that the room was stocked with coffee, juice, water, and a tiny breakfast buffet, with warming pans of eggs and bacon and a platter of pastries. The five of them stuffed their faces and complimented Ralph on the ship frame.

It was a wonder. Six feet long, two feet wide at the widest part, two feet high at the thickest part of the ship. The poles for the masts rose almost another four feet into the air. The ship rested on a base of four thick metal poles attached to a heavy, wide metal plate that would be submerged in the blueberry ocean, when everything was complete. Ralph had made it from the balsawood model she'd given him.

The whole thing was going to sit on a four-foot tall heavy wooden table. Sam wiped her hands on a napkin and shoved the table. It didn't move. She shook it. It was like trying to push a pool table around, it was so heavy.

Well, at least their table was perfect.

"All right, guys. Let's get the frame up on the table and fit the liner into it."

"What are we going to do about the tablecloth?" Donia asked.

"Rubber mat underneath," Kaley said, tossing a folded square of rubber on the table.

"Won't it ruin the table?"

"Not our problem," Kaley said.

"Wait!" Sam said. She unfolded a corner of the mat and sniffed it. "Ugh. It smells like robot butt."

Dale grabbed the mat out of her hand and smelled it, too. "It's PVC, not rubber."

"Don't care," Kaley said.

"Is there anything we can do to get rid of the smell?" Sam interrupted.

"Take a couple of days."

Sam looked at Kaley sadly. Pitifully. Pleadingfully. "Please?"

"Please what?" Kaley said.

"Please go ask Chef Robert if he has anything we can use in place of this mat?"

Kaley put her hands on her hips. "Why can't you ask him? Did you piss him off again?"

"Or maybe we could just call Danielle," Sam said. Yes, that was it. They would see if the hotel manager of this huge, high-class hotel had the time to drop everything and help them find a rubber mat. Danielle could probably just pick it up from the kitchen, anyway...oh, shit. There was no way Danielle was going to pass the opportunity by to send Robert over, just so she could see the fur fly.

If she went to Robert herself, at least she could talk to him without Danielle smirking over her shoulder. She sighed. It felt like her body was collapsing in on itself.

"Sam..." Kaley said. "What?"

"Nothing," she moped.

Kaley lifted one eyebrow.

Sam clutched her head with her hands, staring up at the ceiling, and trying not to notice that she was turning beet red, because if she thought about it too long, she was going to have hysterics, the laughing and the crying and the locking herself in the bathroom and all that, and she just didn't have time for it. "I don't want to talk about it. And I don't want to talk to Robert. And yes, I know, if I make one of you go talk to Chef Robert, you're going to weasel the whole story out of him anyway so it would be less embarrassing if I just talked to Chef Effing Robert by myself..."

She inhaled, and there was the click of a door latch closing softly.

She looked at Kaley and the others, who seemed shocked and guilty-looking. Dale, behind her, sniggered.

"He's standing right behind me, isn't he?" she asked.

Kaley had both eyebrows up and the corners of her mouth turned down. "You're such a diva," she gasped, then burst into laughter.

Sam turned around slowly...watching sections of the wall come into view, one after the other. Some day, she thought, I will look back at this and laugh.

Yep. Robert was right behind her. Looking stone-faced.

Sam inhaled, grabbed the rubber mat off the table, and said, "Do you have anything we can use to protect the table that doesn't smell like robot ass? Thank you."

It didn't help that Kaley burst into fresh cackles.

Robert leaned forward, took the rubber mat out of her hand, and smelled it noisily. He coughed and grunted. "I'll see what I can do." He turned around, grabbed the handle, and left.

Oh, no, Sam thought. I've hurt his feelings. She wasn't sure how she had come to that conclusion, but she had, and she was sure of it. At least, she was convinced of it. Maybe it was fine. But she'd been yelling about being embarrassed about something having to do with him...she'd be embarrassed, anyway, if someone she'd been making out with the day before had been shouting at the top of his lungs about how embarrassing she was.

She drooped and turned around.

Kaley said, "That wasn't so bad, was it?"

"It was," Sam said. "It was horrible."

Kaley snorted.

Donia cracked her knuckles. "Well, if it means we have the Sam meltdown out of the way..."

"What's that supposed to mean?" Sam asked.

"You always have one meltdown," Donia said. "One. Not more than one, not less than one. Just one. It's always better when you have the meltdown out of the way, first thing. Then we can all focus."

Sam sighed again, feeling like there was no hole big enough for her to hide in. "Really?"

"Really," Dale and Ralph said. Not Kaley, thankfully.

"Get on with it," Kaley said.

Dale grabbed another bear claw and shoved it in his mouth. "Can't do anything until Robert shows up with another mat, eh?"

Sam straightened her back, rubbed a loose hair back, and said, "Hardly." She pulled out her list of tasks. "First thing. We need to get it down to about sixty degrees in here. I hope you all brought a sweater."

· · · · • · • · · · ·

The ship was a pain in the butt to build, and almost every second of it saw Sam swearing that she was never going to take on another chocolate sculpture again. Ever. No matter how big or small.

One of the bus boys came back with a rubber sheet they'd been using in Robert's kitchen to keep a pastry cart steady. It was cleaned but smelled, ever so slightly, of mold. Sam insisted on cleaning it with bleach and dish soap and leaving it out to dry while the room chilled and they unloaded her materials.

The chocolate of the main deck, which she'd carefully molded (making the mold herself, damn it) and prepped to look like wood, had cracked in a jagged line from one end to the other and had to be remolded back at her house.

The rudder cracked, too, but not until after they'd finished redoing the main deck.

The cockboat had bloomed on one side, white speckles of chocolate that looked like mold. They wiped it with water and a toothbrush and had ended up with an interesting texture. Then they'd spent an hour arguing over whether they should do the same thing with the rest of the boat. Sam had had to put her foot down: *NO.*

The molding chocolate, which she'd prepared with glycerine, had gone grainy and oily at the same time, and refused to stick to the mesh on the side of the ship.

Donia dropped a plastic mold full of pirate figures and broke them all.

Ralph Mooli noticed a loose weld on one of the sides of the ship and wanted to reweld it, which would have melted everything they'd attached to the frame. Sam refused to let him use epoxy glue, which would have smelled. They wired it solid with jewelry wire.

Kaley had a fit where the smell of chocolate suddenly made her nauseous. She ran out and vomited in the hallway. She had to spend the rest of the day with vapor-rub under her nose and wearing a mask.

Donia kept telling stories about her time in the service and how she would have handled the project if she were in charge.

Danielle kept asking if they were done yet, so she could send in photographers to take publicity photos. Sam offered to let the photographer in for a couple of candid "in-progress" shots, and he sneezed on the remade row of pirate figures, at which point, Sam started giggling and couldn't stop, and Ralph threatened to pull out all the film on the camera, which only made her laugh more, because it was digital.

The gold leaf disappeared for two days.

Robert came into the room about once a day to hover for a few moments, a minute at most, but Sam ignored him. She wasn't trying to be rude. But she was in cooking mode. Even worse, she was in patisserie mode, and was therefore not entirely sane.

At one point, she'd finished carving off the extra chocolate from the big-breasted mermaid figurehead attached to the bowsprit. She didn't dare look away for even a second; it was bad luck.

"Somebody get me a heat gun," she shouted. The one spot where she'd scraped away a trimming was dull-looking. The heat gun slapped into her hand, and she carefully heated the side of a palette knife, then used it to melt down the dullness around the mermaid's shoulder into a bit of a shine. "Do you think a little bit of gold leaf on her nips would be a bit much? Too tacky? What's it like in the movie?" she asked.

Robert's voice murmured in her ear, "Definitely tacky. Do it anyway."

She spun around, aiming the heat gun at him, but he was gone as though he'd never been there.

· · · ● · ● · · ·

After unmolding the third set of pirate figures, Sam discovered that the package area of Jack Malpeque was...blue.

"Dale!" she yelled. It was, all things considered, a logical accusation.

Dale made a 180-degree turn, stumbled on the plastic, and slammed into the door with his shoulder, cackling as he escaped. They all burst into laughter.

Sam sank into one of the chairs, her shoes crunching on the plastic they'd had to lay over the carpet. If her friends were any indication, she was a mess. Kaley had white chocolate running through her hair, making her look like she'd seen a such a terrible sight that she'd come away marked for life. It would have been Bride of Frankenstein hair if it weren't tied back in a bun.

Donia had bandages on the first two fingers of her right hand, from gouging herself with a chisel, trying to carve extra grooves into the "wood." Ralph Mooli's arms were sparkling up to his elbows, from painting gold leaf on the cannon muzzles.

She hoped housekeeping knew a trick or two for getting chocolate out of the soundproof wall; Kaley had thrown a fistful of molding chocolate at Dale at one point, and now there was a brown smear down one of the panels.

Her eyes burned. She needed sleep and water and more sleep. There were two days left until the festival, and she could hear all kinds of ruckus going on past the wall. They were going to have to open up the doors soon, so the organizers could finish decorating this end of the room.

She looked back at the ship.

It was magnificent.

All they had to do was put up the rigging, add the sails, flock the bottom of the ship with the white chocolate mix to suggest the spray from the ocean...well, they still had a thousand little details to take care of, but at least it looked like a ship.

The only thing keeping her from calling it an afternoon was the knowledge that something else would go wrong. It had to. She wasn't quite tired enough to not care, either.

"Okay, break time," she called. "I'm going to keep working, but...we're almost done here. Go take a break. Hell, go home for the night."

Ralph Mooli threw down his paintbrush and cheered. Donia cracked her neck, making it sound like a threat.

"I'm sorry he screwed up your pirate," Kaley said.

"Don't worry about it. It's Dale. I knew the risks of asking for his help when we started." Sam yawned, crossed her arms, and laid her head on the table. "Ugh. I need a coffee."

"You need some sleep."

"So do you," Sam mumbled.

"This is a hotel," Kaley said. "Why don't you use a bed?"

"Because Robert..." Sam cut herself off.

Kaley whistled under her breath. "You and Robert, huh?"

"Not really." Sam was too tired to be embarrassed about it. "He stuck his tongue in my ear and I ran. I went nutso."

"Your marriage isn't going to magically reappear, Sam. You have to move on."

"Don't wanna."

Kaley patted her back and moved away. In the chill of the room (which chill, at times, had been the only thing keeping her awake), it was easy to tell when someone was standing next to you, and when they weren't, just from their ambient body heat.

Sam felt herself slide down into sleep. Just a nap, she thought. With her eyes closed and the room quiet but for the banging on the other side of the soundproofing wall, the smells of it all sank into her. After an hour in the cold room, she'd been unable to smell the chocolate anymore, not until she'd gone home for the night, taken a shower, and picked up her stiffened, dust-choked clothes to put in the wash.

But now the dark chocolate was like earth to her nose, the glorified smell of walking on wet, leafy dirt under oak trees. Like hiking in a forest. She actually craved chocolate then, after days of the thought of eating the stuff turning her stomach. She wanted it hot, though, a mug of Mexican-style chocolate, hot and frothy and full of cinnamon.

Her hands twitched, and she knew she was almost dead asleep.

Coffee and chocolate. It would revive her. She imagined holding it in her cold hands.

The door opened, and she groaned in her sleep; not a sound passed her lips, unless it was a snore.

Whoever it was saw her and sucked in a breath that was almost a gasp. Someone who wasn't expecting her to be there. Someone who wanted to be in the room with her chocolate ship, alone.

Sam tried to will herself to awaken. She hadn't precisely forgotten that she'd received another threat on her ship, but it hadn't been foremost in her mind over the last few days, that was for certain. However, it seemed like the best she could do was a bare crack of her eyelids. Light flooded her vision, and for a second, she couldn't see.

The door clicked. By the time she had her eyes fully open, whoever it was, was gone. She dragged herself up, groggily stumbling to the door, and looked out into the hallway.

Nobody.

She blinked a few more times; nothing was out of place, as far as she could tell, but she was the only one left in the room.

She checked the coffee carafe, but it was empty, as she'd known it would be. Well, it was as good an excuse as any. She tapped her fingernails against the side of the carafe, thinking.

A trap. She could set a trap and see what, if anything, fell into it.

She pulled her camera out of her purse and set it to recording videos at a low resolution. She'd drain her battery and fill up her memory card, but she'd have some peace of mind while she refilled the coffee. She put the camera on the far side of the room, aimed it at the pirate ship, and grabbed the carafe.

·········

She didn't know where else to get coffee but from Robert's kitchen, and she was too tired to care about the potential humiliation involved. As she walked down the back hallway, she saw that someone had left a set of chocolate-coated footprints down the carpet. Crap. Danielle was never going to speak to her again.

A woman passed her, squatted down to the floor, sprayed something on the dusty spot, put a cloth over it, and rubbed it with the back of a large serving spoon. All in a day's work. She didn't even glare at Sam as she walked by. Sam looked down at her clothes. Her sweatshirt was a ratty old thing that her mother had given her in high school that read, *There's no crying in COOKING*, and it had a smear of chocolate that ran from right under her chin and into her armpit. She must have leaned into the railing on the ship while she was adjusting the sugar skeletons that had been climbing up the other side. Shit. She'd have to check it after she got back.

She smelled the kitchen before she saw the door. Pushing her way through, she saw Kaley talking to Robert.

Oh, God. Here it comes.

"Hi, Robert," she said. "Would there happen to be any coffee brewed? I don't think I'm going to make it without some caffeine."

Kaley was wearing a hockey shirt. Not her real hockey shirt, the one that had been signed, but one with the same number. She and Robert were talking about Avalanche players. Kaley punched her fist into her open hand, saying something about a butterfly that went completely over Sam's head.

Robert waved a hand over at the espresso machine. Sam leaned her head against the front of the machine. Maybe if she wished hard enough, the espresso would just make itself. Or maybe not.

Everything was set up and ready to go but the milk. Milk...she didn't really want milk, she wanted cocoa. Not a mocha. A real Mexican hot cocoa that just happened to have espresso in it. She wondered what would happen if she frothed cocoa with the milk frother.

She powered on the machine and started grabbing things. Nothing had been moved around too much since she'd quit working there (she would have been surprised if anything had).

She brewed the espresso and set it aside. *Froth, froth, froth. I am wroth with froth.* Sam filled the pitcher halfway with hot water, honey, and lumps of white and dark chocolate. She used the steamer to heat the water without pulling bubbles out of it, just mixing everything together until a sludge floated to the top of the water.

Then, she frothed.

It looked like soap. She laughed, and frothed some more. The froth splattered a little, and she moved in front of it, so nobody else would be caught in the flying debris. Not soap. Like an egg cream. The smell was wonderful, full of all kinds of things she'd dumped in: cinnamon, vanilla bean seeds, ancho chili. Exhaustion was making her more than a little loopy. She turned off the foam, wiped the frother automatically, and poured the eggy froth into a latte mug. "Needs a cherry tomato on top."

She took a drink, looking into the kitchen. People were staring at her, so she waved. The bubbles were tight across her tongue, breaking into larger and larger bubbles. She knocked the mug against the counter, making some of the larger bubbles pop, humming to herself.

Oh! The espresso. She poured the espresso down the side of the mug, swirled it a few times, and drank.

It was good. Could be sweeter. She missed the taste of milk to even things out. She wasn't sure about the chocolate. Maybe unrefined beans would be better. She would have to check the fat content. Or, she could look up what Mexicans traditionally did to thicken it. *Idiot.* If she hadn't been so tired, she would have started there first.

At any rate, the drink woke her up. Kaley was gone already; Robert was looking toward the door.

She tried to give him the rest of her drink: time to get back to work. "Here, try this. Where's Kaley?"

"She went back to the room," he said, smiling a little at her. "We need to talk."

Sam pushed the mug at him until Robert grabbed it with both hands. "Later. After the show, all right? I'm so tired I can't think straight."

Already, the smell of him was creeping up her nose, making her nervous. She had to get out of there before she got more nervous than tired, and said something she would really regret.

"Later, then," he said. He took a drink, frowned.

"Think about tomato," she said, and escaped.

· · · • · • · · · ·

Back in the room, Kaley was waiting for her.

"I talked to Robert," she said.

"I saw that," Sam said. She grabbed the camera and turned off the recording, then started playing it.

"What are you doing? Taking pictures? We're not done yet?" Kaley said.

Sam skimmed through the video on fast forward, but didn't see anyone come into the room but Kaley. "Just testing the camera," she said. It was strange the way sometimes lying came easily to her, and sometimes it was impossible.

"So what did you and Robert talk about besides hockey?" Sam asked.

Kaley didn't answer, and Sam looked up. Kaley was fussing around with some of the licorice and opened the lid of the container with the leathery marshmallow sails in it. "Should we really put up the sails today? Tomorrow might be safer."

Sam grinned. If Kaley was willing to let the topic slide, so was she.

The door whipped open, and Dale came in.

Dale and Kaley had been doing fine...but they hadn't spoken anything more to each other than "hold this" or "have you seen the icing bag?" since they'd started working on the ship together. Mostly.

"Hey, Dale," Sam said.

He looked around the room, saw Kaley, and stuck his nose up in the air. Snorted. When they were annoyed, they really looked like brother and sister.

"You haven't seen my bag, have you?" he asked.

"Nope," Sam said.

"You didn't take it, did you?"

Kaley said, "I haven't touched your bag."

"It's not here."

"You heard me the first time."

Dale banged back out of the room, slamming the door behind him.

Sam's hands stuck out on either side of the pirate ship, trying to keep it from tipping over—which was stupid; if it was going to tip over, then it was going to take a lot more than her tiny hands to keep it upright. The chocolate weighed a ton, even without the frame.

"Things are pretty bad, huh?" Sam asked.

"About the same," Kaley said.

"Huh. They look pretty bad."

"Yep."

Sam knew where her loyalties lay, but she wished things were different. Dale, although a complete mental teenager, was a good guy to work with. Plus he knew a lot about chemistry and physics, so he was a good guy to ask food questions, if you wanted an answer that would tell you more than any reasonably sane person could ever want to know.

Sam wasn't reasonably sane, so they got along well enough. But Kaley was her friend, her rock, her sanity. Kaley came first.

"If you want to date Robert, I don't mind," she said.

"Where did that come from?" Kaley asked.

"I'm just saying."

"We were just talking!"

"How many men do you 'just talk to'? How many?"

"Stop trying to set me up with every man we meet."

It was an old argument that left their hands free to start picking up bits and pieces of chocolate.

Sam picked up the Jack Malpeque pirate figure. "Blue," she sighed.

"Let me guess. Blue Balled the Pirate."

"That sounds like his level of humor." Sam picked up a palette knife and tried to pry off the blue bit, but it was melted firmly in place. "I just wonder how he did it without me knowing."

"You said that he wanted a bigger package," Kaley said. "Just put some more on top and hit it with the heat gun to make it look shiny."

"My luck, it would fall off while he was here," Sam said. "No, I'll just make another one. The rest of them look okay."

"You shouldn't let him get away with it," Kaley said.

"I'm not paying you guys enough to be able to fire you," Sam said.

"Fine. Just don't give him the bonus, then."

"No. If there's a bonus, we split it. End of discussion."

Kaley sighed. "I just wish this were over."

"What? The ship? Go home already. I can take care of what needs to be done tonight."

"No. The thing with mom and dad. I wish—" She sighed. "I feel like we're teenagers again. Stupid and mad."

Sam took the lid off the sails and stroked the one on top, the one that would go on the foremast. The texture was perfect. She shut the container; better to wait for the sails until tomorrow. Maybe it would give her time to work on the rigging. Shoestring licorice. Augh! There had to be something better. More like rope. Just because it had seemed brilliant a few days ago didn't mean it was brilliant now.

"Why not just give him what he wants?" Sam asked. She'd never asked it before, and she was pretty sure Kaley would rip her head off for it, but she had to know.

But Kaley didn't seem to mind. "It never does any good. If you're nice to him, he just turns around and rubs it in for the rest of your life. He thinks when you give in to his pestering, it means he's won a victory, because he's better than you."

Sam couldn't see it, but then Dale wasn't her brother. "He doesn't think that."

Kaley snorted. "He sure acts like he does."

Sam laughed nervously. "Who am I to be talking about people getting along, after all. Come on." She pulled her phone out of her purse. "It's seven o'clock. Let's get out of here."

"You're right. Out to eat somewhere?"

"Crap. Food. I was thinking about a bath, or at least a shower. I am going to be cleaning chocolate out of my mattress pad for weeks."

"Just get a new one," Kaley said.

"No," Sam said. "I like that one."

"Do you ever throw anything away?"

Sam sighed. "Literally? Yes. Emotionally? Never."

"You have to get over him sometime."

But Kaley didn't know Harry like Sam did. Never would. It must be all the chocolate that was making her feel so maudlin.

Sam packed everything up, then waited for Kaley to step out, so she could lock the door with the key that Danielle had given her.

Kaley looked at her funny, and Sam said, "Just in case. You know, with all the people in the main hall."

She was probably just being paranoid.

· · · · · · · · · · ·

She was on her way home from a new Middle Eastern place they'd tried out when her phone rang with Harry's ringtone; she'd changed it from *I Will Always Love You* to *Bad Romance* a few months ago in a fit of pique. She pulled over to the side of the road, checked her hair, smiled at herself in the mirror, and picked up. "Hello?"

"So, uh..." Harry drifted off. "Where have you been tonight?"

Sam found herself, like usual, trying to read his mind. Then she yelled at herself to knock it off; she was done with the duty of reading his mind anymore. One of the benefits of getting divorced. "Harry. Just say it. I don't have the energy."

"Are you seeing Robert?" he blurted out.

A noise came out of Sam that was halfway between a hiccup and a snort, with a sob thrown in underneath. *I will tell him exactly the truth*, she told herself. *No more, no less. It doesn't matter what he knows or doesn't know. We're divorced. I can do whatever I want now.*

"No," she said, then cursed herself for being an idiot. *No? No was the truth? No was a technicality.* "I mean," she sighed. "Robert asked me to come into his office for something, and we, um, made out for a while. But then he stuck his tongue in my ear and I hoofed it out of there like a virgin donkey at a redneck convention. Bad simile. Sorry."

Harry laughed, deep in his throat. "He stuck his tongue in your ear." It wasn't a question.

"Gah. Don't remind me. I feel violated."

"So..." Harry took a breath. "Sorry. I'm trying to spit things out. Really I am. I know we're divorced and you can do what you want. It's none of my business anymore."

"Harry, I miss you."

"I know," he said.

"Please come back. I'm so sorry."

"No," he said.

"I don't understand."

"I know you don't. But it's important to me not to be with you."

Sam leaned her head against the window. "I'm sorry. I shouldn't have asked." The lights of the oncoming cars were bright, and the SUV shook as a semi drove past. She spent too much time pulled over on the side of the road, trying to survive drama. She should just stop answering her phone until she got home, took off her shoes, and poured herself a drink. It would make days like this a little easier.

Harry grunted. Well, at least he wasn't still mad at her about his tires.

The conversation had drifted into silence. Sam had a lot of experience with it: sitting on the phone, saying nothing to Harry, being unable to hang up. Neither of them being able to hang up.

"Harry, I'm not trying to be rude, but I have to go now. We still have a lot to do on the ship, and I need to get sleep. Call me after the festival, all right?"

"How's it going?"

Sam gritted her teeth. "Look, I know you must have talked to one of them if you know that something was up with Robert. You already know how it's going. Just let me get off the phone already. It's horrible; it's one train wreck after the next. Fortunately, I knew that it was going to be freaking impossible, so I got some really smart, talented people to help me out, and it's going to be just fine, okay? My only regret is that you weren't there to pick holes in everything I do and make me constantly second-guess myself."

He didn't say anything. She hung up the phone so she wouldn't have to listen to any more silence.

CHAPTER 10

Finally the day of the festival arrived.

At six a.m., Dale called and she hit the screen call button; she was busy.

He left a message:

"Sam, pick up. Saaaam, pick up. Pick up the phone. Sam. I know you're awake, you can't possibly be asleep this late today. Pick up the phoooone."

Sam grabbed her phone, answered the call, and stuck it against her shoulder as she stirred her rice pudding. "What?"

"I knew you were awake."

"You're quite the detective."

"Aren't I just. I need to get into the festival area."

"What for?"

"I want to check one more thing. I'm nervous." Dale had spent until four a.m. screwing around with the pump for frothing the blueberry-white chocolate mix at the bottom of the pirate ship, which had become slightly melted around the bottom due to certain temperature adjustments that had to be made at the last minute.

Not that Sam could talk; she'd spent all night taking down the licorice whip rigging and replacing it with tan candyfloss twisted around jewelry wire and flocked with a little white chocolate here and there to suggest bird droppings.

She hadn't slept, but she hadn't planned on sleeping anyway. Sleep was far down on her list of priorities, after "survive chocolate festival" and "set fire to remains of pirate ship while screaming at the top of her lungs" and "eat something that wasn't chocolate." On top of everything else, which she should have predicted, her face had broken out into a million zits, and she had had to use so much base and cover-up that her face felt like it was crawling with bugs every time she changed her expression.

"Tough," she said.

"Well, if something goes wrong, it'll be all your fault," Dale said.

"It's all my fault anyway."

Dale's voice changed from bossy and abrupt to wheedling. He probably thought he was being charming, the idiot. "Nothing will go wrong. I'm just being paranoid. The ship looks fantastic."

"No, Dale. I am not handing over my keys to you. I don't trust you. Especially not after Blue Balled the Pirate."

"Aww...I thought he was funny."

"He was funny. But I had to totally remold that character. Now go away."

"I'll see you at eight."

"Wear that chef coat I bought you last year for that catering job."

"Can I wear the toque?"

"Yes, you can wear the toque, too." Sam knew she was just letting herself in for a bunch of stupid puns, but he'd put in so much work...he deserved to be able to laugh at the way other people didn't laugh at his jokes once in a while.

"I think it's dusty."

"Spray it with compressed air or something."

"Hm. Compressed air *is* good for dust, isn't it?" He hung up.

Sam rubbed her eyes and went back to her rice pudding, giving it a stir and ladling in some hot milk. Rice pudding was a blank slate, a journal with nothing written in it. But it had to stay sweet, or else it would just be risotto.

Eggs? She could temper an egg and beat it into the milk. No. She wanted the challenge of woman vs. starch right now. And no chocolate.

She rummaged around the kitchen and lined up her troops. "Some of you might not make it out alive today," she announced. Honey. Thyme. Pitted niçoise olives. Cherry balsamic. Chocolate-covered espresso beans. Sugar cereal with marshmallows. Ceylon tea. Almond butter. Panko. "You, boy," she pushed the black olives out of line. "This is a man's job. Go home until you grow a pair of stones." She made the jar tip-tap its dejected way back to the cupboard.

"Waah!" the olives cried.

"Suck it up, you fruit!" the cereal shouted.

"Silence!" Sam yelled. "You! Chocolate-covered espresso beans! While normally I appreciate your life-giving properties, your kind is not wanted here! We have had enough chocolate to last us a lifetime! Or at least until Monday! Get out of here, catch up on paperwork, take a few days off to see the ladies around town. Do you get me?"

"Sir, we get you, sir!" She chucked the espresso beans back in the cupboard. "Hm...panko. Some starch-on-starch action would be nice. But no! Too classy for this breakfast. This is a breakfast of champions, not a gourmet's feast!" She chucked the panko and the tea back in the cover. "And that lets you out, too, Ceylon! But I think a high-class risotto with tea and clotted cream is in your near future! English Breakfast risotto. I wonder if I can work in cucumbers with that. And jam. Jam and cucumbers. Ugh."

She pointed a finger at the cereal. "Cereal! You disgust me! You're a slob. Give me fifty."

She tipped the bag of cereal over (she mostly ate it during PMS), lifted one edge of it up a little, and gasped for breath. "Can't do it, Sarge!"

"Back to the cupboard with you!"

She pulled the almond butter and cherry balsamic out of her bedraggled line. "Volunteers! HAHAHA! You know what we like to do with volunteers."

She added a little honey and thyme to the pan and put everything else away, humming tunelessly.

She had no room to make fun of Dale, after all; she was just as bad, if not worse.

She let the rice pudding cook for as long as she could stand, then scooped some of it out of the pan into a small bowl. The rice was getting old, and she needed to pick up another bag at the Asian grocery. She knew that risotto and sushi rice weren't the same thing, but she couldn't help buying these gigantic sacks of sushi rice. They were just so seductive.

She swirled in a few drops of the balsamic and a spoonful of the almond butter. The almond butter made the pudding taste just a little salty, even though there wasn't any salt listed on the label, and she'd only added a pinch to the rice. The cherry balsamic added a little sparkle. The almond butter also added earthiness, richness. Very nice.

She made another bowl but didn't finish it; her stomach started to clench up, and she knew if she ate another bite she'd throw it all back up again. She put the pudding in a plastic container in the fridge and tossed the pan in the sink.

It would be less work if she washed it right away. And she hated leaving behind a dirty kitchen.

But it was part of her ritual for getting ready for things that terrified her. She left the dirty dishes out and the counters unwashed, almost like a promise that she'd be home again someday to clean it up.

No matter how bad things went today, she'd have something to do when she got home, which relieved her a little.

Her plans for when she got home:

- Cry a little.

- Wash dishes (maybe at the same time).

- Call Kaley on the phone and cry some more.

- Call Harry. No, she wasn't going to call Harry.

- Blog about how her catering business was over.

- Delete her entry two seconds after posting it.

- Write another entry but leave off before she was done.

- Get drunk, alone in her own home. (She interrupted her mental list to look through her liquor cabinet. She was out of the good rum, and only rum would go with a pirate ship. However, she didn't dare pick up rum on the way to the festival or the way home, because she would end up drinking in the SUV, and then she would get pulled over, and then she would get arrested for driving drunk with an open container, and they would probably confiscate the rum. So she set the fixings for a gin & tonic in the fridge. She didn't feel like making tonic cubes. The hell with it.)

- Cry herself to sleep.

- Eat Sunday brunch with Kaley and Danielle at the Rose, plus anybody else who would go, because complete and utter flop or not, or complete humiliation from Robert or not, yum, and their bloody Marys were a total hangover cure, too.

Having planned for the worst, she proceeded to get dressed, carefully did *not* smudge cover-up on her chef coat, dug her toque out of the top of her closet (ack, it had dust on top...how embarrassing), and left a message for Dale, begging him to bring a can of compressed air with him.

She called everyone else and made sure they were awake and didn't need to be picked up, assured them that Dale would bring some compressed air to brush their hats off with, too, and checked her email.

That bastard had left her another comment:

UR SUCH A KLUTZ LOL SAY BYE TO YOUR SHIP

Sam slammed her fist down on her grandmother's desk and cursed a blue streak as wide as a fat man's ass. Who was out to get her? Who?

Well, screw that. The whole place had been locked up when they left, with a security guard watching it. Her crew was going to be watching over the ship. She was not a klutz. The ship was going to go over like a fluffy cloud on a sunny day. People were going to love it, damn it, and she was personally going to kick the ass of anyone who had a single negative thing to say about it.

You could mock Sam. But you could not mock her babies. She wouldn't tolerate it.

She threw everything on her checklist into the SUV, hoping that the jerk who was leaving her nasty comments would accidentally trip and fall in front of her while she was driving down the Interstate.

She slammed the door and thought, What if it's one of my friends? What if it was someone like Dale, someone with no real sense of humor, that is, no sense of when to stop, just sending dumbass comments because it was funny? And the soufflés falling was just a coincidence?

But two. Two sets of soufflés.

Ugh. What if it was Harry. Again, you can post a comment from anywhere, and he'd probably know how to disguise who posted the comment. Not malicious...just not funny.

The problem, if she left out the notion that actual sabotage was intended, was finding one of her friends who could cope with the idea of writing "Ur" for "you're." Spelling snobs, every one of them. Except maybe they were doing it deliberately.

Sam shook her head and pulled out of the driveway. She was, literally, getting nowhere. And suspecting her friends! Good grief. Her mouth felt like it was full of dryer lint, she was so disgusted with herself.

·· · · ● · ● · · ·

A few minutes later, she was at the Rose with another mental list:

- People who want to see me fail, either because they hate me, or for my own good.

- People with rotten senses of humor.

- People who could tolerate poor spelling, overdone Internet acronyms, and awkward grammar.

- Saboteurs?!?

- Coincidence

- Karma (*What did I do to deserve two sets of fallen soufflés?* she wondered. *I mean, was I Hitler in a previous life or something?*), bad luck, being born under an evil star, etc.

- Some previously unknown physical property of eggs which negatively affected the soufflés but could *get me published in all the modernist cooking journals I would be totally famous squeeee!*

• Turn right at the parking garage, you fool. Right! Right!

Now, if this were a mystery novel (which, she reminded her-self, it very well might be; you never knew when you were a character in someone else's book), she would be at the point where there was one person who fit all the categories (clearly a red herring), many people who fit some of the categories, and one person who fit none of the categories. A bell-curve distrib-ution of dessert and desertion.

She groaned at the workings of her own mind and put the SUV in park.

Nobody fit all the items on her list, more was the pity. She probably had put too much crap on her list, anyway. Well, except an unknown Internet psycho. There was always the off-chance that she was being stalked by someone she hadn't even met yet. Lame.

The only person who didn't fit anything on her list was Kaley. But she just couldn't imagine suspecting her friend, unless it was making sure that she and Harry didn't get together again, and even then, she'd probably just call Sam an idiot and leave it at that.

Almost as though she had summoned her magically, Kaley appeared at the side of her SUV and tapped on the glass.

"Ready?" she said.

Sam shook her head and grinned. "Feeling stupid and reckless enough to get on with it, though."

"That's my girl."

Kaley was wearing her hockey shirt again.

"Did you even wash that?"

"It's bad luck to wash your hockey shirt during the season."

Sam wrinkled up her nose. "Ewww."

"I'm just messing with you. No, I was going to wear something else, but I put it on this morning and it didn't look right. Nothing was right. So I dug my lucky shirt out of the laundry. Got a problem with that?"

"Nope," Sam said, thinking of her crazy conversation with her ingredients this morning. "Whatever gets you through."

Kaley gave her a hug, banging her hard on the back. Must be a hockey-player hug. Hockey players are so tough they can give hugs...manly hugs.

They both grabbed a bunch of bags out of the back of Sam's SUV and headed into the elevator. Sam looked at the two of them in the elevator mirror and stuck her tongue out at Kaley. Kaley waved back.

Whoever the soufflé killer was, whatever they were trying to do, it wasn't Kaley. Sam felt bad about taking Kaley even a little bit for granted, but she couldn't help it. Kaley was solid.

They reached the top floor and crossed the street to the hotel, rattling the whole way to the restaurant entrance. There was no way Sam was going to walk all the way through the hotel to get to the ballroom; she still had to pick up her badge, and she didn't want to have to argue with the people taking tickets at the ballroom door.

And Robert usually wasn't in so—oops.

Robert was standing at the door to the hallway that led to the back of the ballroom. Standing at the door…or blocking it. He nodded at the two of them, looking for all the world like he was taking a casual break, even holding his fingers out by his side, like he was holding a cigarette.

"You brought your truffles?" he asked. On top of everything else, she'd entered the truffle-making contest months ago, before she'd known she was going to have to cope with a six-foot chocolate pirate ship.

"I brought the ingredients," she said.

"You won't have time to make them," he said.

"I will. I'll do a demonstration."

"You have to enter them now."

"No. I don't have to enter them until noon. I checked the website this morning."

What was his problem? Why didn't he get out of the way?

She handed him a couple of bags. "Look, instead of standing there and arguing with me, why don't you make yourself useful and carry something."

"You ladies," he said. "Always biting off more than you can chew."

She wanted to take him by the shoulders and shake him. "Robert, I don't work for you anymore. Knock it off. Go worry at someone else. If you want to worry, then be nice about it, for crap's sake. It's just a bunch of truffles."

Robert's eyebrows went up, so far up they disappeared under the front edge of his toque. "Just a bunch of truffles."

"You, me, a bunch of chefs that we know, some people who run small businesses in town...come on. I have bigger fish to worry about whether they're going to jump out of the frying pan and into the fire. A boat? Remember our boat?"

She bumped him with her hip until he started walking down the hall.

"Truffles? Little. Boat? Very big," she said. "In fact, the only reason I'm not having a meltdown right now is that I already got it out of the way. Also, I have a plan in place for whatever inevitable failures I manage to incur today. I'm ready for a flop. Truffles? Who cares. I'm just screwing around on the truffles."

"My reputation..." he said.

"Your reputation is that you have a stick up your ass," Sam said. Yeah, she was going to regret this day later, but because she was already planning on it, the sting of it wasn't as bad as it normally would be. "It's chocolate. We could pass out complete and utter crap, and the ladies would be fine with that. Do you not understand? Chocolate is a drug. Good drug, bad drug, it's still a drug. This is the equivalent of a grown-up kegger party. Stop being so serious."

Kaley coughed out a laugh. "Do you really think that?"

"Hell, no. But that's my story today, and I'm sticking to it." Her mouth was running, and there didn't seem to be any way to stop it. At least she wasn't stressing out the way Robert was, by getting mean about it.

Robert leaned over, kissed the top of her head, and set down the bags outside her door. "Good luck."

"Thanks."

And then he winked at Kaley, which made her blush, which made Sam laugh into the lapel of her jacket, trying not to make any sound.

"Not a word," Kaley said.

"When did you get home last night?"

"Not a freakin' word."

Sam left it at that and unlocked the door.

· · · • • ● • • · · ·

The room was full of people setting up booths, arranging bunting, and wrapping baskets in cling film.

Sam looked around; she knew about a third of the people there; there were quite a few out-of-towners with glossy fliers and stacks and stacks of truffles and petit-fours on trays, ready to sample and sell.

Flyers, she thought. *I should have made flyers.*

Already, the room was full of chatter and movement, people wandering through the rows of booths, picking up business cards, hugging each other like they hadn't seen each other in years.

Sam and Kaley had just put down their bags when Danielle called, "Sam! Kaley!" and let out a splitting whistle.

Sam passed a woman who was hanging up the most luxurious-looking chocolate-colored silk scarves and promised herself one, if things went well. *What am I thinking?* She laughed at herself. *Thinking that things are going to go well. I should promise myself a scarf if things go horribly. That way, I can be sure of getting one.* She stopped to touch one, and it felt as beautiful as it looked.

Danielle ducked back inside a door beside the low stage, and Kaley and Sam followed her inside.

"Jack," Danielle said, and Kaley squealed.

"Sorry," she said. "I just got too excited."

Sam couldn't blame her. There he was—facing a mirror, stretching out his mouth into a gigantic circle, closing it, stretching his jaw from side to side.

"I hate doing my own makeup," he said.

"Sam Genoise, Kaley Lugano," Danielle said.

Jack spun around. Sam knew that if she tried the same maneuver, she'd toss herself right on the ground. "Ladies." He bowed, grabbed Kaley's hand, and planted a kiss on the back of it. Kaley tittered.

Sam found herself possessed by the urge to pull on his nose to see if it was real or a fake. *Probably real. But it was so heavily* covered in makeup, she couldn't be sure. When Jack Malpeque took her hand, it was shaking.

"Don't be nervous," he said, smarmily. "I won't bite...hard."

"Oh, for God's sake." The words popped out of her before she could stop herself. "You're such a cheesehead."

Danielle cackled and even Kaley had to laugh. But Jack bowed again, sighing melodramatically.

"Alas, I'm wearing the costume and the makeup. This is what you get." He turned to Danielle. "Who are these people? Friends?"

"These are the two who own the catering company who made the ship," Danielle said, standing a little straighter and looking coyly above their heads.

"Really?" Jack balled his hands into fists and did a little jump, looking like a kid of about six. "You made the ship? You made the ship?"

The hair on the back of Sam's neck stood on end. "Er, with a lot of help? And good advice? You should see the framework that Ralph Mooli put together to keep it from falling apart."

He clapped. He actually clapped and did a little jig. "I'm having someone come down to shoot some film of it. I'm going to stand in front of it like this," he crossed his hands over his chest, "and say, 'Avast ye devil scum! Yar!'"

Sam looked at Kaley, who looked at Sam. Then both of them looked at Danielle, who grinned and tossed her hair over her shoulder.

"Didn't I tell you I know everyone?" she said.

Sam wasn't sure whether to run back to her ship or what. "Um...I have to go. I need to get my hat blown."

Jack's eyebrows went up. "Really? I've always wanted to blow a hat."

Sam gasped as Danielle and Kaley laughed. "Oh, great. Foot in mouth again."

Jack held out his hand and pinched his fingers together. "Hat?"

Sam shook her head. "It's back at the booth."

"Then let's *do* go to your booth. Tell me, are you going to enter the truffle contest? What are you selling? Although I suppose you've been too busy to get anything elaborate up."

"We'll be making them throughout the day, as a demonstration."

"What?"

Sam bit her lip. "Shrimp bisque."

Jack hooted. "You're insane!"

"They don't have to be sweet. They just have to have chocolate. Also, my ex assures me that the only reason he stayed with me as long as he did was for the bisque."

The rest of the room went quiet as he came out; then people rushed toward them. Even though some of these people were at the top of their profession—well, as much as anybody could be said to be at the top of a profession while not living in a major city—they were still flocking around the movie star chattering away and shoving things at him to sign.

Danielle whistled again and yelled, "Signing in fifteen. Now back off and get your booths set up! We only have half an hour left, people."

They backed off, much more slowly than they had arrived, still excited. They were all a little crazy, trying to get themselves worked up enough to survive the crowds that would be shoving and pushing all over the place in just a few minutes.

Dale had arrived and was fussing around with something on the pirate ship.

"Dale, you bastard!" Sam shouted, climbing right over the table that was sitting in front of the ship to protect it from being jostled (although you could drive a tank into that table and not shake the ship on top of it).

Dale turned tail.

"Aha!" Jack drew his sword, leapt up on the table, and ran along it, chasing Dale along the room, toward the hall.

"Stop him!" Sam yelled. Dale was up to something, damn him.

The door to the back hallway opened just as Dale was about to go through it; one of the line chefs pushed a cart covered with truffles through just as Dale ran headlong into it, plunging face first into the chocolates. The woman screamed as Jack slashed at Dale's hind end, whipping him with the end of the stage sword.

Dale rolled off the car, yelling at the top of his lungs and covering his backside with both hands.

Something rolled away from him...something brown.

Something about the size of a chocolate figurine of Jack Malpeque. Broken in half.

Jack swooped down and picked half of it up as the line cook went running. "Unhand me, scallywag," he said. "Well, if it isn't the image of me myself."

Dale tried to grab the other half, but Jack nailed it with the tip of his rapier, crushing it into the carpet and breaking it into smithereens.

"Oh, no," Sam said, dropping to her knees. The figure was ruined.

From down the hallway, a mighty voice yelled, "What?" so loud it echoed off the textured walls. The floor seemed to rumble as footsteps raced toward them.

Robert's face appeared above the cart, looking down at the ruined truffles.

His ruined truffles, apparently.

He exhaled. Inhaled. Exhaled. It was like watching a blacksmith stoke a fire. Sam crawled backward. She tried to say, "I didn't do it," but nothing came out but a squeak.

Robert looked at her and his eyes widened. "You..."

Dale took the opportunity to grab the end of the cart, whip it around, and shove past Robert, fleeing down the hall. Robert caught a glimpse of the smeared creams and crushed rosettes across his chef jacket, and roared again, barreling down the hallway after Dale.

Sam bent over and picked up the pieces of the shattered pirate gently in her hands. It was too late: she couldn't even leave the building, because she hadn't made her truffles yet.

She sighed and stood up, carrying the pieces back to their booth. Behind her she heard the snap of chocolate, and then Jack's voice saying, "Hm. Tasty."

Sam looked up at the pirate ship, knowing that there was no way that the tableau would look complete without the figure of Jack in his pirate costume.

But there was another figure on top of the ship.

Another Jack.

Kaley gasped and clapped a hand over her mouth. Her shoulders shook.

There, in perfect detail, was another rendition of Jack Malpeque.

A familiar rendition.

"Oh, no. Not Blue Balled again," she moaned.

Unfortunately, Jack heard her. "What's that supposed to—" Then he started to giggle, tiny little *hee hee hee* giggles. He stopped, opened his mouth, blinked a few times, and took a deep breath. Let it out again. Closed his mouth. Blinked.

Then thumped the table and started laughing so hard that black streaks down his face. He gasped out the words, "Blue Balled," and then started laughing again.

Danielle stood beside the ship, looked up and said, "But it's the skeleton who has the boner," and walked over to Jack with a perfectly straight face. "I trust the package is to your satisfaction?"

Which just got him started again. "I'll run you through!"

She patted his hand. "You can try, dear. You can try."

It took them until Robert returned to get themselves back under control. By then, Jack was sitting behind a table, signing pictures of himself with an unreadable scribble.

Sam and Kaley finished setting up the booth, which, either by luck or Danielle's say-so, was right next to Jack's signing table and the ship.

"I could, um, paint his crotch to be the normal color," Sam said.

Jack waved his hand and signed another picture. "This is the most fun I've had in a month. Please don't."

"All right," she said.

Robert stopped in front of her table. "They are ruined."

"What, every single one of them? I'm so sorry, Robert. I don't know what got into Dale."

Actually, she could see the chain of events very well; she knew exactly what had gotten into Dale: mischief and arrogance. The desire to slip one more practical joke past her. But it was more politic to pretend otherwise. Robert didn't need to hear the whole story, not at that moment, anyway.

"Dale's an ass," Kaley said.

They looked at each other, something unspoken going back and forth between them. Sam backed away and watched Jack signing photographs of himself. After a few signings, she realized he was writing all kinds of nonsense on them. A few of them were really "Jack Malpeque" or "The Black Pirate," but some of them seemed to be "Blue Balled the Pirate" and some of them were just complete gibberish.

Then Robert said something to her, and she missed it completely. "Excuse me?"

"I said, 'Do you have room in your booth for one more?'"

She frowned at him. "Well, no, to be honest. We're going to be making truffles, after all. Unless you can talk Jack out of part of his table. Did you want to set up to make your truffles out here so you can see what's going on? Wait. Don't you have a table already?"

Robert puffed out his cheeks. "I thought I would experiment a little. And my table is all full already. Kids making roses, that kind of thing." He waved his hand toward the table for the Rose.

Sam wanted to go over there and see everything they'd made, up close and personal. It looked truly elegant. Several sculptures lined the table, far more refined and precise than anything she and her team could have made in a million years. Sheets of candied sugar so clear you could see through them. A stained-sugar glass display of St. George slaying a dragon, with a rose under both their feet. A chocolate woman swinging her chocolate child around by the hands. Mountaineers climbing a snowy Pikes Peak.

And yet...Robert seemed so depressed.

"We have room," she announced. "However, no stealing the bisque, and no trying to talk the recipe out of either myself or my assistants."

"Done," he said.

"I certainly don't need an extensive amount of table," Jack said, his feet up on the tablecloth in front of him. He'd run out of fans for the moment, although the doors were almost ready to open. "Have six feet or so."

Robert went back down the hallway.

"Where are Donia and Ralph?" Kaley said.

Sam pushed her hands against her stomach; she'd been so tied up in everything else that was going on that she hadn't noticed. But Kaley was already on the phone.

Motive.

Method.

Opportunity.

She just felt awful. The Horrible Internet Troll had lashed out against them.

Or was one of them. No. That was too crazy to even think about. She really didn't touch either one of their lives so strongly that they'd be willing to do...what?

What was going to happen today?

"Donia's not answering," Kaley said. "Trying Ralph."

Sam paced back and forth. She was going to have to get to the bottom of this. The Horrible Internet Troll seemed to be acting out against her friends now, too. She reached down into her cute red purse and pulled out her phone. She was about to dial Donia when she noticed the mail icon at the top of the screen.

It was the Horrible Internet Troll. She just knew it.

It was a bunch of social networking messages from people wishing her luck on the ship—she'd posted a picture of it last night, scratch that, this morning—she scrolled past them, still looking for the message that was going to kick her in the gut.

Instead, she found a message from Donia that said, "Running late—be there at ten."

"Donia's running late," she told Kaley.

"When?"

"Ten."

"I'm not getting any answer from Ralph."

"I don't have a message from him."

Motive.

Method.

Opportunity.

Damn it! It's just jitters, waiting for people to start coming through the door. Stop thinking like that!

The only person who could have reasonably sabotaged the ship was Ralph. What else was there to go wrong? Well, the chocolate could fall off the sides, for one thing, but she'd mixed the chocolate herself. It was either a) hard with a pleasant snap or b) clingily molded to the sides of the ship. It wasn't going to just fall off.

But what if Ralph had done something to the framework?

Why on earth would he? He didn't hate her or anything. He wouldn't make money off her business failing or anything like that. He had no personal stake in it...but if anything happened to the framework, he'd be obsessed over it, trying to find out what had gone wrong.

Maybe he was crazy, subconsciously sabotaging himself.

Sam laughed to herself. If anyone was subconsciously sabotaging themselves, it was her. Maybe she should start recording herself in her sleep and make sure she wasn't sending herself nasty comments out of the depths of her fractured mind.

"Still nothing," Kaley said.

Sam checked her phone again; there was another message.

From her blog.

WHOS GOING 2 HELP U NOW? ROFLMAO.

Sam threw her phone hard, at her purse. "Mothersauce! Mother-effing-sauce!"

Kaley looked at her out of the corner of her eye, then switched off her phone. "Nothing. His phone is turned off."

"I got another message." Sam grabbed the tablecloth in her fists, squeezing it like she was a human potato ricer.

Kaley bent over and picked up the phone. "Do you think—?"

"Do I think it some kind of threat? Yes. Do I think it's some kind of threat against Ralph? I don't know. Yes. I think it is."

The purple cloth started making the heating pad on the table slide toward her.

"Whoa there, missy," Jack said. "You're about to have a very hot accident."

Sam looked down at her hands. "I'll kill him," she said.

"Who?"

"We don't know. That's the problem," Kaley said.

"Him or her," Sam said. "Someone has been threatening my desserts. They've already murdered two sets of soufflés. Two dozen soufflés. Flat. Oh, yes. They mean business. But so do I."

"Threatening your desserts?"

Sam's phone rang, and she snatched it out of Kaley's hands. "Yes?"

"Sam?" Ralph Mooli's voice crackled from the speaker.

"Oh, thank God, Ralph. We were worried about you. Where are you?"

"The hospital," he said.

Sam gasped. "Are you all right?"

"No...the brakes went out on my truck." Ralph lived up in the mountains; this was serious business.

"Oh my God."

"I broke a leg, hon. I won't be in. I'm so sorry."

"Ralph, don't be sorry. I'm so glad you're all right...well, you're not all right, but..." Sam blinked back tears and tried to hide them from her voice. "What was wrong with the brakes? Did you find out? How's the truck? Where did it happen?"

"On the way down the mountain. I don't remember much of it. A guy in a moving van stopped and dragged me back up. He left behind a bunch of boxes on the side of the mountain, and someone ran them off the road. I feel bad about it."

"Oh, Ralph."

"Truck's totaled. I'm lucky to be alive."

The tears did come then, and she sniffed them back. "Oh, Ralph. I feel so bad, getting you mixed up in this. Can I come see you this afternoon?"

"I'll probably be out," he said.

"Out of the hospital?"

"Out out. They have to knock me out and put everything back together. Tomorrow I should be back together again. And awake."

"Oh, Ralph," she said again, feeling like she was an idiot for being unable to think of a single other thing to say. Kaley was squeezing her arm; the front doors were opening, and a line of people was coming through. Robert was setting up a warmer on the table next to Jack. "Everything is just fabulous on our end, Ralph. Don't worry about a single thing over here. I'll see you tomorrow and tell you all about it." She got his room number, wrote it on a napkin, and hung up.

"He's in the hospital for a broken leg," she said. "His brakes went out coming down the mountain."

But Kaley was hurriedly straightening the tablecloth, setting out fliers, and putting the double-boiler on the heating element. "Do you think it was the Soufflé guy?"

Sam shook her head. "I don't want to think about it right now."

"This isn't just a bunch of soufflés."

"I don't know what else to do," Sam snapped. "I need to cook for a while. I'm too confused."

If it wasn't Ralph then who was it?

Unless he hadn't meant to break his own leg. Sam slammed her knuckles into the sides of her head. Kaley squeaked, grabbed Sam's hands and pulled them down, then shoved an apron at her. "All right, all right! Get this on now!"

"But my hat's still dusty!"

"Forget about the hat! They're here! It's time to cook already!"

Chapter 11

Within a few moments, Sam was tempering chocolate on the slab of marble left over from her kitchen remodel and chatting with customers.

"Unfortunately, the person who made the internal structure for the ship couldn't be with us here today. But his name's Ralph Mooli, and if you're interested in custom work, I can give you his number," she told the woman in line in front of her as she dipped the Thai-coconut truffle in the milk chocolate with a fork and rolled it out onto a silicone mat.

The woman reached for the truffle, and Sam pushed her hand toward the row that had already cooled. "You should try the ones that have had a chance to cool a little," she said. She didn't know why, but the customers always wanted the ones she had just made, and after the first two had squished chocolate and filling all over their fingers and dropped them down their fronts, Sam had started watching for their grabby hands a little better.

She glanced over at Robert. He was making these elegant little truffles whose tops were adorned with pretty little fillips of chocolate, each one identical to the next. "You make me so jealous," she called over to him. "Your truffles look perfect."

He shrugged. "Just jellies. Blackberry, blueberry, that kind of thing. Why Thai?"

"Why not?" she asked. "The only strange thing in it is the fish sauce."

The woman stopped with the truffle already in her mouth. Her hand flew to her lips, ready to spit it out.

"Just joking," Sam lied, and the woman smiled, showing chocolate teeth.

Kaley snorted.

She dropped another truffle on the silicone mat, and a hand shot out in front of her, snatching up the warm, gooey truffle and dragging a trail of chocolate behind it on its lace cuffs.

Jack slid back into his chair. Sam looked at Kaley, whose mouth was still open. "He...jumped..."

"I do at least some of my own stunts," Jack mumbled, or at least, that's what Sam thought he mumbled. He wiped his mouth with the back of his hand and put his arm around a woman so her friend could take a picture of them in front of the ship. Fortunately, Jack had allowed Sam to position "Little Jack," as they'd taken to calling him, so that his frustrated state wasn't so obvious in the photographs.

Some of the guests noticed, pointing and laughing, but it didn't seem to be a big deal.

Donia still hadn't arrived, and Dale apparently didn't dare show his face again, with Robert sitting right next to them.

Right next to Kaley.

Well, if it was Robert who was sabotaging everything, he'd better rethink his position. Kaley needed this business to work just as much as Sam did.

Sam's phone beeped at her; she'd received another message. She smiled at the guest in front of her, whose hand was hovering among the different types of chocolate, first aiming toward the Thai, then the bisque (with not many takers), then the white-chocolate blueberry. "Excuse me," Sam told her. "Take the bisque."

A text message was waiting for her. From Harry. She sighed.

"Hope its going well," he said. The phone chirped again. "*it's." No. Grammar-correcting Harry was not the Horrible Internet Troll.

She dropped the phone back in her purse. The woman had taken one of the truffles and put the whole thing in her mouth; Sam couldn't remember how many truffles were in each row, so she wasn't sure which one it had been.

"Omma," the woman said, or *Oh my God*, in sticky truffle-talk.

Ah. The bisque.

Sam nodded. "It doesn't seem like it ought to work, but it does. It has more to do with the chocolate than anything else; I actually use the same chocolate on the Thai truffles, too."

The woman swallowed and grabbed a handful of business cards. "Do you make the soup by itself, too?"

"Sure," Sam said.

"How much for a quart? A gallon? Do you sell soup by the gallon?"

Sam laughed. "I can. Call me after the festival. Did you have an event in mind? Or do you just want to freeze it for later?"

There was a thump behind her as Robert punched the table.

Kaley stuck her tongue out at him. "She's mine. And so is her bisque."

Sam looked at Kaley's truffles. Row upon row of perfection, and the customers who ignored Sam's end of the table gobbled up Kaley's confections readily: lemon cream, peanut butter, rose. The rose ones reminded Sam of, oh, what was it called? Turkish delight. She dipped and scooped her truffles, ignoring the fact that the woman who had liked the bisque truffle was trying her other ones, too. They were only supposed to pick up one per ticket, but Sam hadn't been paying attention. Kaley had, which was probably why they weren't going to go out of business—as long as Sam didn't manage to sink them before they really even got started.

Kaley was the brains, Sam was the other kind of brains. It should work. It really should.

It was funny, really, that they got along as well as they did, with as much as they envied each other and were embarrassed that that other person envied them for something that came naturally.

Then there was a thump behind them, and Sam looked over her shoulder. It was Donia, dropping a camo duffle bag on the floor and wearing workout clothes. Kaley handed her an apron.

"Sorry, guys," she said. "I had to run back up the mountain for something." Donia lived up the mountain, too. "Where's Dale and Ralph?"

Of course she didn't know.

"Ralph's in the hospital," Sam said.

"Oh, no! What happened?"

"His brakes went out as he was coming down this morning."

"Really? He just had those done. Two months ago."

Why would she know that? Sam wondered.

Donia sniffed and cleared her throat into her elbow. "Is he all right? Anything broken?"

"A leg. They're going to have to knock him out to set it and whatever. It sounds pretty bad. But he talked to me on the phone earlier."

"Good," Donia said. "Hey, why aren't the waves moving?"

Sam had a minute of pure horror: they'd completely forgotten about the waves! It was supposed to have been Dale's job to make sure it was running properly and that the levels weren't getting too low, but of course he wasn't going to brave Robert for that.

Kaley shook her head. "We should just leave it off. We don't really need waves, anyway."

"You're just saying that because it was Dale's idea," Donia said cheerfully. "He put Blue Balled back up there after all, didn't he? That's why he's not here."

"You knew about it?" Kaley asked, because Sam's mouth was hanging open.

"Sure! I even helped him out a time or two."

Jack let out a few high-pitched peeps that sounded suspiciously like giggles, then coughed, covering his mouth with his fist, until he got himself back under control. "Ah, the drama," he said, as bright lights flashed around him and he posted in front of his namesake.

Sam rolled her eyes. "Twit."

"Wench."

Donia went behind the ship, where the switch for the motor was.

Kaley said, "Seriously, Donia. Leave it off. The stuff has cooled off...we don't want to burn out the motor."

There was a slurping sound from behind the table. "It's fine." The motor started, and Sam froze, waiting for the smell of burning rubber, sparks, explosions...anything was possible.

Nothing happened.

The motor hummed, and ripples of chocolate-blueberry goodness started to ripple around the ship.

"It doesn't look like anyone's been eating this stuff," Donia remarked. "How about I start passing out sample cups or something?"

Sam frowned. A lot of the pretzels and things that they'd set out for people to dunk in the ocean were missing, but the level of the white-chocolate-blueberry sea hadn't dropped much, and they had a lot of extra made up. "Might as well," she said. "See if Danielle can get you paper cups or something."

"Okay!" Donia stepped back around the ship and looked around for a while, then stood up on a chair. "Danielle!" she shouted, waving both hands over her head.

"Hey, baby," Danielle shouted back, and Sam saw her leave the table with the silk scarves, holding a package. She charged straight into a clump of about twenty people all standing around and sampling some chocolate wine and disappeared, even though she was wearing some high pumps. The clump jostled, and Danielle emerged from the other side, walking almost at top speed.

Sam said, "Watch my station for a second," to Kaley and ducked around the table, grabbing her purse from the floor. She was going to get that scarf before Danielle bought them all.

· · · • · • • • · · ·

A few minutes later, Sam had the package with the scarf in her purse (she didn't dare wear it; she'd just dip it in her chocolate) and was back at her station, happily dipping a row of Thai truffles.

Dipping truffles was a mindless, soothing task, even though it annoyed her that she couldn't get the swirls on top to match up perfectly or blobs of chocolate from congealing at the bottom of hers. *Om*, she thought. *Yuuuum.* This is my meditation. My stress relief for the last few days.

She actually enjoyed talking to the guests, as long as she knew she couldn't trust them farther than she could throw a hot truffle. It was nice talking to people who loved what you were doing, even if they didn't entirely agree with your philosophy of making truffles as surprises instead of just comfort food to stuff in your face on a bad day.

And the unpleasant ones? All she had to do to keep a smile on her face was imagine them with a face full of post-chocolate-overdose zits.

Donia was bringing over more guests than ever by passing out the ocean dip.

Hm…ocean dip. Maybe she should call her bisque truffles "ocean dip" truffles. No, because then someone with a seafood allergy would pick one up and have a reaction, and Sam would just kill herself. Maybe she should have her customers fill out a questionnaire before she let them try anything. That way, she could make the perfect recommendation…

Danielle was standing next to Jack, having their picture taken by someone with a professional camcorder, with a big microphone on it and everything. A woman with the most thoroughly blonde hair that Sam had ever seen in real life was standing next to them, asking questions.

Sam stared at them, but didn't see any news program logo. It must have been the friend that Jack had mentioned earlier.

She sniffed. Something smelled wrong. Smoke? Did she smell smoke?

No...she looked around and failed to see any plumes of smoke or anything. She couldn't tell what it was...she couldn't really smell it, but it wasn't smoke.

Other chocolatiers were looking around, too, from place to place. Robert was smelling his hands, bending over his bain-marie and smelling his chocolate.

Of course! The smell snapped into familiarity. Somewhere in this room, chocolate was burning. Sam bent over and smelled her two pots of chocolate, then checked Kaley's. Nothing. Someone's water had run out. They'd notice in a minute.

Donia came by and said, "You're supposed to turn in your truffles for the contest now. Hand them over."

Sam checked a clock: *noon!* "Oh, thank you. I'd completely forgotten." Sam dished up five of each truffle on a platter and handed it over. "You're a lifesaver."

The smell of burning chocolate was getting worse, and all the cooks were lifting up dripping pans, shaking their heads, and looking around. Even the guests were starting to notice.

Sam looked around the room, then tried to catch Kaley's attention, but she was talking to Robert. Sam glanced back at the interview as Danielle hugged Jack so hard that he winced.

Behind him, however...it was like a nightmare come true. Something was wrong with the ship. The side of it was drooping, sloughing away from the metal framework.

Sam shoved Kaley out of the way and ran over to the ship. "Get out of the way!" she shouted. "It's sinking!"

Which, when she thought back on it later, might not have been exactly the best thing to say.

She ran behind the ship, grabbed the electrical cord, and yanked it out of the socket.

Sparks started to shoot out from the cannons with loud pops, and some of the guests said, "Oooh," like it was some kind of firework or something.

A loud bang echoed through the room, and the back of the ship blew open, exploding fragments of chocolate throughout the room and throwing a brief flash of fire out the hatches. The rigging, twisted candyfloss, started on fire in patches, spreading to the leathery, dried marshmallow sails dusted with cocoa powder.

Then the front of the ship, which was supported by a one-inch pipe welded to a metal plate, started to tilt downward. The pirates and the undead skeletons slid forward across the deck. A few of them tipped over the rail, past the mermaid, and clattered on the table.

"Nooooooo!" Sam cried.

The sank further, then suddenly plowed through the lined box holding the sea, splitting it wide open, and onto the table.

The blue chocolate ocean spilled over the side of the table and onto the floor. The pipe holding up the back of the ship snapped, and the back of the ship splashed into the white blueberry chocolate, splattering it everywhere.

"Grab it before it tips over!" Sam shouted.

The ship leaned toward Danielle and Jack Malpeque.

Great, she thought. *Great way to start a business...by killing your biggest supporter and a movie star.*

She saw Robert try to grab the front of the ship. "Ow!" he yelled, jerking back his hands as though the ship were smoldering hot—which was exactly what it smelled like.

Jack yelled, "All hands abandon ship!" and pushed Danielle out of the way...straight at Sam as she ran around to the front of the ship.

Sam kept them from falling to the floor, somehow, and watched as the ship started to roll toward Jack.

Jack ducked; the side of the ship slammed into the table he'd been using to sign pictures on, and Robert's bain-marie, complete with three types of chocolate, flew into the air, splashing near-boiling chocolate straight toward Sam and Danielle.

Sam shoved Danielle one way and fell over the other way, covering her face with her forearms.

It was all so fast.

She rolled to her feet. Her arms were covered with burning patches of hot water and chocolate, and her front was soaked and splattered. The smell of burning chocolate was getting worse.

She looked around for Danielle, who seemed similarly splattered but not seriously hurt.

Kaley was still standing at her station, frozen in place, saying, "Robert? Robert?"

The table creaked and started to slide to one side as one of the legs went out from under it. The weight of the ship was knocking it down, twisting it out of shape...Suddenly, Jack rolled out from under the table.

"Man down, man down!" he shouted.

Kaley unfroze, running in the worst possible direction—straight for the table. "Robert?"

The leg went out from under the table, and it dropped down toward the floor—stopping short with a groan.

"Robert!" Now Danielle was running, too. Jack grabbed her arm and kept her from charging under the table, but there was no one to catch Kaley.

She knelt by the side of the table, trying to pull Robert out from underneath as the ship slid down the table toward them, dragging the tablecloth with it and scraping noisily.

"Kaley!" Sam shouted.

Kaley saw the ship coming, squatted down, and slammed into the side of the table.

She didn't knock the table over or anything requiring superhuman strength. All she did was tilt the table.

The gigantic burning chocolate pirate ship tilted with it, crashing into the Sweet Granadilla Catering table. Their table went ass over teakettle and threw chocolate, hot water, and filling sky high—but not toward the guests.

The giant ship was finally on the floor, chocolate ocean everywhere, guests with wide eyes tasting the chocolate on their shirts and nodding at each other. The marshmallow sails had been nicely toasted in spots, blackened in others, and the bare wires of the rigging gleamed black under their burnt-sugar coating.

Blue-Balled was tangled up in some rigging that had come loose, and swung next to the mermaid, his face butting her breasts.

Kaley pushed the table off Robert. "Are you okay?"

He groaned, and she knelt beside him.

Jack grabbed Danielle, dipped her, and gave her a big smooch as she came up again. Cameras flashed. He must be grateful just to be alive.

Sam felt her world falling apart. She wanted to die. She wanted to call up everyone who had ever believed in her and apologize, and then she wanted to just die.

She'd almost killed someone. She had no idea of what she was doing, and it was all her fault. Her stomach clenched. Her brain went around and around in circles: *I could have killed someone. I could have killed someone.*

"I'm so sorry," she said. And then, somewhere, under all that mess of chocolate, her phone rang. *Bad Romance.*

Harry.

Sam rubbed her hands on her apron, not sure whether she was making things better or worse, and walked around the melting ship to the side of the table. Her purse was completely splattered, but her phone had survived. She answered it.

"Harry?"

"What's wrong?" he said.

"I think I'm going to be arrested for attempted murder." She hung up and tossed the phone at her purse. It bounced off and skidded into a pile of chocolate.

CHAPTER 12

The first ambulance left with Robert and Kaley, who told the EMTs bare-facedly that she was his fiancée. Nobody argued with her. Kaley glared at Sam, who hung her head, as the doors closed on them and they raced away.

"Cheer up," Donia said. "He'll be in the same hospital as Ralph. You can visit them both at the same time."

Sam sobbed into her hands, which had finally started to hurt from the flying, burning chocolate that had splattered them.

The other EMTs were checking over the guests making sure they weren't burnt. They'd already caught up with Jack and Danielle, who were both looking a little patchy. If she didn't escape soon, they were going to stick bandages on her, too, even though she didn't want any. Didn't deserve them.

"Good grief," Donia said. "Stop acting like this is all your fault, you ninny."

"It is all my fault," she said. "If I hadn't screwed up on the ship..."

"Screwed what up on the ship?" Donia asked. "You didn't have anything to do with it. It was clearly electrical. You should be pissed at Dale, not blaming yourself."

"What?" Sam asked.

"Well? Wasn't the wave machine the only part of the whole set-up that was electrical? That was the only thing that could have possibly happened. Dale was a dumbass and did something that shorted out the wiring. The frame conducted the electricity, which fried the chocolate and everything else. And the heat must have messed up the solder that Ralph used. See? A perfectly reasonable explanation."

Sam wiped her face. "But everything about this ship is my responsibility. It's going to be in all the papers. How I almost killed Robert Langoustine and Jack Malpeque. I'm useless. This whole company is useless. I should just quit."

"Ah-ah," Donia said. "I don't want to hear you going down that road. There is no tragedy so overwhelming that you can't bounce back from it, if you put your mind to it. I'll pretend you didn't say any of those things."

Sam let the EMTs catch up to her and put all kinds of bandages on her arms. Miraculously, she'd managed not to burn her face except for one patch under her chin. They checked her chest, too, which was embarrassing, but apparently her clothes and apron had managed to protect her enough that she just needed to put burn cream on it.

Just as she was pulling her shirt down, Harry showed up, parking right behind the ambulance and jumping out.

As he ran to her, she said, "It's all right. I'm just being melodramatic again, as usual. I'm not going to be arrested. It was all an accident. But I think I'm out of business now. Who would want to hire me?"

Harry grabbed her and hugged her.

"Ouch."

He backed off. "Sorry. You're burned? How did you get burned? What happened? Why are you going out of business? What's going on?"

Sam sighed. She didn't want to deal with Harry and his incessant questions; she should have just let the phone ring through. But it was too late to take it back now. "Harry, just shut up."

He clamped his lips together and looked angry.

Well, too bad. She hadn't asked him to come, and, in fact, didn't want him around. Not really.

"The ship started on fire, some of the welds must have broke, and the whole thing tipped over. They think Robert might have broken some ribs, but everyone else is pretty much okay. And it's all my fault."

He shook his head.

"Oh, yeah. And Ralph Mooli totaled his truck and broke his leg coming down the mountain this morning, so I feel bad about that, too."

"You can't—!" Harry snapped off his words again and walked around in a circle, taking breaths. "I'm glad you're all right."

"Mostly all right."

"Whatever. Where's Dale?"

"What?"

"Dale. I want to go look at the ship. See what went wrong."

"Dale, ah, Dale ran off."

"Just now?"

"No, earlier. Long story. He didn't even turn the machine on. Kaley told Donia not to do it, but she wouldn't listen."

Harry shook his head. "I saw pictures of that frame. It should not have been possible for it to tip over like that."

"Donia thought the solder might have melted."

"No way," he said. "No way." He was still pacing.

Sam wondered whether she should tell him about the messages she'd received. Maybe not. They'd just set him off. He'd be so angry that he couldn't even speak.

And he'd be angry at her.

Well, she deserved it, didn't she?

Sam sighed. "Harry, there's more."

"What?" he snapped at her, and she took a step back.

"Sorry. I'm not trying to be scary," he said.

It didn't matter. "I got a couple of messages this morning. Threatening ones. On my blog."

Harry froze. "What? Did you call the cops? Why aren't they here now? Where—"

"Harry!"

He stopped. This was going better than most of the arguments they'd had for years. Incredible.

She hunted around until she found her chocolate-covered purse and pulled out her phone, opened up the first comment, and handed him the phone.

He read it.

She found the other one, opened it.

"I don't understand," he said.

"Me, either."

"Logically...It should be me," he said.

"That's what I thought at first," she admitted. "I mean, part of me still wants to suspect you. But I knew it wasn't you. I was just mad."

"That's why you tracked me down at the brewery."

She nodded. "But you were out of town the first time. When the soufflés fell."

"That was just a bunch of soufflés."

Sam said, "How would you feel if someone were fooling around with your beer? And then said, 'Well, at least they didn't dick around with something important, like the money.'"

Harry actually bared teeth. "Point taken. But."

"Yeah. But."

"You checked out Robert?" he asked.

"I don't think it was him."

"But you checked him out? Made sure he had an alibi for the time?"

"No," Sam said. "He didn't do it. Because now he has the hots for Kaley, and there's no way he would have set things up to get crushed under a table by a chocolate ship."

"That doesn't make sense," Harry said. "You know what would make sense?"

Sam rolled her eyes. "Okay, okay, I get it. I'll find out where he was during the soufflé class."

"We have to go look at that boat."

They went back inside. Chocolate tracks were everywhere, ground into the carpet.

The cleaning staff is going to hate me, too, Sam thought. A couple of hotel staff tried to keep them out of the room, but Sam led Harry down the back hallways and let herself into the room using her key.

She hadn't seen any cop cars, but there were a couple of policemen there, standing next to the ship, and a couple of people in blue suit things over their clothes, poking around.

She heard the word "gunpowder."

"What?" she said. She walked over to the ship, where two technicians in white suits were bending over the table with the "ocean" base. The blueberry-white chocolate sauce had gone all over the place; dark chocolate smeared everywhere that the ship had slid and scraped. The blue from the blueberries was going to be a bitch to get out. Sam squinted her eyes shut, crossed her fingers, and hoped that the hotel insurance would cover it. Otherwise she was screwed.

Who was she kidding? She was screwed. She was just screwed. She'd be lucky if she ever cooked in this town again.

She opened her eyes again to see what the technicians were talking about. They pointed at the metal plate that had been the base of the support on the front of the ship, their fingers moving to the left, to the right. Part of the dark chocolate covering the plate had been removed, and a few flags were stuck into the chocolate as markers of some kind.

The cleaned area of the plate showed a line of scratches all the way across it, a circular area where the post had been, and one twisted, flattened piece of metal. The circular area showed arcs and blobs where the welding had been, and was shinier than the rest of the plate, even the parts that had been cleaned.

"I'm sorry, miss," one of the technicians said. "You're not supposed to be here. You're going to have to step away."

Sam walked over to where Harry, Danielle, and Jack were standing back by the wall. "Sam!" Danielle shouted.

"Oh, Danielle," Sam said. "I'm so sorry. I don't know what went wrong."

Danielle squeezed her hand as she stood next to her. "Honey, you don't know the half of it."

"What?"

"They think they found gunpowder in the cannons."

"Dale," Sam said.

Danielle nodded. "That was my thought, too. But it sounds like the charges were big. So big that—well. Beyond the level of Dale's stupid pranks, anyway. Where is he?"

"No idea," Sam said. "I'll try calling him."

She pulled out the phone again and dialed, held it to her ear.

Dale answered after a few rings. "Am I still in the doghouse?" he said.

"Dale, did you set up..." Sam looked around, wondering how much she should say. They probably shouldn't be in the ballroom, anyway, if there was going to be a police investigation. "Dale, nevermind. I gotta go."

It was shitty, suspecting your own friends. But she couldn't seem to help it.

The cops released Harry pretty quickly.

But they had a lot to talk about with Sam. At least it wasn't as bad as being interrogated by Harry.

She told the officer, Detective Parsons, everything she could remember, and showed him the threatening messages she'd received. He had her forward them to him, and she was glad that she'd kept the others.

Finally, he'd asked her if she suspected anyone.

She said, "Honestly, I was feeling so paranoid that I suspected everyone."

He nodded. "Understandable. But was there anyone in particular?"

Shit, she thought. *Who haven't I suspected?*

"No," she said. "And now—it seems so serious. That ship could seriously have hurt someone."

"Who benefits if something happens to you?"

"My friend Kaley, I suppose." It was out of her mouth before she could stop herself. "She'd have the business all by herself. But that's just stupid."

"Why is that?" he asked, patiently.

Sam tried to think of the most cold-hearted, practical reason that Kaley would never do anything like this. "She'd have no idea how to figure out how to blow up the ship, for one thing. And for another, well, I'm the one who talked her into quitting her job and working with me. Why would she want our catering business to fail?"

She was just making it worse, wasn't she? Making it sound like Kaley would be better off if the business failed, so she could go back to working for a company again. Job security.

The officer wrote a few things down on his pad and said, "Can you tell me how to contact Dale Lugano? We still need to get a statement from him, I think."

She gave him Dale's phone number, and he let her go. She couldn't help but be relieved that it was going to be him who had to talk to Dale, not her.

Her phone rang. Dale's number.

She ignored it.

· · · • · • — · • · ·

Of course it was in the papers and on TV. And all over the Internet.

It was a good thing that she'd planned ahead for tragedy, because she felt immensely comforted by the fact that she had everything all ready to go when she got home. The message light on the house phone was flashing. It rang as she came in the door.

It was some idiot wanting to talk to her, a total stranger who claimed to be from some website she'd never heard of. She unplugged the phone and wondered how hard it would be for people to get her cell phone number. Well, she'd find out.

She watched the news and drank a gin and tonic; they played the clip where Jack had bussed Danielle, both of them covered in chocolate. And then they played the interview that the blonde woman had taken from Jack.

There was one sound bite that got stuck in her head. They'd taken it totally out of context. In the full interview, he'd said, "I just love that [beep] ship. And Sam, she's just [beep] nuts." They'd trimmed it down to "And Sam, she's just [beep] nuts" and stuck it with a picture of him looking worried, like she had deliberately tried to kill him or something.

After a while, she finally felt brave enough to check her website, which had been mentioned on the TV program. Sam had no doubt that by morning she would be portrayed as a sex maniac with a kink for food and a craving for death.

She logged in. Ugh. She had three hundred emails, with more pouring in every time the screen refreshed. At least her ad revenues were going to go up.

She opened up a new post and started to type...but remembered she wasn't supposed to talk about this stuff until the police could find out more. Also, she was tipsy already and tending toward drunk. She took another sip of her second gin and tonic. Mmm, cold and delicious.

Her fingers hovered over the keyboard for what seemed like hours. She had no idea what to say, what not to say. In the end, she typed, "I'll talk about this as soon as I can, I promise. Please hold emails and comments until I can get things together," turned off comments, and posted it.

Then she read through the rest of the comments, spending just enough time to open them and make sure they weren't more threats. Lots of support, a few jerks deriding her. No LOLs.

· · · ● · ● · · · ·

Kaley didn't call, and didn't call, so Sam called her. Not at home, but on her cell phone.

"Hey...Sam," Kaley said.

"Hi. Are you okay? How is Robert?"

"Oh, he's okay. A couple of broken ribs. But okay."

"Kaley, I'm so sorry. This is all my fault."

"Sam, shut it."

Sam shut it. She was waiting for the worst: for Kaley to tell her that they had to close down the business, that there was no chance in hell that they were ever going to work together. It wasn't going to work out. It would be like breaking up with someone. Almost as bad as breaking her marriage. Maybe worse; Harry wasn't going to be there to hold her together.

"I'm the one who's sorry, Sam. It was Dale."

"Dale? Dale did that?"

"Who else could it be?"

Sam wasn't sure what to say—say what she really thought and defend Dale; keep her mouth shut and let him get ripped apart by his sister; agree with Kaley and try to rebuild their business...

But Kaley hadn't finished talking. "I know he's an idiot. And I'm sure he didn't mean for things to turn out the way they did. He's always like that, Sam. Always. But he'll never apologize, and he'll never take responsibility. It was meant as a joke, so fuck you if you can't take a joke. He likes you, so he plays his little jokes on you. And never thinks about what's going to happen if anything goes wrong."

"You don't think he sent those emails, do you?"

Kaley didn't answer, and Sam started to wonder if she should hang up or not. "Um, Kaley? Are you still there?"

"I don't know," Kaley said. "If he was behind the soufflés somehow...why send the threats? But who else would know? It doesn't sound like him. Especially since this guy isn't bragging about it afterward. Only before. Why send the threats? Why not just…do these things?"

"It could be more than one person," Sam said.

"Yeah, but why? And who would know what Dale was planning?"

Why?

Why would anyone threaten her desserts?

Suddenly, it crashed down on her, and she gripped her phone.

"Sam? You okay?"

"Someone is threatening our desserts, Kaley. It isn't Dale. Because how do you bribe Dale?"

"With food," Kaley said. "It's the only thing that let me survive high school."

"Exactly. I can see Dale screwing around and getting in deeper than he thought he would. I can see him setting up a joke and messing it up like that. But threatening food? You know he had to have been bribing people from outside the ballroom at the Rose to bring him truffles. He probably had some kooky story cooked up for it, too."

"Maybe," Kaley said. "Seriously, Sam, you're scaring me."

"I'm going to get whoever this is," Sam said. "I'm going to set a trap."

Chapter 13

Easier said than done.

Sam waded through website after website detailing classic confidence schemes. Some of them sounded easy enough; some of them had so many technical terms that she gave up on them before she'd finished reading them all the way through. But none of them seemed to give her what she wanted, which was an easy way to find her troll.

After several hours, she rubbed her eyes and tried to blink away the dryness, but there wasn't anything she could really blink with; her eyelids stuck onto her eyes, making clicking sounds as she forced them open and closed.

She logged off, turned off her screen, and went downstairs.

It had been two days; it was time to stop being a drunk and put her big-girl pants on (literally).

She plugged in the phone and drank a glass of water, skimming through the messages.

Detective Parsons had left her a message: The collapse of the ship hadn't been an accident; the ship had been deliberately rigged to fall off its supports. He was also unable to reach Dale and wanted to know if she had any ideas where he might be.

Later on, Dale had left her a message.

"Sam, this is Dale. I just wanted to let you know that I'm sorry. I...found out what happened. I just want you to know that I didn't do it. I never would have wrecked that ship. Never. All I did was switch the figures. That was just too damned funny, you know? I hope you're not still mad about that, and I hope you believe me. I don't know what happened. I really don't. Everything seemed fine when I left last night. You were there. Did you tell them that? That you were still there when I left?

"Anyway, I'm not going to answer my phone for a couple of days, until things settle down. I know you'll understand. Tell Kaley—shit. Well, don't tell her anything. I'm sure she's already blaming me for everything. But hey! From what I hear, it sounds like things are working out for the best for her, anyway. She went off in that ambulance with the chef, anyway. Too bad for you. I thought you had the hots for him, but first come, first serve, right? Ha. Serve."

Sam wrinkled up her face.

"Anyway, I'm sorry I wasn't there to help, and I'm sorry if something I did contributed to that train wreck. I can't believe that the motor we were using to make waves in the blueberry sauce did all that. There just isn't enough energy. I'll try calling again later, maybe on Wednesday, if you're still talking to me. Um. Bye."

The machine beeped, and Sam's finger hovered over the delete button. She left it, and kept skimming through messages until she reached the end, then called Detective Parsons. She couldn't figure out how to play the message for him without hanging up on him (which she did several times), so he agreed to come over and take a recording of the recording.

So. Going with the assumption that it wasn't Dale, how was she going to catch the bastard, whoever it was? Should she bring the cops in on it?

She snorted as she opened the fridge and rummaged around. Oh, there were things to eat, and she could have whipped up any number of things out of the pantry. Nevertheless, she stood there and could think of nothing that sounded good.

"No wonder people drink themselves to death," she said. "They can't think of what to eat."

Well, as long as there wasn't anything she wanted to do, she might as well come up with the things she least wanted to do and get them over with.

Immediately, she thought of Harry.

Yep, she thought. He's the last person on my list. But I should go see Ralph and Robert, too.

After a few minutes, she decided that she was going to see Ralph and Robert and leave Harry until later.

Much later, she hoped.

· · · · • · • · · ·

"Hello, angel," Ralph said, one leg propped up in the air and reading through a magazine. "Where are my cookies?"

"I didn't bring any," she said. "I didn't feel like cooking."

"There's a first."

"Oh, Ralph—"

He raised his hand. "Don't apologize for any of it. That's just silly. I've heard that the frame was damaged somehow."

"That's what Detective Parsons told me. Sabotaged."

"I met him. He wanted to know where I went off the road, so he could get a look at the skid marks, if any, et cetera."

"Did he say it was related?"

"Oh, no," Ralph said. "How could he? I could have a reporter in my pocket and be ready to sue him. But he certainly suggested it, in a perfectly deniable kind of way. I think he was trying to find out whether I suspected anyone of hating me."

"Does anyone? Hate you?"

Ralph smiled, one corner of his mouth up, the other down. "I'm sure there's a few casinos that have my name on their list, and more than a few exes. But no, no one enough to make me run my truck off the road. Or to wreck a chocolate-covered pirate ship. They'd be more likely to hold me at knifepoint unless I turned the whole thing over. What happened to it, anyway? Did it get eaten?"

"No, more's the pity." Sam sat beside the bed, collapsed over the acid in her stomach. The weave of the chair seemed too rough. Didn't people who were sick need smoother chairs? She scratched her fingers back and forth over the seat.

"You can go now, you know." Ralph waved his hand. "You're still feeling far too guilty to have any kind of decent conversation with me."

"I'm sorry."

"See?" He grinned at her. His stubbly white hair was getting too long, making his face look different. Or maybe it was the pain and stress that was getting to him.

"Do you need anything taken care of at your place?" she asked. "Your plants or anything?"

"Thank you, sweetie, but you'll have to talk to Danielle about that and see if she wants any help. I believe she has taken charge. I gave her a detailed list of instructions last night, and I don't feel like writing them out or talking them over again."

"What do you want to talk about?"

"Tell me how it went, of course. Danielle was telling me all about it."

She laughed up at him. "If she's told you all about it, then you don't need anything else from me."

"She wasn't there for all of it. And I'm bored. So tell me." He tossed the magazine toward the bedside table and missed. The magazine slapped onto the floor.

"Do you want some coffee or anything? Water? Tea?"

"Tea…" he said. "No, bring me some water. They're bound to have nothing but underbrewed Lipton, and they'll be annoyed that you sent them after that. At least the water here is good. Water. With ice."

She grinned and jumped out of the chair. "As you wish."

Ralph mock-frowned at her, and she skipped out of the room. She always felt better when there was something she could do.

· · · · • · • · · · ·

She knocked on Robert's open door just as he was groaning and trying to rearrange his pillow.

"What?" he snapped.

"It's me, Sam," she said.

"You ridiculous thing, go away," he answered.

She clenched her jaw and stood up straighter. The hell if she was going to apologize to him.

"No," she said.

"What do you want?"

"At first I wanted to visit you and see if there was anything you needed, but now I just want to annoy you." She walked into the room, dropped her purse on the floor, sat in the rough chair, and put her feet up on the edge of the bed.

"I need to be alone."

"Are you sleeping with Kaley?" she asked.

"It's none of your business." He'd turned around and around so much that his hospital nightgown was in a twist around him, and she could see the bandages and bruises on his side. He jerked the blankets up further.

Sam said, "Yes, actually, it is. My business." Which, really, it wasn't, but she wasn't about to let him think that she thought that. Hopefully, he'd tell her, just to get her to leave him alone. Although if he pressed the call button, he could have her tossed out of his hospital room in a second.

"No," he said.

"No, you aren't sleeping with her, or no, it's none of my business?" Sam kicked the side of the bed a little, jiggling it. She'd suffered far too many insults from this man to put up with crap from him now.

He grunted. "Stop that."

"Talk."

"No, I'm not sleeping with her. I'm working on it, though." He smiled a little. "She reminds me of my mother."

"Yuck," Sam said. "She is—"

"Oh, shut up. She's constant. Consistent. Utterly disciplined in dealing with errant geniuses."

"I am not a—"

"I wasn't talking about you. Her brother. You should have seen the homicidal look in her eyes when she talked about him. I wouldn't be surprised if he were dead in a fortnight." He started to put his hands behind his head and winced. "I can't stretch out, I can't get comfortable. She's thoughtful and sincere."

"Look, I've known Kaley forever. You couldn't possibly know her well enough to make a comprehensive list of even her best qualities. What makes you think you're worth her time? You're an insulting pig who's going to cheat on her within a month."

"No, my dear. My entire career with women has been in preparation for her."

Sam rolled her eyes. "Really? How many women have you slept with? Or tried to sleep with? A hundred? Two hundred? How long ago was it that you were drooling all over me?"

"Don't be insulted."

"I'm not. We're talking about Kaley here. You're a slut. Why should I stand by and let you seduce her?"

"She will bear my children."

"You are such an ass!" Sam laughed. "You are the least convincing pig I've ever known."

"But I have the *most* delectable bacon."

She couldn't help it. She laughed again. "Well, all right. Lord knows that I've cried on her shoulder enough to be willing to repay the favor when you inevitably break her heart."

"I will not."

"Either you'll dump her, or you'll cheat on her, or, God help her, you'll stay faithful, and that will make her the most miserable of all."

He pinched his eyebrows together and tried to look hurt. "Really? What a cruel thing to say."

Sam looked at him through the corner of her eye, pulled out a nail file, and started cleaning under her nails. "And if you steal her away from my business, I'll kill you."

"How catty."

She stabbed the nail file through the sheet near his hand. He jerked his hand back.

"Sssss. You should have seen what I did to your sous-chef after he pinched my ass the second time."

Robert cleared his throat and tried to shift his weight a little bit away from her. "I did, actually. It was obvious exactly which kind of fork you had used, too. You're lucky he didn't press charges."

Sam leaned back. "You know, I guess I am. Although it wouldn't have been too hard to come up with something to hold against him so he'd withdraw them."

Robert shook his head. "The two of us, we would have been...delightfully evil together. But I'm afraid it's too late for me. I have sworn to become a better man."

"Good luck with that."

"Have you heard how the judging went?" he asked as she picked up her purse and stood.

"No. I assumed they canceled it, after all that. God, I must have lost them a fortune."

Robert reached over to the bedside table and handed her the newspaper. "I realize that you have been grieving for whatever it is that you evil women grieve for, feeling sorry for yourselves, but I wouldn't hold that against yourself."

The headline read, MALPEQUE DIPS AT CHOCOLATE FESTIVAL and showed a split picture—on the left, Jack was dipping Danielle; on the right, he was smooching her while she had this ridiculous grin on her face. They were both splattered with chocolate.

The article said almost nothing about the collapse of the ship. It *did* mention who won the truffle contest, someone from Fort Collins who Sam didn't know, with a boring-ass *chocolate fudge truffle.*

Oh come *on.*

The newspaper article did mention that a lot of people were quoted as saying that they enjoyed the festival and would be back next year.

And that was it.

"What?" Sam said. "But the ship meltdown was all over TV last night. Surely they know."

Robert shrugged. "Most of the article was written before the reporter ever attended the event, if they attended at all. No, don't be concerned. Danielle told me that most of the guests got a good laugh about the shipwreck."

"They weren't laughing," Sam said.

"Would you even have noticed?"

Probably not. "It wasn't something to laugh about; look at you!"

"Yes, and they'll send me home in the morning. They just wanted to make sure that I didn't have a concussion or any swelling in the head—ah, ah." He swayed his huge, gnarled, toughened chef's finger at her. "Say nothing about the size of my head."

The finger that had dipped in a thousand sauces, she thought, then laughed at herself, catching the double entendre inside her own head. "I wasn't about to."

"Liar. Now go."

She finished leaving. Robert was fussing with his pillow as she softly closed the door. She felt oddly better for picking a fight with her old boss. Maybe they could be friends someday, colleagues instead of intimidated student and haughty teacher. Maybe they were already, and she just hadn't noticed.

·········

And then it was time to see Harry. Sam got in the SUV and drove to the brewery, parking around the side (and out of view) out of habit. She walked around to the back of the building to make sure his SUV was there. It was. She peeked inside and saw that it was in its normal neat-but-dirty state. Harry hated to leave trash lying around, but he didn't mind an inch of gravel on the floor or so much gray dust on the ceiling that the only undusted spot was in a streak where his head brushed as he got out of the vehicle.

It was cold outside, so she went in, not bothering to let the air out of his tires this time. If he had to run away, well, that was his option.

The bartender, Brady, was pouring a big pint of pale as the door closed behind her.

Sam frowned. "That's not for me, is it?"

"Yep. If you want me to answer any questions, you have to drink it. The entire pint. New IPA."

"I don't like IPA," she whined.

"Sure you do. You just don't know it yet."

"I don't liiiiiike it."

"Tough." Brady, truth be told, was a hundred percent on Harry's side of things. He'd been divorced when he was younger, about five years ago, and still wasn't over it yet, seeing women as evil beings who would mind-control you at the drop of a hat so it wasn't perfectly obvious when they weren't cheating on you. Brady was probably most of the reason that Harry had actually made it out the door and moved into the apartment above the brewery, as hot and airless and awful as it was (it didn't even have a hot plate, the one time she'd been in it).

Nevertheless, she liked Brady and couldn't hold it against him. And he didn't hold it against her that Harry had left her; after all, she hadn't cheated on Harry, just been impossible to live with.

She sat on the stool nearest the door, trying not to elbow the man next to her, who held up his mostly-empty glass full of something more gold-colored than not. Probably an amber of some kind. She checked the chalkboard to see what he was drinking. "You're serving honey mead? And I have to drink IPA?"

"Have one of each." Brady waved his hand across the top of the taps. "On me. But first you have to drink the IPA."

She pulled the pint across the bar, listening to the glass rumbling against the wood grain, and took a sip. She glanced up at the chalkboard to find out what she was drinking, and Brady put his hand across her face.

"Just drink." His hand was clammy and smelled like lime.

She sighed and drank. "Grapefruit. Almost like retsina. Don't even ask me what kind of hops these are, because I don't know. Honey? Walnuts? Whoa, the walnuts really popped out there. Something else. I don't know?"

"Good enough," he said, taking his hand off her face.

It wasn't bad, actually. What she really hated about IPA was the extreme hoppiness, but this was more balanced, in an unbalanced kind of way. She sighed. It was almost like Harry had been working on an IPA specifically for her. The fact that "Crazy X IPA" was chalked on the board was also a clue.

"Well? Aren't you going to finish that?" Brady asked.

Sam leaned on one elbow. "I can't just drink it all down in one gulp, Brady. I'll pass out." Damn it, the beer was making her feel maudlin already, thinking over good times with Harry. She drew nonsense patterns on the bartop until Brady picked up her pint and stuck a coaster underneath it.

"It'll get warm."

"It's good enough beer that it'll drink warm," she said without looking up. She drank some more. Now would be the perfect time to say something nostalgic and sentimental about Harry, like, *I just can't get over him*, or *I wish he were still mine*, and then give up and drive home.

Except if she finished the beer, she'd be here for an hour or more. She'd heard that Harry had added food lately, and she wanted to check it out. In a totally non-threatening, non-judgmental way. Right. "I'm hungry. What's good?"

Brady hummed, walked off (he was wearing boots) into the kitchen, and came back with something that smelled sharp, full of vinegar. She looked up at it. Salad with strawberries and red onions and balsamic vinegar. "Interested to know how well that goes with the stout, thank you," he said. The salad plate was too big for her to eat it at the bar (she'd just keep elbowing the guy beside her), so she picked up everything but the coaster and went back to one of the big overstuffed chairs to eat.

They were stained and smelled like beer. So be it. She plopped down in one and waited until the leather hissed and deflated, settling her into the perfect spot. She put the beer on a tin-topped table beside her and ate.

The salad wasn't original, but she had to admire the thought behind it. Fruit on a salad. She and Harry had been fighting about that for a while.

Maybe that was the real reason that Harry had left her. She'd tried to force one too many new ideas down his throat.

She crunched her way through her salad and drank her way through the IPA, not seeing Harry anywhere. He'd probably already escaped, run off in the SUV.

What did she even need to talk to him for?

She didn't want to think about it.

She stabbed a piece of spinach viciously, nailing it to the bottom of the bowl with a clink that echoed off the wall at her. She was going to think about it, damn it.

She wanted to ask him for help.

She had been determined to handle this on her own, in her own way. Look what it had got her. Two hurt friends and no answers. Probably more than two hurt friends.

This time, though, she wasn't going to drop it in his lap and walk away. She was going to stand with her head high and ask him for help, but only on the things that he was actually better at than she was. She wasn't going to ask him to do everything for her.

What was she going to even ask him?

She sighed and swirled a strawberry in some balsamic. No idea.

Brady stopped by. Somehow, she'd emptied her glass. "Mead?" he asked. She shook her head.

He took her glass and went away. She mentally cursed herself for telling him not to bring any more. But it was Brady; he'd just assume that the merrier, the better. She finished the last of her salad and stood up. She'd just hide in her SUV for an hour and then drive home. It was a stupid idea. She'd just...

Wait. A giveaway. She could put up a giveaway on her blog; if the Horrible Internet Troll entered, she could just have him win and get some kind of contact information out of it.

Nobody could possibly be that stupid.

But what could it hurt?

Tickets to one of her classes? No, she didn't want to do that. What if someone out of town won?

She put down her bowl and smacked herself on her head just as Harry brought her another IPA.

"That good?" he said.

She opened her mouth to say exactly what she thought about it, not to be mean or anything, but just to give him her honest opinion. "They went well enough together that I passed up the mead," she said instead.

"I see that."

"It was a trap, wasn't it?"

"In a way, in a way. A hope. If I can get you to drink a whole pint of IPA, it must be good."

"Nice name."

"Well." He looked pleased with himself.

She took the fresh glass away from him, and he sat next to her, another IPA in hand. The leather of the other chair whooshed air as he settled. They both drank.

She wanted, more than anything else, to let him know that she missed him, that it delighted her that he was playing around with flavors like this. How silly was that? But they were her feelings, and the things she wanted. Having him leave her had made her feel stupid and shallow, like she had to be happy every waking minute, or at least melodramatically sad. She couldn't have a normal life without him. She needed him. She didn't need him at all.

She sighed and drank some more. He smiled at her, and she wondered what was going on inside his head.

"I need help," she said. "There are things about this whole situation—not you, the thing with the Horrible Internet Troll."

"The what? Oh. The stalker."

"Whatever. I need to know whether or not, or how much, this person is mixed up in everything. I have to find out, and I want to track some things down, but I don't know how to do them."

"Have you tried—"

She raised a hand. "Please, can I just trust you to listen to me first? Without interrupting?"

He put his beer down and faced her fully from the other chair, affecting such a serious-looking face that she had to smile; in smiling, she realized how much she'd started frowning just a second ago.

"Stop that. Just...listen first, and then think out loud."

He shrugged and grabbed his beer. "Go."

"I want you to try to track down the Horrible Internet Troll's address from an anonymous email. I gather that it's difficult, so I'm not expecting much. And I'd like you to help me figure out the best way to try to get him to volunteer his information. I was thinking of running some kind of contest where I physically had to mail something, or have him show up. I don't think it'll work, but that doesn't mean that it's not worth trying, because it's the kind of thing I normally do anyway.

"If that doesn't work, I'd like to make sure that it's public, the next big project that I do. And I want to figure out how I can get proof that someone's screwing around with my desserts, and who it is. Oh, crap. How could I have forgotten? I might have a recording on my phone."

She grabbed her purse and jerked it open. A waft of chocolate came out; she was going to have to pick up another purse soon. This one was just too stained. She grabbed her camera and opened the recording that she'd left.

Chances of actually catching someone screwing around with the ship: practically none.

But she had to check. She wanted to know. She was going to wish she didn't know, if it turned out to be one of her friends, but she wanted to know.

She fast-forwarded through the movie until she saw someone come in the room. Then she stopped, rewound it a bit, and played it at regular speed.

Kaley came into the room, wandered over to the ship, fiddled with it for a second, then went over to the small table where the breakfast food had been sitting. She picked up a stale bagel, bit into it, made a face, and tossed it in the trash. Then she sat at one of the chairs and stared into space for a while, nodding to herself.

After a few minutes, she got up and left the room.

Sam rewound the image, watching it again, studying details.

Kaley hadn't spent long enough near the ship to have sabotaged it; besides, it would have been hard to do a lot to the ship at that point without making it obvious.

Sam watched her walk over to the ship, look at something more closely under the ship, then pick it up. She tossed it in the garbage, then brushed her hands on her jeans. They were already smeared, so it wasn't like she was doing any more damage than she'd already done, but Kaley looked down at the pair of brown smudges on her pants and snorted. Sam could almost read her mind: *Great, just great.*

And then she grabbed another bagel, threw it away, etc.

From over her shoulder, Harry said, "You don't think she did it, do you?"

"No," Sam said. "Kaley? Come on. But I have to wonder what she found under the ship. I wonder if it was just a piece of chocolate or if it was something important."

"You should ask her."

"She's all tied up with Robert right now."

"Robert," Harry said, with a smirk on his face. "That was pretty fast on his part, wasn't it?" He walked back and sat down in his chair, took a swig of beer.

"Look, if you're not going to sleep with me, shut up about it, all right?" She fast-forwarded through the rest of the recording, which wasn't much before her crappy camera ran out of memory. Luckily, she'd left it at the lowest setting, because she'd rather have a lot of crappy digital recordings than ten seconds of high-quality perfection.

Nobody else came into the room before the camera ran out of memory.

Which meant nothing, really.

Sam started to watch the movie again, but her mind wandered elsewhere: the sight of the plate at the bottom of the ship.

She reached into her purse (it was probably leaving smudges on the floor, but it didn't bother her; Harry's place wasn't the kind of place where you worried too much if you left a little dirt behind. Clean, yes. Stain-free, no. The fact of its current cleanliness was enough for Harry; he thought the splotches on the concrete floor added character. Eventually, he would just paint over everything, and that would add even more character) and pulled out her notebook. She had little notebooks all over the place, grocery list notebooks. They were perfect for a) grocery lists and b) for when you woke up in the middle of the night or in line at the DMV with the perfect idea for a new recipe or flavor combination. Harry had always insisted that he never dreamed, and thus never had to worry about it, and in fact could jot down notes on his smartphone if he needed to, but Sam needed to be able to write things with a pen in order to put them into her head long enough for her memory to kick in.

She drew a circle. She didn't know how big the supports on the ship had been…three-quarters of an inch? She wished she'd been paying more attention when Ralph had told her, but she hadn't. Three-quarters seemed about right.

She tried to remember the way the cleaned-off metal plate had looked, when she'd caught a glimpse while the cops were looking at it, and sketched a black area on her circle where the twisted piece of metal might have been, before it had flattened onto the plate. At least half of the pipe had been cut away, which would have taken something around, oh, at least half an inch in diameter.

She drew a circle with a dot in the center, giving it about half an inch all around next to the support.

She wiggled her pen around in a circle over the dotted circle, pretending it was a whirling blade. She hummed the sound of its motor under her breath. Then she moved her pen, still making circles, over the circle of the support rod.

She wasn't positive, but it looked like the arcs she was making over the support rod would match the pattern of the marks that were on the actual plate. Someone had cut through the rod with a spinning disk of some kind, she thought.

"Harry, what's about half an inch in diameter and whirls around really fast and could make an extremely flat cut through a solid piece of metal?"

"A Dremel, I suppose."

Who would have a Dremel?

She drew the outline of the ship on the next sheet of paper, complete with the supports and the metal plates. She drew little lines to show where the cuts were. Then she drew arrows at the back of the ship, said, "Bang!" and rushed the paper out to arm's length, to show how the explosion would have pushed the ship.

Forward.

As the ship was pushed forward, the mostly-cut-through supports tipped forward, and the ship...hm. From the way the ship had tilted forward, looking like it was sinking, she'd have to say that more cuts had been made in the front support. The front of the ship had gone down, and the support hadn't really dragged along with it. It had snapped off completely, letting the front of the ship dive dramatically, which was why she'd said it was sinking, because it was.

"What would you use to fill a cut in a metal rod so it wouldn't look like it had been cut through?"

Harry was frowning at her. "Lab putty. It's silver."

"Can you get some that isn't silver? That's dark brown?"

"No," he said. "Maybe."

"What does it do in heat?"

"Nothing. Once you let it dry, it stays solid."

Sam groaned and looked up at the ceiling. "What looks exactly like chocolate and melts exactly like chocolate? Chocolate. With some of this other putty stuff on top."

"What?"

"The cannons went off right after I smelled the burnt smell. It was burning chocolate. That's why all the chocolatiers' noses were going haywire. Because they could all smell the chocolate burning."

She knew she was going too fast; she shouldn't be talking out loud around other people at this point. There was no way she could explain what needed to be explained, not fast enough. But the ideas kept coming and coming, one right after the other, and she had to say them out loud, because she couldn't keep it all inside and still be able to think the next thought.

Poor Harry.

"So. There should be wires that lead to the frame of the ship, and they'll look like, oops, I didn't wire the cannons correctly for when we wanted to fire them, and that's the reason that the chocolate melted on the side of the ship. Ha ha, dumb blonde at work. But I didn't wire any of the cannons, Harry. They were never intended to go off.

"And maybe the cuts were never supposed to be seen. It was just supposed to look like everything snapped, maybe because of bad welding. Except the technicians actually looked at it. I mean, they were doing their job, but maybe they weren't supposed to be really doing their jobs, not because of bribery or anything, but because it was all just an accident. Maybe he didn't know that he was leaving cut marks. The way everything looks is the way it looks because we already know the way it's supposed to look."

Which didn't make a word of sense, but that's what she had. "Do you see? Does that make sense?"

"No."

She tried to calm down, so she could put one word in front of the other, but it was just not working. She noticed that there seemed to be no sound in the room other than Harry not understanding her, and her sub-brilliant explanation.

"It's Dale, Harry," she said, trying to cut to the chase.

"What?" he was saying that a lot.

"Dale. He sabotaged the ship. Nobody else would have the know-how or the tools, and nobody else would think that what they were doing couldn't get noticed."

"But why? And what about proof? You can't just accuse someone of doing something based on the fact that they might have done it. You need to have proof."

Sam took a breath. "I..."

And then it all fell apart. All the sounds in the room came back with a rush. People chatting, silverware clinking on plates. Slurps. The long belch of someone at the bar, and appreciative laughter. Brady, for whatever reason, telling someone *Hey now*. Footsteps on the floor. The men's room urinal flushing. Someone shifting on a high, vinyl-covered stool, their skin making a rippling noise.

A waitress who looked about ten years old brought over a platter of pints to a four-top. Her arms didn't look strong enough to hold the platter up. She bent forward to put the beer on the table and showed skin between her black t-shirt and the studded belt at the top of her low-cut jeans. Sam watched Harry watching her and felt her face flushing, from embarrassment or jealousy or whatever.

"Pixie," Harry yelled. "Pull your shirt down or I'm making you wear an apron over it."

Pixie stood up in a flash (or lack thereof), turning her back to her boss. One of the men at the table behind her chortled and stuck his hand out, but Harry snapped his fingers at him to catch his attention, then waggled his finger and shook his head before he could touch the girl.

Pixie stuck her chin up in the air, thinking that the snap was for her, snorted, and walked over to the bar. She left the platter at the bar and went into the back. When she came out, her shirt was tucked in again, but it was just going to come right back out, Sam knew.

"I don't know," she finally admitted. "I guess I'll just have to confront him."

"You can't go confronting someone without proof," Harry said. She knew he was remembering arguments they'd had along those lines. *You're not telling me something. What is it? Nothing.* And of course they hadn't been telling each other things, by then. A lot of things.

"My suspicions aren't baseless."

"I never said they were," he said, meaning that that was exactly what he thought.

"Who do you think did it?" she asked.

"Let me talk to him."

"Why? Don't you think I can handle it? It's *Dale*."

"If he did this, then what makes you think you can handle it?"

"Oh, so now you're saying he did it? Now you're agreeing with me? Now that you have a chance to be all manly about it?"

"I'm not saying he did it or he didn't do it," Harry said. He picked up his beer glass, but it was empty. "Pixie!" he shouted again.

"What!"

He cleared his throat and held up his glass. She looked upward with an *oh-woe-is-me* look, then went back to the bar.

"I said, I'm not saying he did or didn't do it. But you're in no mood to handle it rationally, either way."

"So I'm irrational now."

He was leaning forward with his hands clasped loosely in his lap. "Yes."

The thing was, he wasn't wrong. She didn't want to admit it; admitting it would mean that she would have to calm down. It felt like another piece of her confidence was falling away—ah, what the hell was she doing, coming up with things like this, based on what might be, which might not be the case at all.

What if one of Robert's line cooks, jealous of her and her reputation with el chef grande, was behind the whole thing? It would be far more likely than blaming Dale.

Her head hurt; her teeth throbbed. She was her own worst enemy. She was the one who was pushing people away from her, with her nutty way of approaching everything. Kaley was going to get tired of working with her soon, nothing consistent, everything two steps away from chaos, never knowing whether an event would go well or would end in tragedy.

"Kaley said it was Dale, too," Sam said.

"Does she have proof? Or is this just the two of you throwing around a bunch of blame without knowing for sure?"

"Without knowing for sure," she said.

"This isn't the kind of accusation you can guess about," Harry said. He didn't look like he was trying to lord it over her, was the thing. He looked uncomfortable, like he had heartburn. Shifting around in his seat, puffing out air, hunched up in his shoulders. He looked small.

Harry was worried about her. For her. He was tearing down everything she said because he was worried. If she was wrong, she'd lose her friendship with Dale forever. She'd look like even more of a nut than she was now. She might even set the cops onto Dale with no evidence, nothing to go on, and they might blow it completely out of proportion. He might go to jail over nothing.

Would she be able to live with herself?

She sighed, picked up her glass, and drank the rest of it, just as Pixie arrived with another pint for Harry.

"Took you long enough," he told her. She blew a raspberry at him, and he smiled, turned back to Sam without a second glance. "You want another one?"

"I better not. I have to drive."

Harry held his beer out to her. She wasn't sure what he wanted but she was sure she didn't feel like hanging around to find out what it was.

"Sorry," she said. "I just can't. I feel like a big, stinking pile of rat turds. A pile of rat turds that has been a long time in the making. And I need to go home."

He was still holding the beer out to her. "You know, that's what this stuff is good for."

"For you, maybe," she said.

"Something to eat?"

She was still hungry, but she wanted to make something with her own hands. "I need to cook."

"Ah." He stood up; she stood up with him. He bent over and grabbed her purse and her notepad, stuffed the one in the other, handed them to her.

She took the straps and started walking toward the door. One foot, the other foot. Not begging, not asking, not even hoping that he would follow her. Not wanting.

She walked away. It felt better than being walked away from. Maybe because she wasn't screaming or panicking or doing anything other than wanting to go home. She walked herself sober; it took a while.

· · · ● · ● · · · ·

The answering machine light was flashing at her as she dropped her keys next to the phone and her purse next to her keys, but she ignored it. She had no desire to listen to anything that anyone was likely to say.

It promised to be a bad night, full of depression, woe, and cold. She put her hands on her face but couldn't tell which was colder, her hands or her cheeks. She needed something hot.

She started a kettle to boil. Drinking would make her feel warm for a minute, then leave her feeling worse than before. A branch clattered against the black windowpane, then scraped back and forth. The heater kicked on, spraying out a blast of cold air from the vents. She stepped closer to the oven, but the oven was cold.

The story of her life.

She gave up, went upstairs, and got ready for bed. She just wanted this evening to be over. Let her business fall apart before she lost all her savings, go back to her day job, etc. Cook for fun instead of for work. She tried to think of what jobs she had coming up. Well, no cooking classes until January. On Monday, she was going to have to start working on the batches and batches and batches of cookies that she was delivering for various places—including her and Kaley's old office. Closer to Christmas she had two dozen Yule logs to mess around with.

She spat toothpaste in the sink and smiled. She had plans for the Yule logs. She had run into a pop-up book during her last trip to the bookstore, and she desperately wanted to make either a pop-up log or a log that had some kind of pop-up feature. Totally edible. Totally incredible.

She had no idea how she was going to pull it off, and that made her grin even wider.

She'd begged off a trip back to see her mother for Christmas. She felt bad for her mother...but not that bad. Maybe it was a sign of the times, that evil daughters would rather cook Christmas dinner for complete strangers (strangers to her mother, that was), but Sam couldn't force herself to do it, when she had such a good excuse: cooking an Italian feast for Danielle and her mother, who was from Italy.

A complete and utter disaster awaited her, surely. But Danielle had asked her specifically to do it. Beside her mother, Danielle's bosses, the owners of the Rose, would be there. Looking for revenge.

Sam's devil-may-care smile faded from the mirror. She was going to have to really beg for their forgiveness. And that was just for the carpets.

Sam dragged out her saggiest, worn out, lamest pair of pajamas, the ones that she'd had since college, with the stupid black and white squares all over them. The black had faded into gray, and the white had faded into another shade of gray. The first time she'd washed them, they'd turned an entire load of her and her roommate's laundry dingy.

She wore them when she was feeling low. When she wanted to wallow. Which, most assuredly, she did. Not for her the sexy lingerie this evening, with no one to show it off to. Not for her nakedness, which was both suggestive and bitterly cold, with no one to snuggle up to. Not even for her favorite pair of pajamas, fuzzy and bright and with the power to seal her up in warmth like a fur blanket.

No. It was time for the bad pajamas, and nobody could stop her.

She tossed the blankets back, slid into bed and the cold sheets, and covered herself up. She rolled back and forth for a few seconds, pulling the blankets around her and tucking them under her just so, almost like a sleeping bag made out of quilts.

Then she did the same with her head, rolling it back and forth until she had made her head a shallow nest of comfortable feather pillow fluffs.

There. She was in.

She relaxed in the darkness. The heater turned off, and she heard tree branches scraping on the side of the house again. She was going to have to hire someone to cut them off, or else climb up a tree or a ladder or the house and cut them herself, and she knew if she did that, she'd be splattered on the ground with a broken leg inside of five minutes.

So many things she didn't dare do.

She relaxed some more, consciously sending thoughts of sleep into her feet, her legs, her back…

Her stomach growled.

She ignored it and considered her shoulders, how much better they would feel if they were more relaxed.

Her stomach growled again.

It wanted calorie comfort and would not, damn it, be denied.

Sam sighed and tossed off the blanket. There were stupider things she could think of than trying to argue with her stomach, but not while she was hungry. She put her feet in her slippers (which were hiding under a pile of chocolate-infused clothes) and went downstairs in the dark.

The kitchen seemed much friendlier, for some reason, as she turned on the lights.

The answering machine light was still blinking at her.

What she wanted, was soup.

Humming to herself, she dragged ingredients onto the counter. Duck breast, chicken (mostly) broth, tiny mache leaves…sesame oil. Promising.

She threw together a mix of salt, crystallized ginger buzzed into powder using the food processor, five-spice powder, and some white pepper, and rubbed it into the cut skin of the duck breast. She heated the broth, infused it with some shallots, ginger, and…*oh, let's throw in some lemon peel, what the heck, don't have any lemongrass today*. She almost added some powdered galangal, but smelled it first and decided not to.

She considered what would go with the soup...figs? Dried apricots? In broth? Woman, are you mad?!? Okay, no dried apricots. Figs.

Figs. In soup.

It would be shallow soup, she promised. The figs would just stick right out the top.

Figs? With Asian?

She ran the taste of five-spice powder and ginger through her mind and compared them to the figs.

Figs and slices of duck, yes. In a salad. But this was salad with broth over it, damn it, and it would work.

Hot broth over figs.

Maybe if it were sweet.

Why not make it sweet?

What, with sugar?

Sweet chicken broth. Well, now that it was in her head, she was going to have to try it.

She added some mirin to the broth...it wasn't right. Not bad, but not right. She turned around in a circle with her hands out, touching her cupboards, running through what was inside them. Without thinking, she reached out for something and added it.

Tasted the broth. Sour, sweet and sour now. Maybe?

She combined the taste with the figs. Overwhelming, except...it was broth, not sauce. She'd have to try it, anyway.

She'd wanted to leave the duck in the salt mixture for twenty minutes, and she still had five minutes left, five to midnight.

Harry couldn't complain about her keeping him up, anyway. The only time he'd actually complained was the time that she'd decided to bake a cake at three a.m., and that was probably only because she'd sung misremembered Aretha lyrics at the top of her lungs with the mixer's paddle attachment in front of her face.

"If you're going to sing at three a.m., at least learn how to spell," he'd said. And slammed the door to the stairs.

She smiled, then sighed. If she didn't find something to do, she was just going to eat those figs.

Those deliciously quartered figs.

Instead, she jabbed the button on the answering machine. Even listening to Kaley saying that she was quitting the business and going to work for Robert instead was preferable. Or Dale saying that he'd heard that she suspected him, he was totally offended, and he was calling the cops with proof that she was a complete airhead and had accidentally caused the whole thing. Or the cops calling and saying...

Something snapped her out of her reverie, and she started listening to what the answering machine was saying. Well, not really listening to what the actual words were, but to the fact that it was Jack Malpeque saying them. He was babbling, and not angry, as she had half-expected as soon as she recognized his voice.

She restarted the machine message and started to listen to it, but no, no, what he was saying wasn't making any sense.

She tried a third time.

"Hello! This is Jack Malpeque. Listen, do you remember me? The pirate at the chocolate festival that you almost killed with a chocolate ship. Hah. At any rate, Danielle assures me that the cops are saying that it wasn't an accident. Actually, I said that wrong. The cops are saying that it wasn't negligence on your part that caused anything to happen; the ship was deliberately sabotaged. So either you were trying to kill me, or someone else was trying to kill me, and Danielle says it wasn't you."

Sam spent a few seconds wondering why on earth Jack would think someone was trying to kill him, then remembered that he was, really, the most famous person in the room.

She spent the rest of the phone message wondering whether this was all a setup by an enemy of Jack's. Literally trying to kill him.

Well, he was the only person that could be guaranteed to be sitting in front of the ship; it was right on the little paper maps of the maze of chocolate booths that had been passed around at the door. Sam gasped as she remembered that her new scarf was still stuffed at the bottom of her purse. She pulled it out, rubbed it on her face. It smelled like chocolate, but seemed to be unstained.

Ahhh! She heated up a pan and dropped the duck breast in it. She couldn't possibly expect herself to be able to focus while she was hungry.

Except she wanted to be able to listen to the message all the way through...she pushed the button again.

Jack continued: "...Given that you don't want me out of the picture, whatever that picture may be, I have a proposition for you. Not that kind. A food proposition. This is going to take some explaining, so excuse me if I run out of recording and have to call you back.

"You see, I have a new movie coming out in February, a big science fiction action blockbustery thing. But in February. I ask you, is there a worse time? But the director pissed off the producer, and the producer, I name no names but feel free to look it up, has literally cut his nose off to spite his face here. February."

Literally? she thought. But tried to keep focusing.

"We're going to lose millions. Hundreds of millions. The studio is, let us say, furious. But with all the political games that have been played around here...to make an unnecessarily long story filled with sex, blood, and...other things, much shorter, let me just say that the movie's in February. *Pirate Moon IV.* I take my shirt off. It's lovely. That is, what they can do with digital imaging these days.

"And...there was some point here, wasn't there. And I want to join in with the general pissing off of people by throwing a party at my chateau in the mountains, a humble little abode that can sleep fifty people if necessary," she could hear the preening in his voice, "and not inviting the producer. Maybe. We'll see how the results are from opening weekend."

He took a deep breath. "And I would like you to cater it. Now, I know, if I were you, I'd feel like the name of Jack Malpeque was bad luck for you. Especially if someone's trying to kill me! Wouldn't do to have your work undermined by unknown miners, would it? Not a second time! But this is going to be just too tempting for you to resist. You see, I want you to cater the feast from the end of *Pirate Moon IV*. It's an alien feast. Completely alien. And completely inedible; the set designers made everything, and then the animators added more, and I didn't get to taste a damned bit of it. And so...I want to recreate the feast. To eat. To serve to my illustrious guests. There's a bit of a battle to reenact as well. But that won't be your problem.

"I have here, right in my hands, footage. Footage of the feast. So even if you don't want to do it, if you're already booked, which is my greatest fear at this point, even greater than death, please tell me you'll watch this with me. Because it is simply amazing, and I love to make women gasp. But of course you are totally safe with me. Do call back."

He hung up.

Beep!

She shook her head and checked the duck, but it wasn't ready yet. His message had seemed to go on for longer than it really had.

The machine went on, playing a second message: "Aha! My phone number is—" he rattled it off. "I may not answer right away, I really don't like phones, they're interruptions. But tell me a time to call you back, and I'll make a point of it, although I'm a bit of a flake when I'm not on the job. Ahh, I don't have to do anything else until March. It's so good. But I'll probably get bored and—"

Beep! Out of memory. *Beep!*

At least he'd left his phone number at the beginning. She laughed and flipped the duck breast over.

Ah, but what was she thinking? She was just going to have to call him back and tell him that she couldn't do it, that someone was out to get her, not him, and that she was a spaz who couldn't be trusted in the first place, and that her business was falling apart and she was going to try to beg for her old job back.

On second thought, how depressing. She'd have to get his email from Danielle instead; she'd just break down over the phone. But she'd love to see that footage. It would be something to tell her grandkids, if she ever had any kids or even ever had sex ever again, in her whole life. But to tell someone's grandkids that she had, once, watched part of a Jack Malpeque movie with him, unless he just sent it as a file via email, which would be the smarter thing to do, really, so she had watched part of a Jack

Malpeque movie before anyone else except for the people who had worked on the movie and the publicity people or whoever watches a movie before it's released, and then said, "Sorry, that absolutely fantastic project you want me to do? I can't do it. I'm too chicken."

Lame!

No. She would do it.

The duck informed her that it was done, so she pulled it out of the pan, let it rest while she poured off the fat, and deglazed the pan with a little of the black vinegar. She slashed into the duck across the grain, thin, flexible slices of juicy love topped with crisp skin, added them to her wide pasta dish along with the mache and the figs, then poured the broth over all.

Garnish...she quickly turned a few pieces of crystallized ginger into strips, put them on top of the duck closest to the center of the bowl, and poured the deglazing (unsieved) juices over that, black over pale yellow.

She smelled it. Good. Perhaps not rapturous, but good. She had a sweet spot for black vinegar, if you could say such a thing. The black vinegar plus the duck...that had promise. Duck plus ginger plus vinegar almost smelled like too much.

She didn't bother with a spoon, just picked up the bowl, held it at eye level for a second (the duck fat was already rising up to the surface of the broth), and slurped.

The mache hit her tongue first, peppery. But was it really the mache, or was it the vinegar plus the ginger? The ginger had hit her nose first. But not her tongue. She breathed out everything in her lungs, then breathed in again. Cinnamon? Yes, from the five spice. And the fat on her tongue, she could barely taste it. It almost tasted like it was more under her tongue than on it.

She slurped again, reaching out with her lips to pull some of the mache into her mouth. The tiny little stem was a tease of crunchiness. She grabbed one edge of the duck toward her mouth, complete with a pile of ginger still on it, and shoved it in with a slurp of soup. The ginger went straight up her nose; the meat melted in her mouth.

The skin, though. Was already getting soggy.

Sam grabbed a pair of chopsticks out of her drawer and stood there, slurping and shoving food in her mouth, until it was all gone.

It wasn't perfect, but it made her feel better.

She *would* take the catering job. So there.

CHAPTER 14

In the morning, she realized that she had already changed her mind. She wasn't going to do the catering job. She wasn't even going to tell Kaley about it, because she didn't want to influence her decision. Kaley was just going to have to make her own mind up about whether she wanted to go or stay. Giving her a tantalizing tease of what could have been, if Sam hadn't been such a klutz, a jump-to-assumptions nutcase, would just be cruel and misleading. It would come across as a plea.

And Sam had to...she didn't know, start to treat herself with a little respect. She didn't want to have to beg Kaley to stay.

She got up, got dressed, and prepared to face the day. For a minute, she couldn't remember what day it was. Monday.

Her day off.

Which meant that she had nothing to do, and Kaley wouldn't have to show up unless she felt like it.

Ugh. Sam didn't know if she could face it, a whole day of nothing to do but think. Unless she cooked, and then she wouldn't have to think. A good idea, really. Fantastic. Spectacular.

But what to cook?

Normally, Sam didn't have any problems coming up with something to cook.

She looked around the kitchen.

Nothing sounded good.

Maybe she should go up to the computer and take care of her backlog of Food Slut stuff. Write a few more blogs, so she wouldn't have to think about anything the rest of the week, during Cookie Madness.

No, that sounded terrible, too.

She wandered around, wanting to cook, not wanting to cook. Wanting to be productive, not wanting to be productive. Until noon.

By which time, her stomach informed her, if the only way she was going to find peace was to call Jack and get it over with, she had better do it already.

So she did, dialing from her cell phone, so he'd have the number. She'd leave a messa—

"Hello?" he asked. "Is this...Sam Genoise?"

"Yep," she said, as though his answering his own phone hadn't scared the crap out of her. "I just got your message."

He waited for her to say something else, but she didn't, and then he didn't, and she'd spent far too much time on the phone not talking to Harry to be so easily pushed around, so he broke down first.

"What do you think?"

"I'd like to see the clip first. I mean, so even if I turn it down, I can tell my grandchildren."

He laughed nervously. Tittered. "Ah, yes."

"What, you don't have it?"

"It's not that. But I'm afraid I don't know how to give you directions to my chateau. I don't know where it is, you see. That is, I know where it is, in that I know how to get here."

"Don't you know the address?"

"I never give it out. I don't even get mail here."

"You don't have a mailbox?"

"No."

Sam rolled her eyes. "At some point, go to the place where your driveway leaves the main road. There will be numbers there, so the ambulance can find you if there's an emergency and you call 9-1-1."

"9-1-1!" he shouted. "Hang on..."

"Stop!" she snapped. "Do not hang up and call 9-1-1 just to find out where you are."

"I wasn't going to really," he said, but she didn't believe him. "Joking. Ha ha."

"When would be convenient?" she asked. The words coming out of her mouth still astonished her; she sounded like she was completely cool, calm, collected...fake! Totally faking sounding like she wasn't a spaz...in front of a world-renowned actor. She wasn't fooling him a second.

And what was she saying?!? She was supposed to be telling him thanks but no thanks...

"Now?" he asked. "Today? I'm bored, I tell you. Bored. Hang on, I'll walk out to the road...you know, maybe I'll drive out to the road. I'm not sure I remember the name of the road, and I may have to, er, backtrack until I find more signs. But that's a good point. I did wonder what that little sign was for. Good thing I didn't take it down. Back in five. Five! Maybe ten. Don't go anywhere."

"This is my cell," she said. "I'll keep it at hand."

"Hmph," he said, and hung up.

What a strange man. She automatically dialed Kaley's number, her thumb taking over before her mind had a chance to worry or decide whether she should tell Kaley or not.

However, she did almost hang up when she realized that Kaley wasn't on her own anymore. She might be...with Robert. No. It was noon. If she was (they were) still asleep, that was her own lookout. So she let the call go through.

"What's up?" Kaley asked.

"Is this a good time?"

"What are you talking about? Why wouldn't it be a good time?"

Curiosity pounced on her from behind. "Where are you?" With Robert?

"At home?" But the real question in her voice was, "Who are you, my mother?"

"Sitting down?"

Kaley sighed. "It's bad news, isn't it?"

"Jack wants us to host a party for him in February."

Suddenly, she knew what she wanted for lunch, a caprese. Unfortunately, this was not a reasonable wish, because there was no way she was going to get decent tomatoes this time of year, and she didn't have any mozzarella around anyway, nor nearly enough fresh basil from her little plant, so what was the point?

She opened up the fridge and looked into it. No...oh, the hell with it. It was a munchy cold kind of day. She pulled out a bag of little gingersnaps from the freezer that she had intended to make into...she couldn't remember what exactly, but the bottom of some kind of cookie appetizer, with—

"Cream cheese frosting," she said. "Oh, yeah."

Kaley hadn't responded to the news about catering for Jack Malpeque. But cream cheese frosting *could* elicit a response from her.

"Cream cheese frosting on what?"

"What do you put on top of tiny gingersnap cookies with cream cheese frosting on top, if you're going to put it next to regular appetizers to surprise people? I can't remember whatever it was that I was going to do with these things."

"What kind of party? Because February is when..."

They both kept up on this kind of thing.

"Yep. *Pirate Moon IV* comes out. Apparently there's an alien feast at the end."

Kaley sighed. "You can bounce back from anything, can't you?"

Sam was not in a mood to be depressed anymore. "Yep. As long as I can find something completely insane to lose myself in, sure. He says he's going to call back in a minute and give me the address of his chateau up in the mountains."

"Not a cabin. A chateau."

"That's what he called it."

"Yeah, okay."

"Wanna come?"

Kaley paused again. "...No."

"Why not?"

"I'm not invited."

"Don't be silly."

Tomato roses? Slice of cucumber? Mache leaves? Parsley? Ooh, mint leaves.

She could make a cookie wreath, with bits of dried fruit and mint leaves. Which would be pretty, but would it be any good? Oh, not gingersnaps...cookies with the same flavor profile as red velvet cake. It would have to be cookies, or the whole thing would fall apart when you picked them up.

Kaley said, "I can't, Sam."

Sam's heart clutched inside her chest. Here it was, the moment when Kaley told her she was quitting, really quitting.

"I can't do this anymore," Kaley said.

Sam took a breath, and said, "I'm going to convince you to keep working with me. You can't stop me."

"It's too much."

"I don't really care what your argument is, Kaley. You belong with me, and with this business. The only one allowed to fall apart on a regular basis here is me. And that's because I'm me, and I never really mean it."

Until she'd said it, she hadn't realized it was true. But there it was.

"And I'll promise to knock it off. No more working myself into such a state that I'm like, oh, everything's falling apart."

"You're not listening," Kaley said.

"Didn't I just tell you that I wasn't going to listen to you?" She mentally reviewed the last few seconds of conversation. "No. Okay, Kaley, as long as you talk about giving up on me, I'm not going to listen to you."

"I'm not giving up on you," Kaley started to say.

"Shhht. Not listening. If it's not my fault, then it's not your fault. If you're bad for the business, I'm worse. If you weren't here, I'd drive this into the ground in a heartbeat, and I know it, and I value you and working with you more than words can say. And I'm expecting a phone call so I'll call you back later bye."

Beep!

It wasn't fair, but there you go. Sam made a batch of cream cheese frosting, pulled a few more things out of the freezer to start them thawing, and tried to think of what she could do for the top of the frosting. She wanted something brightly colored, something innovative...but she kept coming back to the crystallized ginger.

From the counter, her cell phone rang. She answered. "Hello?"

"Jack. Have you got a pen?"

"Sure," she said, sticking her finger in the frosting.

"It's fifteen fifty-five North Umberland Road," he said. "Do you know it?"

She wrote 1555 N Umberl on the counter, in frosting. "Nope. But I can find it."

"I don't know, it's pretty impossible."

"You left the ambulance sign up, right? I'll be fine."

He sighed. "Well, give it a shot. I'll be here all afternoon."

Instead of assembling the cookies and frosting, she stirred the ginger into the frosting and left the cookies in the bag. Chips and dip. A few minutes later, she was headed up into the mountains on the highway, a bag full of goodies and small bites beside her.

Jack's house was difficult to find and out past Leadville and Turquoise Lake besides, but the GPS got her as far as the head of North Umberland Road. She drove past the driveway twice but got it on the third time around, which was pretty normal for her, anyway, or it had been before Harry got her the GPS. The trees were thick around her, the road steep and winding, the smell of pine thick inside the SUV. There was snow on the road, but nothing she couldn't handle.

The driveway led up and up and up, until she reached the chalet.

Crap. It wasn't a chalet, it was a freaking resort.

The roofs were as peaked as that of an a-frame, but there were four sets of them. The whole front of the house, facing down the mountain, was covered with windows; it would be bright and cheery and impossible to eat at sunset, with all the sunlight coming in. Large posts braced the overhanging roofs, which were slathered with snow as creamy-looking as frosting. She followed the driveway, which had been freshly plowed, up to the house, found a wide spot, and parked.

The place was a freakin' postcard, and Kaley was going to kick herself for not coming. Sam pulled out her camera (she'd switched bags, finally) and took a shot or two, just for bragging rights.

She couldn't see any doors on the first level (all garages), so she climbed the steps to the porch, which rose just above the pile of snow at the end of the driveway, and rang the doorbell.

The air smelled like woodsmoke; a cheerful tail of smoke ran overhead like the cute puffs of a choo-choo train. Sam hefted the bag of goodies again; as always, she'd brought too much food. Maybe she shouldn't have brought any. She shifted from foot to foot as her breath steamed. The light was starting to get creamy; she wasn't going to be able to stay that long, if she didn't want to drive home in the dark.

An older woman opened the door and bawled, "She's here, Jack."

"Mom!" he said. "Could you not open the door like you're my mother?"

Sam grinned and stuck her hand out. The woman shook her hand and stepped backward, still holding the door. Sam stamped her feet, knocking off as much snow as she could, and took one step inside, then one step to the side. Jack's mother closed the door, pulling on the handle to make sure the door had latched.

Sam loosened the zippers on her boots, slipped them off, and left them by the door.

Jack might be a Hollywood movie star, but his mother was from somewhere where the doors blew open if you didn't shut them tight and you took off your shoes when you came inside a house. It made Sam feel better.

"The kitchen's this way," his mom said, as footsteps ran toward them.

Jack was preceded by a giant white dog that looked like some kind of bear with a long snout. The dog ran quickly across the room with him but stopped a few feet away, leaning toward her, stretching out his neck to be patted like a little kid pleading for a cookie.

Jack looked less like himself out of costume than in it. She squinted at him...no, he *was* wearing a costume. It was just a normal-looking one. He had black-rimmed eyeglasses, longish hair, and just a touch of stubble. He was wearing a wool cable-knit sweater over a dark green shirt, blue jeans, and red-and-ivory socks. Clever. Now he looked casually sophisticated. It was exactly the kind of outfit someone from out of town would think that mountain-folk wore, because that's what they wore in the movies. She smiled at him, and shook his hand.

He smiled awkwardly.

The room was big, with gigantic antler-horn chandeliers hanging from the ceiling, stone walls, and wood floors covered with all kinds of subtly-patterned rugs. The floors weren't as cold as she'd expected, under her socks. The room was a little chilly, but not annoyingly so; she'd been to cabins up in the mountains that were far colder at their best. Paintings hung on the walls, modern-looking stuff thick with paint that she didn't know what was, but still looked good. No mirrors, no clocks, big timbers running across the pointed roof, a balcony across the inside of the room leading onto several doors; upstairs bedrooms, probably. The furniture looked suede but felt like cloth when she brushed against it.

A bland, formal-party kind of room.

"No, Mom, this way," Jack said.

"I know where the kitchen is," his mother said.

He stopped. "I want to show her the theater. Where the movie is."

"She brought food."

He stopped. "What did you bring?"

"Don't be so greedy," his mother teased. "And aren't you going to introduce me?"

He rolled his eyes. "Sam Genoise, my mother. Mom, Sam Genoise."

"I have a name." She looked like him, only shorter, with the same nose but thinner eyes, white hair in almost exactly the same haircut. Dressed like a normal person would dress at home, in worn gray sweatpants, socks and slippers, and a thick, dark blue sweatshirt over a fuzzy turtleneck. Her hair hadn't been brushed recently, and she had dog hair on her sweatshirt.

"Introductions," Jack announced. "I'm Jack Malpeque, that's Cheryl Malpeque, Sam-probably-Samantha Genoise, and you, darling mutt, are Lennie."

The dog's ears twitched as he heard his name, and he held out a paw.

Cheryl jerked her head toward an arched doorway, and Sam followed her. She didn't trust the dog with some of the things she had in her bag.

The kitchen had stone tile floors and thick counters and lots of cabinets with lots of cabinetry all over them. They looked like a horrible pain in the ass to clean. It was the kind of kitchen designed by someone who liked to design dining rooms. Two islands with a total of eight cream-colored dining chairs around them.

Spotless, though.

Lennie stopped just outside the door and put his head over his paws, trying to look like a harmless lap dog.

Sam put the bag on the counter and started pulling things out. "Pardon, but a lot of the things that I had on hand were, uh, intended for a cooking class on aphrodisiacs. We were experimenting."

"Experimenting?" Cheryl asked.

"Oh, they aren't particularly effective. Historical more than anything else, and not terribly original. But fun. May I use a few pots?"

Cheryl walked her around the kitchen while Jack practically danced from foot to foot. Sam prepped the figs and chorizo, boiled water for the ravioli, thawed the bisque.

Ah, well. She was going to have to get over the bisque eventually.

She gave the cream cheese frosting another turn and said, "Oh...I should ask. Are either of you allergic to anything?"

But they weren't. Sam found a platter and set out the cookies. The longer the bisque sat on the burner, the closer the other two of them stood to the range, until Sam had to shoo them off so she could see if it was done.

Finally, it was all ready. Cheryl handed Jack a picnic basket and a bottle of merlot and shooed him into the theater while she and Sam dished everything else into serving dishes.

They walked through the big room and into the theater, which had seven rows of eight seats each, and screen that wasn't as big as most megaplex screens but was easily as big as the screen in the tiny theater in her hometown. The seats were red velvet with wide arms and side tables between each pair of seats.

"You wouldn't happen to have any popcorn, would you?" Jack asked. He had set up a table at the back of the room with the dishes and was delivering glasses of red wine to the tables. Before she could answer—of course she didn't; he'd seen her getting things ready—he ran to a small door in the back of the room, under the projectionists' window.

"It's film?" she asked.

"Digital. But projected," he shouted. "I won't bore you with the technical details; I find it annoys most people, but I honestly find it fascinating. We're living in revolutionary times, I tell you. Revolutionary." He ducked back through the door. "Tell me when you're ready. Should we eat first? It won't distract you?"

"I'm fine," she laughed. She guided the other two through the dishes, pointing out that the truffle powder would be replaced by real truffles and that yes, the bisque was essentially the same recipe that she'd use to make the chocolate truffle filling.

Cheryl skipped the bisque and loaded her plate with figs and chorizo. "I know what I like."

"A nice big chorizo with a pair of fat figs," Jack announced with wide eyes and raised eyebrows.

"Jack!"

He muttered and put his plate next to Sam's, then went back through the door. The lights went off, and Sam's hand froze above her wineglass. The theater, without light, was windowless and pitch black. The next moment, light splashed the screen, and the movie started.

"I apologize; I don't have the entire movie. So I realize this is all out of nowhere," Jack said.

The screen captivated her from the first visual. A room full of aliens lounged like Romans at an orgy. The room looked like something out of the Seventies, with round walls and stone-like grottoes, water trickling from tiny waterfalls on the walls and winding around the room in streams. An alien about the size and shape of a Chihuahua mixed with a gecko clung to the wall next to the waterfall and lapped at it, giggling. Glowing vines drooped leaves overhead, casting dim light and dimmer shadows; the ceiling seemed to be made out of swirling mist that sometimes reached down to caress one of the alien warriors, covered with buckles and leather and bristling with shiny, pointy things.

Half the aliens looked at least somewhat human, in suits, but others seemed like magic tricks, like you couldn't possibly fit a human being inside, or if you did, their limbs couldn't move in those directions. At the head of the room, on a dais slightly higher than the others around her, was the queen (she was the most humanlike; knowing Jack's character, he'd probably slept with her in the first five minutes of the movie, thinking that she was some kind of space slut, and only later had he found out that his fling would lead to epic consequences). Short, ugly aliens who were clearly servants walked around at floor level, carrying large, shiny platters of food from dais to dais.

The queen, a nearly-bare-chested green womanish thing whose upper arms sparkled with gold and blue silk scarves, picked up a blood-colored, dripping fruit with flowing ribbon-fingers, sucked on the juices with her lips while her finger-ribbons did the same, lapping up juices with dozens of tiny, small mouths (the camera zoomed in closer), and said, "Miklos. You say I have been betrayed?" Her voice came out as a literal purr, with a sexy whistle to it. It worked.

The visual switched to Jack, as Miklos, the arrogant Pirate King of Sector Seven, dressed in a torn, dirty, blood-stained spacesuit (the scene was just after an epic battle, no doubt, in which he had accidentally sacrificed himself and looked at least somewhat noble, for the moment) with his helmet beside him, stood in front of the woman in chains so big they were comical. He dropped to his knees, and the chains rattled. "My lady. You are in the direst danger. I swear it."

Jack dropped down into the chair beside her, grabbed his wine, and said, along with his character, "Your son means to see you dead by nightfall, in seven hours."

"Perhaps I wish to die," she said.

"But—" Jack waved his arm, as heavily bedecked with chains as it was, toward the room. Rattle rattle. "What about your people, my lady?"

She sighed, crushed the fruit in her swirling hand, and let her fingers suck up the juice, even as it ran down her arm and onto the silken pillows below her. "If I am crushed, then they will be crushed, too. I tire of this life, Miklos. Even you could never bring back my joy of it. I am ready to die, and my people are ready to die with me."

The other aliens around the room pounded on the dais, making a steady beat.

"My lady," Jack gasped along with his character. "Do I no longer please you? Does my lovemaking no longer give you life?"

But that was Miklos, vain to the end.

The corner of the queen's mouth tilted downward in a way that made Sam wonder if she recognized the actress under all that makeup. At the moment, she couldn't remember who, besides Jack, was supposed to be in the movie.

"You come to me in chains to ask that? No, Miklos! Life has lost its savor and I wish to *die*!"

Jack made a slurping sound and said, "Damn, this is good. What's in it?"

She ignored him. Miklos said, in a whisper that was almost as loud as a roar (and with a close-up that was close enough for her to see that they'd airbrushed his pores but had left his stubble alone): "You can take my ship. You can take my freedom. But you can never insult my lovemaking, my lady."

Miklos jumped up, throwing off his chains (they weren't fastened; there must be a traitor in the midst of the aliens!), and pulling out a secret vibro-knife, cutting down the alien guards next to him with two chops and a stab.

The alien warriors surrounding the queen jumped, leaped, or rolled off their daises, pulling out small weapons that were probably the equivalent of cutting utensils at best, and swarmed toward Miklos. He fought them, left, right, up, down, grabbing a chandelier made out of intertwined tubes of liquid, dropping onto a group of gibbering, one-eyed monkeys, and knocking them under a dais. He sliced through the dais, cutting it in half and letting the food slide onto the floor with a *crash!* and the monkeys scattered. Roaring, he charged toward the Queen, fighting his way through defender after defender.

She reached underneath the silks on her arm and pulled out a blade that was far too long to have fit under them.

"Kill him!" she shouted and she climbed to her feet, her finger-ribbons pulling other deadly weapons out of nooks and crannies about her person to hurl at Miklos. *Where did she keep all that stuff?!?* Sam wondered.

Miklos took a slash from behind and curled backward against the wound. He spun, leapt, and kicked a flying mosquito thing the size of a Saint Bernard into a pile of lumps glistening with slime and gold leaf that were probably food rather than an alien. The alien's skin hissed, throwing up steam, and it coughed and died. Then again, maybe it wasn't food after all.

When Miklos landed, he stumbled and dropped his vibro-blade, and the aliens attacked all together. Miklos collapsed under a pile of growling, snarling aliens.

"Stop!" the queen commanded, and they stopped immediately. A comically pitiful groan emerged from under the pile.

The queen snapped her fingers. "Bring him to me."

The aliens pulled back out of the pile one by one. It was like watching clowns climb out of a clown car, as bigger and bigger aliens backed away, dripping blood, ichor, and colorful sauce. Finally, the camera showed poor little Miklos at the bottom of the pile, flat as a pancake. One of the bigger aliens reached down and jerked him up.

His spacesuit had somehow been almost totally destroyed in the fray, leaving Miklos in tatters and space underwear.

"Somehow, I don't think real space underwear are that sexy," Sam sighed.

"Shh!" Jack hissed, while his mother snorted. "Let us not talk about plumbing in mixed company, which is to say, my mother. And you're missing the dialogue."

"What are you doing?" the queen demanded.

"Testing your will to live," he said. "And the will of your people."

She reached out, grabbed the tatters of his shirt, and pulled him close as the alien warrior released him. "You play a dangerous game, Miklos."

He leaned forward and kissed her passionately. "But I always win."

"What would you have me do?" she asked, when Miklos came up for air, the finger ribbons twining around him, almost of their own accord.

Kinky, she thought. But that was Miklos.

"Feast," he said. "Feast and drink and wench and, er, whatever it is *you* do." He jerked his head toward some amorphous blobs that were quivering nearby, focusing their lasers on him. Then he roared, "And tomorrow, we fight your son!"

The warriors cheered and shook weapons, the queen pulled Miklos even closer, cut scene, fade to black.

Jack got up and turned on the lights. Sam suddenly realized that her hand was still hovering over her wine glass, so she picked it up and drank, then grabbed a cookie and dipped it in the ginger frosting.

"Did you catch all that?" Jack asked.

She shook her head. She hoped he wouldn't ask her how much she'd missed while staring at Miklos's chest.

"So...you need to watch it again, right?" Jack asked.

Sam was about to answer that of course they could, but Cheryl said, "Jack, you've already seen that clip a hundred times. It's so cheesy. I'm sick of it."

Jack grinned at her. "Nobody like your mother to keep you from going crazy from fame. All right, I'll send you a copy to take home with you. But you can't give it to anyone. The producer will kill me if he finds out I have it."

"But won't he be able to guess?" Sam asked. "When he finds out you've had a party? There's no way a caterer could come up with all that off a verbal description."

"By then, it will be too late," Jack said. "Do you think you can do it?"

"You aren't going to destroy all that food, are you?" She poked her fork at a few pieces of chorizo. "I'd hate to make something delicious if it's just going to be a prop in a battle and nobody gets to eat it."

"I should think so. We'll scatter the guests around the room in alien costumes, and eat, and then have Miklos brought in, in chains, etc. A mock battle in which the guests don't have to get up, say a few people charge in from the side, that kind of thing, the end."

Sam tapped her fingernails on the table, thinking. "I have so many questions."

"Ask them, my queen."

She stopped ticking her fingernails and looked at him. Was he trying to make a move on her...in front of his mother?

He bowed with the top half of his chest. "But first, answer me this...do you want to do it?"

Normally, Sam was pretty good at telling whether someone was trying to put the moves on her; her stalker sense would tingle, and her elbows would start swinging. But she wasn't picking up on that now at all.

He was an actor, though. And his mother was in the room.

Maybe she was just jumping to conclusions and he was talking about food.

"I don't know," she admitted. "I mean, I can do it, but I don't know whether I should."

"Why not?"

"I almost dropped a ship on you."

Cheryl got up and loaded her plate up with more chorizo and figs, then left the room. Lennie whimpered, begging for the sausage, and Sam noticed that the theater didn't have any dog hair in it, not that she could see.

"You did no such thing."

"But we've—I've thought about it, and the only way the ship could have been tampered with was if someone had access to it while we were building it. Either it was someone who worked for Danielle who did it...or someone who works for me. What if they do it again?"

She wasn't sure that she bought the idea that someone was after Jack, but she'd go with it for a minute, at least in front of Jack.

"And there's no way we're going to be able to do the grotto like that. Holy cow. I mean, some of the people who helped me make the ship might be able to, but they're not professionals at it. It'd take too long. And..."

Jack waved his hand at that. "Don't worry. I know the crew that built the original set. And the costumes, which I'm sure you're about to get to next—I can get hold of the original costumes or have them made, and I know people who can act out any necessary parts. I'm an actor. I know a lot of people who can create and re-create all kinds of things at the drop of a hat. That's what they do."

"So why me? If you can afford to fly in a whole crew of people to turn your house into a set, why me?"

"You, my dear," he took her hand, still not activating her Stalker Sense, "are a nut. You have found your place in life, and it is doing the odd, unusual, and tasty at the drop of a hat. You turn the impossible into the merely improbable."

"Danielle asked you, didn't she?"

He coughed into his hand, releasing hers. "No."

"You're lying."

"Stop being such a goddamned paranoid," he snapped. "Look, I'm famous and I have enough money to hire people to do crazy things for me when the whim strikes me. Sorry about that. But I don't hire people out of pity or for a favor, unless I was going to do it anyway. Yes, she did mention that you were available. No, she didn't ask for a favor, and no, she doesn't know that I'm asking you to do this. I want it to be a surprise, and Danielle is the last person you talk to if you want to keep something a surprise. Get over yourself! This isn't about you. This is about my project. I want to do the project, and damn it, you're going to work on it with me, because I want this to taste as good as it looks."

He sealed his argument (but totally spoiled the effect of the stormy look on his face) by picking up his bowl of bisque and slurping from it.

"What *is* this?"

"Shrimp bisque," she said.

"What's the recipe?" he asked.

She shook her head. "I never tell."

"Why not? Trade secret? You got it from a witch to whom you sold your soul? What?"

"I promised my ex I would never tell."

"Your ex, huh?" He leaned forward. "Danielle said something about you being a hopeless case. Your protecting the recipes of an ex-husband does indicate that she was right, you know."

"It wasn't his recipe," she said.

"Even better, even better. All right. Let's talk money. How much do you want?"

"I'll have to look at the movie again. I have no idea what this is going to cost to put together."

"Nevermind that. How much do you want? Do you even know what you want?"

Sam snorted and said, "I want five grand and a pony."

"Done," he said. "I'll assume that you'd rather have cash than the actual steed."

"What?" she asked.

"Don't be coy," he said. "It's a perfectly reasonable figure, for what I'm asking of you. And I really think you should plan ahead and hire someone to do professional photos and camera work throughout; actually, I'll include that as part of your fee. You'd be a fool not to try to get a book deal out of this. This is going to be...a once-in-a-lifetime event. Magnificent."

"Or a tragedy," she muttered. He'd verbally backed her into a corner, making her agree to do it. She hadn't signed anything, though, so she told herself she could still back out at any time.

She knew she wouldn't, though.

He was right. This was a once-in-a-lifetime event, and she'd love to fill up her years with a series of them.

A bell rang, and Lennie made a short bark.

"I got it," Cheryl yelled.

Jack frowned. "Who could that be?"

But the theater was soundproofed, and they couldn't hear much, even though the door was open. Jack couldn't control his curiosity, and after shifting back and forth in his seat a few times, he jumped up and skipped out the door.

Sam made sure she wasn't going to knock over her wineglass and followed him to the door of the theater, unsure of whether she'd be intruding.

At the door were Kaley and Harry.

Sam gaped. "What?"

Kaley waved at her. She wasn't smiling, but she didn't look like a woman who was going to quit on the spot. Jack was chattering at her at full speed, lurching from word to word while he bounced on the balls of his feet, and she shifted her attention back to him.

Harry, on the other hand, was looking only at her. He glanced at Cheryl and nodded, shook her hand, but it was Sam that he was looking at.

She walked over toward them.

"But of course you'll have to see the clip," Jack was saying, taking a step backward.

"Just a minute," Kaley said. "Where's the kitchen?"

Jack stood with his hands on his hips, frozen for a second, then started cackling. "You brought food, didn't you?"

Harry said, "And there's beer outside in the snow."

"Beer?" Jack asked. "That wouldn't be…your beer?"

Harry nodded. "I'm a brewer. I have a place in town, The Shandy."

"The Shandy…" Jack leaned backward, crossing his arms over his chest. "I've heard of it, but I've never been."

"You're welcome anytime," Harry said.

Meanwhile, Kaley had gone with Cheryl into the kitchen, and Sam followed them.

"Hi," Kaley said.

Sam knew she wasn't going to be able to think straight until she got it resolved: "You aren't going to quit, are you?"

"No," she said.

Sam waited until she put the bag of food down and threw her arms around her. "Kaley!"

Kaley patted her back. "I'm sorry. I don't know what came over me. You were right."

"Don't be silly," Sam said. "If I were you...well, let's just say I would have had a meltdown before now. Let's just hope that you're a one-meltdown-per-project person, like me. What did you bring?"

Kaley pulled out a bag of treats that was mostly Christmas cookies but included a few variations of puff pastry appetizers: puff pastry with bacon, red peppers, and pomegranate molasses, with a slice of green olive on top; puff pastry around a chorizo cocktail wiener with some of the figs blended into sauce and leaking around the sides (Cheryl grabbed those and started loading them onto a pan to go in the oven); puff pastry with pesto and goat cheese.

"I was testing them out this morning," she said. "I knew I was going to go back to work, but I wanted to make sure that they worked. I mean, I didn't think you would totally throw me out on my ear."

"What made you change your mind?" Sam asked.

"I just kept thinking, 'When am I ever going to have another chance like this?' And then Harry called wanting to know where you were, and it all came out, and he insisted on driving me up here, but I wouldn't let him, because I don't trust his driving this far up in the mountains—" This was news to Sam— "but I finally agree that yes, he could come with me. I think he's jealous about Jack. Everyone knows what a womanizer he is."

Cheryl laughed, and Kaley blushed. "I meant, well, that's what everyone says, anyway."

"Don't mind me, girls," she said. "He's an incorrigible flirt. But then he keeps his mother up in his romantic getaway cabin. So there you go."

Sam said, "Is he dating someone?"

"Oh, no," his mother said. "He's just a big kid. He should settle down and get married so I can have some grandchildren. He'd make a good father. But he's having too much fun running around and being a movie star and getting into mischief. That's the way he's always been. Always the mischief, never the serious trouble. But ever since that friend of his, Rick Alster, died on the set in an accident, he's been a little giddy. Putting on a show, as always."

Sam put down the container of cookies that she'd taken out of the bag, her mind wandering off. Accident?

"What kind of accident?" she asked. "I'd heard about it, but I suppose I didn't really pay attention."

"Electrical," Cheryl said. "He was one of the people who was working on the last *Pirate Moon*. On the feast set, actually. One of the pumps for the fountains went out, and he went to check it. It turns out that there was a short in one of the big set lights, and it had taken out the pump. When he pulled it out, he was electrocuted."

"I'm sorry to hear that," Sam said. "He doesn't act like he's…"

She didn't know what to say. Grieving? Sad? Upset? He hadn't said anything about the feast being a memorial for his friend or anything, but it seemed like it might be.

"Of course he doesn't," Cheryl said. "I know, it's up to you, what decision you make, but this party is really important to him. For what it's worth, I think you'll do a lovely job, both of you."

Sam looked at Kaley. "Just wait until you see this."

"This is going to be insane, isn't it?"

"Just wait."

"You've already made up your mind, haven't you?"

"You have to agree, too," Sam said. She'd just have to make sure that Kaley agreed, that was all, because she wasn't about to turn this down.

Kaley sighed. "I'll do it."

She and Cheryl finished setting out the appetizers and put them in the oven, Kaley handing them to Cheryl and the two of them looking through the oven window. It struck Sam that the two of them might have similar personalities. Two kind, solid women who were utterly reliable, barring the odd "I can't take it anymore!" tantrum.

It made Sam feel even closer to Kaley, knowing that she wasn't made out of stone. After the trays were in the oven, she hugged Kaley again, and went out of the kitchen.

Harry and Jack were still standing in the entryway. Harry was scratching the dog's head, and Jack was talking while Harry nodded. Jack was probably talking pure piffle, but Harry had built up quite the resistance to piffle, living with her.

"Beer?" she said.

Harry's eyes lit up: his eyebrows wiggled suggestively, and he grinned, turned around, and reached around the corner, picking up a grocery bag covered with snow. Sam noticed that the light outside was starting to turn from cream to gold, and she sighed.

"It's getting late," she said. "We should really go."

Jack cut off in mid-sentence. "But you just got here."

"I don't know that I can find my way out of here in the dark," Sam said. "When it gets dark out here, it gets *dark*."

"That's part of the reason I have the house so far out from Aspen," Jack said. "Who wants a bunch of drunk gate-crashers at midnight? Not I. Mom would kill me. But we have plenty of room. You could stay ooo-ver."

He said it like a little kid. Sam had a hard time believing that he was still grieving for his friend, but then again they must have finished filming a year ago or so. Time had passed.

She'd been divorced for about a year or so, herself.

Harry wiggled the bag with the beer. "There's more out in the truck," he said.

Sam gasped. "It's going to freeze!"

And then there was nothing for it but for the three of them to put their shoes back on and run out to the SUV, bringing in Harry's big cooler full of beer, no two bottles the same. He'd pulled out a little bit of everything. For someone who was supposedly fighting jealousy, he was being really generous.

Sam carried in a few more things that Kaley had left out there, including a crock pot full of chowder that she must have forgotten about.

That's what the three of them were, a moveable feast.

CHAPTER 15

Later, Jack showed them upstairs to the guest rooms: a row of four rooms on each side, each one just a little bit stranger than the next. Sam wandered through them. The Elvis Room had aliens. The Toon Room had buxom beauties in black and white, dancing suggestively with woodland creatures with oversized heads. The Noir Room looked more like a detective's office than a bedroom, until Jack grinned and pulled a chain underneath what looked like a side lamp, and a bed lowered out of the wall. Sam peeked inside one of the desk drawers; a half-full bottle of cheap bourbon was inside, along with a dusty glass.

Kaley claimed the Pirate Room, turning her nose up at a room full of Raiders gear. She'd have to climb up a ladder rope to the loft and ride down a hidden slide in the morning, but the bathroom featured a grotto with an enormous tub and a row of identical bottles all marked "XXXRUMXXX."

Sam stopped outside the Princess Room and looked inside. She'd expected something pink when Jack had announced the name, but the place was as stark as stone, with hardwood and long tapestries. Jack led her inside and pulled out the top drawer of a vanity in front of a long mirror. A collection of sharp daggers, hairpins as long as her hand, and tiny bottles marked "Beware" in black-letter script appeared.

Jack leaned toward the mirror. "Mirror, mirror, on the wall. Who's the fairest of them all?" It was actually the first mirror that she'd seen in the house, other than in the bathrooms.

The mirror said, in a Kathleen Turner voice, "Fair? Whoever said you were fair? You're hot stuff, Jack, and don't you forget it."

Jack grinned. "Now you."

Sam leaned forward. "Mirror, mirror, on the wall, who's the fairest one of all?"

The mirror squealed and said, "You are, mistress! You are! Don't break me!" and let out a bloodcurdling scream.

The bed was a stack of mattresses that stretched almost to the ceiling and had to be reached by a ladder that looked like it belonged in a library.

"This one?" Jack asked.

She shook her head. Knowing him, there was probably a damned pea under the mattress somewhere.

They passed the Asgard Room and the Zen Room; Jack noted that he only put people who were being a pain in the ass in the Zen Room, which appeared to be an empty room with a strawlike mat on the floor. Then he pushed on a spot on the wall, and a door popped open; he showed them the rolled-up futon inside. "It's actually very peaceful." He touched a small wind chime near the window. The bathroom was odd, with a showerhead on one side of a half wall and a small but deep tub on the other, facing the mountains. An orchid grew in the window, surrounded by a wooden box full of small river stones.

Sam knew, somehow, that he'd save the best room for last.

He threw open the door and swept his arm across the view, bragging, "The Kitsch Room."

If the Zen room had nothing in it, the Kitsch Room had everything in it. Antiques, collectables—there were so many things that Sam couldn't even figure start to look at any of it.

"Mine!" she said, at the same time that Harry said the same.

Jack backed out of the doorway at the same time as Harry, crossing his arms over his chest. "I'll just let the two of you fight it out, then," he said. As soon as he was out of arms' reach, he turned around and trotted down the hallway, escaping the two of them.

"It's mine," Sam repeated.

"Why should I let you have it? Because you're a girl?" Harry put his arm across the doorway, trying to block her from going inside. She ducked underneath, poking him in the side as she went past. "Hey!"

She skipped into the room, turning and sticking her tongue out at him, tripping backwards across the patchwork quilt. The pattern was so intricate she couldn't even tell what was on it. Teacups. Different teacup patterns.

Harry ran after her, jumping on the bed beside her, throwing her up in the air. She rolled over and scrunched her head down into her shoulders, then started tickling him. "Aha!"

He squealed. "Stop it!" But he was laughing.

She wanted to kiss him, more than anything, but the thought of having him turn his face away—again—made her stomach queasy. So she shoved the thought back and squirreled out from under his arm when he tried to roll on top of her. She ran, not very quickly, to the bathroom, and he chased after her.

She hid behind the door and slammed it shut after he found her. The noise made him freeze.

"What are we doing?" he asked.

She closed her eyes. She didn't want to see the sad, disappointed look on his face as he backed away from her. She'd had so much fun tonight; she didn't want it to end.

She'd have been better off in the Princess Room, after all.

The little hairs on her face felt like they were all standing on end. She waited for the door to open, or the sound of Harry's feet on the thick carpet, or any of a million other signs that he was leaving, or that she was going to have to go.

"You're crying," he said.

She blinked—which meant her eyes had to open—and brushed the tears away. Harry was standing in front of her, looking puzzled, and her heart was breaking. She was leaning against the cold sink. The back of the bathroom door had a hook with plaid bathrobes hanging from it.

She couldn't say anything. It had been a year since they'd divorced. She'd been up and down and all of it, since he'd gone. And still, what she wanted to say were the things that he didn't want her to say, like *I love you* or *I miss you* or *Come home*.

What could she say, if she couldn't say those things? So she said nothing. She sniffed back tears before they could run down her nose, leaving sticky trails down her lips.

It wasn't that she couldn't do it on her own; she knew that now. And it wasn't that she was going to fail. It was a year later, and...the business wasn't doing great, but at least it was hitting the benchmarks she'd had to learn how to set for herself. It was doing good enough, and it would keep doing better, as long as she and Kaley kept working together. Jack's feast would get them a lot of recognition.

She could do it all on her own.

But it was a lonely way to live.

"I'll go," she said. She felt like a wet dog being sent outside, so she didn't mess up the house with her muddy paws and shaggy fur. She stepped sideways, opened the bathroom door, and slipped out.

Harry grabbed her arm. "Don't do this," he said.

"There's nothing else I can do," she said. The tears were welling up in her eyes again. "There's nothing I can say that you won't tell me is the wrong thing to say, and there's nothing I can do that isn't the wrong thing to do. I'm not...supposed to be here with you. I'm not supposed to be around you. I'm supposed to be strong and self-reliant and hopeful and not a mess and totally in control of everything and not a meltdown and not lonely." She rubbed back tears again.

"Stop feeling so sorry for yourself," he said. "You're so melodramatic."

She pulled her arm away from him. "That's what I am, Harry. I'm melodramatic. I'm happy and then I'm sad. I'm not rational all the time. That's what I am, and you keep telling me to change, and then you tell me to stand up for myself. So shut up. You don't even know what you're saying."

He glared at her, and she started to leave again. She didn't know which room she was going to go to; probably whichever one was across the hall.

He wasn't going to stop her. He wasn't ever going to make her stay. He was never going to bend. He was always going to insist that she be someone else. That was Harry, anal-retentive and rational and logical and cut and dried. He wasn't going to change any more than she was.

She got a glimpse of the room as she passed through it. A canoe on the ceiling, upside down. A lamp made out of theater masks. The teacup patterns on the quilt. She touched them as she passed.

"I'll go," Harry said.

"You're always going," she said. "You stay here and see what it feels like to be left behind, for your own good." Petty, she knew, but why bother to be nice? It didn't matter whether she begged or forgave or yelled or tried to keep her mouth shut. It just didn't matter. "You stay where all the memories are."

She opened the door. She couldn't resist just one more dig: "I'm just sorry that we've polluted yet another place by being here together."

"You won't be able to get away from me," Harry said. "He'll hire me, too. And then you'll just have to work with me."

"I've never tried to get away from you," she said. "I'm always the one begging you to stay. Okay. So today I am. A first. Pretty amazing, huh? Too bad you'll never beg me to stay. Because you know I would, and that scares you more than anything else. Goodnight, Harry."

She closed the door behind her. Oh, she was angry. And sad and bitter. But she wasn't going to let him mess with her anymore.

She wasn't sure how, though.

Sam went into the room directly across the hall, the Zen room. It was empty and felt as cold as it looked outside. The moon had come out, shining into the room and making it feel even colder.

She couldn't remember which one of the cupboards held the futon, but she looked inside them, one by one, until she found it. She pulled it out, and it almost fell on top of her.

It was a sad little room, really, with nothing in it but herself and a lumpy mattress. She hunted around some more until she found a duvet and a sheet to wrap around herself. Pillows seemed nowhere to be found.

Using the bathroom was awkward; even with the lights on, she kept running into things. But she found a plastic bag full of toothbrushes still in their packages, a robe on the back of the bathroom door, some toothpaste in a tiny tube. Jack must have guests here fairly often.

She didn't know what Harry thought he was trying to do. Change her. As often as he'd accused her of being crazy or of trying to change him, it seemed like Harry was hell-bent on turning her into someone else. Fine. It was over. She wrapped herself up in her sheet and duvet, and tried to go to sleep.

Old arguments ran angrily through her head, and she blinked them back, even in her dreams. All she wanted to do was run back into his room, apologize, beg, etc. It was exactly what she used to do.

"Stop feeling sorry for yourself. You're so melodramatic."

He didn't want a woman. He wanted a woman who was independent yet who would act like a doormat when he felt like she was out of line. He wanted someone who could laugh but would never cry or have a meltdown. He wanted—

CHAPTER 16

The next morning she was stiff and cold; the Zen room was not for her. She took a shower in the weird shower setup, in which there was no shower stall and she had to sit on a stool because the showerhead was so low. On another day, she would have loved to soak in the tub, but she didn't want to hang around that long.

Breakfast was uncomfortable, with Jack and Cheryl looking back and forth at the two of them, wondering what was going on. But Kaley knew, and ignored them both. And neither Jack nor Cheryl were naïve enough to try to get in the middle of whatever it was.

Harry...well, he was Harry. He acted like everything was fine, completely fine. As though nothing had happened. As though acting like it would make it so. *Oh, that irrational ex of his! Ha ha, wasn't she funny? If only she could see that the way he made it seem like it was all her fault, and his hyperrationality was saner than her so-called irrationality, it would all work out! An ideal, 100% good times partnership!*

Whatever. She ate quickly of bacon and fresh biscuits (Kaley's, she could tell), and packed up.

"Mind if I ride back with you?" Harry asked. "Kaley has things to do."

"Yes, I mind," Sam said. "But if you have to have a ride, then I suppose I better be the one who takes you."

"What is with—"

She raised her hand. "Don't. Just don't. You're the one who wants the ride, you have to put up with the driver. If you don't like it, you can walk."

He sighed.

"And don't be so melodramatic," she said. "Where's your cooler?"

They went back inside and picked it up. Kaley was getting ready to leave, too, and she had a steely look on her face whenever she looked at either Sam or Harry, so Sam didn't ask her friend what on earth she thought she was doing by dumping her ex-husband in her lap. She never should have brought him up here, was what it was.

Sam tried to set her irritation aside as she was saying goodbye. "I'll send you a list of dishes with short descriptions tomorrow," she told Jack. "That way, you can decide whether you want the whole thing or not."

"Right," he said. He spread his arms, and she gave him a hug, then scratched Lennie's head.

Cheryl hugged her and said, quietly, "It'll get better."

"How?" Sam asked. "I've bent over backwards as far as I can get, and he won't budge an inch. Who cares, anyway?"

Cheryl actually kissed her on the cheek, which seemed a little odd, but Sam let it go. "You'll see."

Sam gave her another squeeze, then gave Kaley a quick hug. "See you later for cookie insanity."

Kaley raised her eyes. "Oh, every day with you is insane. Just because there are going to be cookies doesn't mean that it's any different."

"Thanks," Sam said dryly.

And then it was time to get in the SUVs and start driving back down the mountain. Sam looked in her rearview mirror as she left, and saw Jack and his mom waving at them as they drove down the hill.

Jack looked sad, like a dog that had been left behind. Well, she knew how that felt. Lonely houses were hard to get away from. They all had to learn how to sleep alone.

"I was thinking about what you said last night," Harry said.

Sam gritted her teeth, waiting for him to say some snide thing, but knowing that it was her punishment to have to listen to him all the way back to town, unless he got so obnoxious that she really did kick him out of the car.

"Yeah?" she growled.

Harry cut off to stare at her.

"I'm driving," she reminded him. "Maybe you should try to be nice instead of logical for once. It might save you a few miles of really cold feet."

"Why do you—"

She slammed on the brakes, and the SUV skidded forward a few feet. Luckily, she hadn't been driving very fast, and there was plenty of room before the next turn.

"Out," she said.

He crossed his arms over his chest.

"Okay. Then don't speak. You can't seem to keep a civil tongue in your head for thirty seconds, so...just shut it."

She was in an absolutely foul mood, she decided. Maybe she was in a bad enough mood that she could finally push him out of her life, instead of hanging around her, putting her through torture. She was sick of it. She wasn't the one who had dragged him up here. It was his own damned fault.

"Sam," he said.

"What?"

He didn't say anything for a long time.

"You might want to try talking to me like I'm not, you know, an idiot. Why do you always *blah blah blah*," she said. "Whining isn't going to win you any arguments today."

"I'm not whining, I'm..." he cut himself off before she could go for the brakes again.

"You're totally justified in being an ass," she said. "So what? If you're justified in doing something, then I'm justified, too."

"You whine all the time."

"Not while you're driving me down a mountain on an icy, winding road," she said. "And not since you started hanging up on me while we were married."

"I still care about you," he said.

"So? I say that all the time, and it doesn't make a damned bit of difference to you."

Her eyes, surprisingly, stayed dry. Being angry was good for that, because tears would have blinded her and kept her from being able to drive.

"Why are you so stubborn?" he asked.

"Why are you?"

He bit off words again. Part of her enjoyed baiting him, and part of her just wanted to get off the damned mountain, so she could get as far away from him as possible. But none of it was important; it was over. She knew that now.

She went around a hairpin turn; when she hit a straight stretch, she tried to imagine what her next lover would be like. Like Jack? Definitely not like Robert. She'd never be able to trust him, and they'd fight over food constantly. After fighting over food with Harry, that was the last thing she wanted.

"I want to work with you on this job," he said.

"Why?"

"So I can protect you."

She laughed, and her voice sounded crackly and dry in her throat. "Protect me?"

"From whoever is sending you threats. It's not Dale. I talked to him."

"Yeah? What did he say? That he didn't do it? I don't know about you, Harry, but I don't believe every word that comes out of Dale's mouth."

"He has nothing against you, Sam. You're the best friend he has."

That startled her. "Really?"

"Really. He's completely paranoid that you're never going to speak to him again unless he proves that he didn't do it."

She tried to think back to the last time she'd talked to him: on the phone, while he'd been on the run from the cops. Over a month ago. The cops had told her they were closing the investigation for lack of evidence.

She shook her head. "I'll call him. But I don't want you working on this with me. I'm not your problem anymore, remember?"

"I'll work for free. You'll get to keep the money."

"I don't need it that bad. I said, I'm not your problem anymore."

"I hate to see you like this."

"Bitter," they both said at the same time.

"Why are you like this?" he asked.

"Why don't we change the subject?" she said. "You don't actually care."

She stopped at the turnoff for the highway. After this, the road would still be difficult, but at least it would be blacktop instead of gravel.

"I still care about you," he said.

"Then why are you such an asshole?" she snapped.

"I want you to grow up!"

"Grownups are bitter!" she yelled. "Don't you get it? Grownups are bitter and cold and mean and hateful and they say things you don't like and do things that break your heart. You wanted me to grow up? Fine! This is what grownup looks like!"

She was crying again. She didn't dare wipe her face as she went around and around the turns of the road, gradually working her way back out of the mountain.

Ugh. It was going to be hours of this, wasn't it?

"It doesn't have to be...all one way or the other," Harry said.

"You know what? I've been living without you for a year. So don't even drag that old argument out again about how I need to grow up, all right? I can take care of myself. I'm going to do fine without you. I'm going to have good days without you, I'm going to have bad days without you, and I'm going to figure out how to handle Horrible Internet Trolls without you. Just like you wanted." She kept having to sniff back tears. She felt just broken. It was like having him shove the divorce papers at her all over again. No. At least it wasn't as much of a shock this time. Being poked and poked again had become second nature to her.

"I'm so strong," she said. "I'm so strong that I'm going to be able to never want you back. Any day now. My pride is going to be stronger than my desire to be with you, and I'll stop, I'll just stop, and it'll finally be over. I won't have to rip myself apart, trying to figure out what you want and how to give it to you and have you say you want me to figure out what I want for myself when I used to know. I used to know exactly what I wanted, and you wouldn't listen. It was fine. What we used to have was fine. It was you that has never been happy. It was you that has always wanted to go away. It was you who thought I was never good enough or strong enough or non-insecure enough. You're a picky, anal-retentive, overthinking, rationalizing jerk, but I could live with that."

He was regretting riding down the mountain with her. He was regretting ever having laid eyes on her, she was sure.

"Why do you always act like it's my fault?" he asked.

That was it. She slammed on the brakes, pulled off the side of the road, and waited.

"Goodbye," she said. "Get out."

"You can't be serious," he said.

"It is all your fault," she said. "You left. I begged you, and you left. If you wanted to be with me, all you had to do was come back. Now you want me to listen to you whine and pout. I warned you. Get out."

He sat there with his arms crossed over his chest. "I'm not getting out."

"Hitchhike," she said.

"No."

She put her flashers on, popped the hood, and got out, grabbing her purse and sticking her keys inside.

"What are you doing?" he called.

She raised the hood up fully, went into the back of the SUV, and pulled out an emergency triangle, the one that he'd made her stow in the back. She set it up, took a few steps back from it and waited.

A semi drove by, and she waved at it. It didn't stop.

"What are you doing?"

"Getting out of here," she said.

"Please don't leave," he said.

It took her breath away, and she burst into tears. She was a fool; she knew she was a fool; he was going to take it back or destroy it in a heartbeat; she just wanted to hear it; it didn't mean anything.

"What did I say wrong?" he asked.

"Nothing."

A truck rushed by, scattering snow and pine leaves on her legs, pulling at her.

"You're crying," he said. The truck door slammed as she tried to wipe her eyes. A second later, the clicking of the hazard lights stopped, and the other door slammed. The black ice crunched as he walked over to her.

"I don't understand," he said, from over her shoulder.

She turned around and hugged him, just grabbed him hard and kept crying. He shifted from foot to foot, but he didn't try to back off. He patted her on her back. "I don't understand you."

"You don't have to understand me," she said. "You just have to not understand me. I love you and I miss you and every night I have to sleep without you just makes me sad."

"You should be with someone who understands you," he said.

"About the only person who understands me is Kaley, and I'm not a lesbian," she said.

"You could try," he said with a leer in his voice.

She pounded on his arm, but it was all right. A vehicle pulled up beside them.

"Everything all right?" a woman's voice asked.

"She's had a bad day," Harry said. "She'll be fine. Just needed to pull over and...uh."

"Let it all out," the woman said. "All right. Take care." The vehicle sped off, without Sam ever having seen it.

Harry let her go, picked up the orange triangle, and put it in the back of the SUV. Then he pushed the cooler out of the way and had her sit.

"You shouldn't be like this," he said. "You're so...stubborn. And confident. You shouldn't fall apart like this. You're too strong for this."

"I'm not a man. Girls fall apart. Even Kaley falls apart."

"Not Kaley," he said. "You're just making that up."

Sam laughed. "She did. She thinks what happened with the ship is all her fault, too, because she thinks Dale did it, and that makes it her fault. She wanted to quit, and I wouldn't let her."

"What is wrong with you people?" Harry said.

"Nothing. Didn't you know? I have one meltdown on every project. They all said so."

"You've had more than one meltdown around me," Harry pointed out.

"You're a really big project," she said. She closed her eyes, worked up her nerve, and grabbed him by his coat. She pulled him forward and kissed him.

His lips were cold and damp and unpleasant, but it was still like sticking her mouth on a battery. Her lips buzzed from it, painfully, and she didn't think she could let go.

However, he wasn't kissing her back, so she did. She leaned back. "Thanks," she said.

"Can we go back to town now?"

She slid out of the back end of the SUV and shut the door behind her. "Sure." She snorted and wiped her face until she thought she'd be able to see again.

"You're disgusting," Harry said.

She laughed and spat on the ground "Augh! Totally."

They drove down the mountain, back to being—whatever it was they had been, at Jack's house before they had fought. Friends, maybe. Harry talked about the new beers he was working on. Sam talked about cookies.

By the time they reached town, they had decided to have a beer and cookies party for Christmas, at Shandy's, with milk stout and shortbread. And it was good enough.

CHAPTER 17

The feast came down to the following dishes, which, honestly, was nowhere near the number of dishes from the movie:

- Gold-chased roasted alien thingy with Frenched wrists and ankles, supported by gold chains.

- Iced, glowing, jellied worms with silvery skin with smaller, black and oozing wormlets inside.

- Flaming meat ziggurat with red ooze.

- A steaming acid cooking bath into which what looked like live bugs were dipped.

- Edible webs.

- A sabered champagne-like drink that was poured into gobbets of blood.

- A twitching organ that was ripped live out of some caged critter, eaten dipped in green foam.

- A dark-colored egg with swirling patterns on the outside, that was cracked open, with yards and yards of slimy, tubelike stuff pulled out, like a thick noodle in sauce. Or intestines, she supposed.

- Trickling fountains on the walls. Jack wanted booze, but the alcohol would just evaporate. She was trying to work him up to one wall with something sweet, and another wall with pickle juice.

- Piles of edible flowers, dusted with different flavorings.

- Weird fruit. The planet Earth could supply all kinds of freaky things, if she could manage to get hold of them in February.

And maybe a few other things. As she had time. Probably.

Plus, she was totally going to sneak in some relatively normal things, so the picky eaters would have something to eat. They might have to work themselves up a bit, because none of it was going to look exactly normal, but at least they wouldn't be eating bugs.

At first, she hadn't intended to use real bugs, just fake ones.

But then she'd done a little research and found out that honeybee larvae were edible.

And then she'd gone to a meeting of beekeepers who had hemmed and hawed and finally hooked her up with some bee larvae, which was apparently a terrible thing to do to a hive in the middle of winter, but anything that would help improve the cause of honey in the state of Colorado was probably worth it. She took them home in a section of bee's nest, which was honeycomb plus baby bees, in a paper bag so they didn't smother.

Then she called Kaley.

Her mom answered. "Hello, Lugano residence. Marilyn speaking."

"Marilyn..." She was so excited, she couldn't finish her sentence.

"Is that you, Sam?"

"Yes."

Marilyn didn't say anything for a second, then: "Did you win the lottery?"

"No."

"What is it, then? You're breathing so hard it sounds like you're fit to burst."

"I'm going to try to talk Kaley into eating something that sounds really, really disgusting."

"Mmm-hmm." Marilyn sounded amused but not horrified. "What, blood pudding? Sautéed brains?"

"Bee larvae. But don't tell her! I want to hear her when she finds out."

Marilyn didn't say anything for a second; Sam couldn't even hear her breathing. Then Marilyn took a deep breath, let it out in a series of short, silent *hee hee hees*, breathed in again, and yelled, "Kaley! Phooo-oooone!"

Sam turned her head and chortled into her elbow, then got her serious face on.

Kaley picked up a phone, covered the pickup with her hand, and yelled, "I got it." Sam could hear a faint echo to the sound; Marilyn still had the phone to her ear.

"What's up?" Kaley said.

"So I got a new ingredient that I want to use for the feast," Sam said.

"Really. What is it this time?" Kaley sounded guarded, and, really, Sam couldn't blame her, considering what was coming.

Sam looked at the bag on her counter, still carefully folded over. "Something surprising. Something wonderful. Something utterly disgusting. I have the bag on my counter right now."

"What?"

Sam opened the bag—rustle rustle—and broke off a chunk of the nest. It was about as thick as a brownie and smelled a lot like honey and a little like dirt. She bit into it, bracing the phone against her ear.

There was sweetness, there was wax...there was the squish of biting into the bee larvae.

"What are you doing?" Kaley asked. She sounded worried. "Oh God, please tell me it's not something poisonous."

The taste of the bee larvae spurted into her mouth and across her tongue. The taste was bland. Creamy but bland. She was totally going to have to do something to liven it up a bit. She poked around with her tongue until she'd separated out the larva. She squished it around a bit. It wasn't very firm. Firmer than a salmon egg, not as firm as a grape. It would probably be nice with some banana-lime-coconut sauce, which should make it look nice and slimy, too.

"Sam? Sam? Are you all right?"

Sam swallowed. "I'm fine. You just heard the sound of me eating my very first bite of bee's nest, including a bee larva."

"A what?" Kaley shrieked.

Sam giggled. She could hear the soft sound of Marilyn trying not to laugh on the other line, which made it even worse.

"Sam, are those things even edible? Shouldn't you be at the hospital right now? You don't know if those things are full of pesticides, do you?"

Sam accidentally dropped the phone as her head rolled around on her shoulder. "Oops." She put the rest of the nest down, picked up the phone. "Sorry, I was laughing too hard. I'm fine, Kaley. I got the nest from a bunch of professional beekeepers who said exactly the same thing, 'Make sure you get your bee's nests from professional beekeepers who know their bees. Never eat wild bees' nests.'"

"They let you eat their bees?"

"I had to talk them into it, but yes."

Inside the bees' nest, one of the larvae slid out of its half-eaten cell and flopped on the table. It moved, but not much; it wasn't designed to be a bee escape vehicle or anything. She picked it up and bit it in half. Translucent, wormlike...not much texture or flavor to it.

"What are you doing? What are you doing? Are you eating another one?"

"I'm nah eadding nudding," she said.

"You spit that out. Spit it out!"

Sam laughed, spraying bug juice on the counter, then swallowed. "Oooh, what's that? Is that...a pupa?"

"I don't even want to know."

She took out a paring knife and cut the cell out, carefully letting the white, half-formed buglike thing fall out of its cell and onto the counter. She squatted down to get on eye level with the bug. "Interesting. You can see all its little legs and stuff. And these grayish eye blobs."

"Ugh!"

"I think I'll eat it."

Honestly, while it had been fun eating the larvae, she wasn't too sure about the pupa. It looked like a bee, only kind of clear and white, where the larva had looked more like a wet gnocchi than anything else. Her stomach twisted a little.

"No!" Kaley shouted.

Well, even if she turned around and threw it up again, it would be worth having eaten it, just for the effect it would have on Kaley.

Before she could think about it, she picked it up and shoved it in her mouth, chewing with her mouth open so Kaley could hear it.

Ehhh, it was kind of a letdown. The bee still tasted kind of milky and bland, and even though it looked like a bee, it didn't really have the crunchiness of a crushed insect exoskeleton yet. More like yam noodles or bean threads as far as texture went.

She chewed and swallowed. Fortunately, it didn't wiggle or anything on the way down, or she might have chucked it back up.

She didn't say anything, thinking about whether she should try them cooked, because she could totally see deep-fried coconut bee larvae, with that little bit of crunchiness to them, being quite the snack, like shrimp.

Finally, Kaley said, "How was it?"

On the other line, Marilyn lost it, cackling as psychotically as an old witch in a candy factory.

"Mom!" Kaley shouted. "Get off the phone!"

There were a few more seconds of laughter, and then it cut off.

"Jeez, Mom," Kaley muttered to herself. "Get a life."

Sam couldn't remember starting giggling, but she couldn't seem to stop, either.

"Well?" Kaley asked.

"Kind of disappointing, really," Sam said. "I was expecting something weird. No. It's a little bit sweet, like, um, scallops maybe? Somewhere between grapes and salmon eggs for squishiness. The pupa was just about the same. Just looked weirder. I want bananas and coconut with this stuff. But maybe that's just me thinking Thai, which is where I heard about this from, a Thai website."

"You're going to kill me, one of these days."

"Not a chance."

"Do you really want to put these in the feast? I mean, nobody's going to eat them."

"Here's the plan. We use them as one of the things that you can dip in the fake acid bath. We'll make Jack practice eating them. So when we get to the party, he can say, 'Oh, by the way? These things that look like bugs that I said were only fake? They're really bugs.' And then pop them into his mouth and chew them with his mouth open. It totally worked on you, and you couldn't even see them."

"Ugh," Kaley said.

"Want to come over and try some? These aren't going to last very long. I have to experiment with them right away."

"No. Just no."

"Come on. They won't bite, and I promise that I won't make you eat them."

"No. You'll try to talk me into it."

"I said it wouldn't make you. I didn't say I wouldn't try to convince you."

"No. I do *not* trust you."

But Sam knew that Kaley would have to let her guard down sooner or later, and then it would be frozen bee larva puree in her ice cream. Hah.

· · · • · • · • · ·

She apologized to Dale for ignoring him, let alone not trusting him. As always when it came to something having to do with squishy stuff like feelings, he blew it off but used it to get her to work on a weird project with him: he'd built an outdoor pizza oven, using a stretch of balmy Colorado weather, and she had to build him the perfect Neapolitan.

It was strange looking at him and thinking, *I'm his best friend in the world.* For a moment she didn't know how to act, but it was Dale. They argued about whether it was really necessary to roast the tomatoes first, what kind of salt to use, whether barbecue sauce would be a good idea, etc. They molded a Han Solo figure out of butter and black food coloring, and filmed it melting and bursting into flames in the five-hundred-degree heat.

· · · • · • · • · ·

The feast came together slowly but inevitably, one failed experiment at a time. At first, she refused to call Harry for help.

But then she had a problem that she couldn't solve on her own: Jack had compromised on the fountain on one wall, and allowed pickle juice, as long as she could find a way to make it taste good in relatively large quantities. But the other fountain, somehow, had to be alcoholic.

Harry would know.

She knew Harry would know.

Harry would know that she would know that he would know. And so on.

Harry had called her to tell her that he wasn't getting anywhere with the address, and that was fine.

And she had survived the beer and cookies party just fine. The other people at the party seemed to have a harder time with it than she and Harry had had. And Christmas. Well, she hadn't gotten him anything, but he called her anyway, and they'd talked for a few minutes. She'd promised to come over to the bar and had. The regulars had sung carols like, "All I want for Christmas is a Keg of Beer (A Keg of Beer, A Keg of Beer)," "Let it Brew," "I've Been Dreaming of a Hefeweizen," and "The Twelve Brews of Christmas." And they all wore cute little reindeer antlers with red noses, except for Brady the bartender, who wore a Groucho Marx glasses-nose-and-mustache contraption with a Santa hat instead.

It was easier, having given up, and she went home feeling warm instead of lonely.

So. It should be the easiest thing in the world to ask him what she could use for the other fountain.

She stood in the kitchen next to the phone with her elbows on the counter, trying to convince herself that she wasn't crawling to him for help.

It wasn't working.

Why was it, she could ask Kaley or Dale or Donia or Ralph or anyone else for help, and it was almost killing her to ask her ex?

Because he'd made such a big deal about it.

Stand on your own.

No. Why should she? He wasn't standing on his own; it wasn't like he could run the brewery single-handedly, especially now that he had food there.

But what did he mean then, if that wasn't what he meant?

Ugh! It was like plowing through a book of fourteenth-century poetry, trying to figure it out. It just made her head hurt, trying to figure out what secret code he was using.

Grow up.

He ran a brewery, for God's sake. If that wasn't screwing around with something less than adult, she didn't know what was. A candy shop, maybe. And it wasn't like she wasn't being responsible: she was running her own business. Just like he was.

You know what, I'm going to call him anyway, she thought. I don't give a shit what he meant anymore. I just don't. If he wants to have a meltdown over whether I'm going it alone or standing on my own or being a grownup, fine. That's his problem. And then I'll ask someone else.

She picked up the phone and dialed his number.

"'Lo?" he said. People were chanting something in the background that sounded a lot like *Chug chug chug*, then cheering.

She shouted, "Harry, I'm stuck on something for the feast involving booze. You got a minute?"

"Uh....yep. Sure. Let me get out of the noise first, though." After a few seconds there was a thump, and the cheering cut off, mostly.

"I'm supposed to make a booze fountain, and I'm afraid all the alcohol will evaporate and it'll taste flat."

Harry laughed. "I've converted you. I've totally converted you."

"What?" she said.

"That's beer. And it's bubbles you have to worry about, not alcohol. The alcohol won't evaporate that fast. You don't have to worry about it. Does it matter what kind of booze you use?"

"No."

"Then plan on using some young red wine. The Tudors did it in England all the time, back in the day. They had giant public wine fountains. The fountain aerated the wine, letting it breathe."

"How long is it safe to leave it like that?"

"I don't know. Until it turns into vinegar. You should be fine for the feast. Don't use anything aged, though, or it'll go off really quick. Anything that benefits from aerating would be good to use...I suppose I could find some white that would work, if color's a problem."

"I think the stuff was red in the movie, but I'll check again. Hm…"

"Okay, just let me know. I better get back to it."

"Thanks, Harry."

"No problem." He hung up.

…and that was that. She put the phone down.

It was all in her head, wasn't it?

Sure, he was hard to deal with sometimes, but who wasn't? It was like two blind people trying to pull each other to the eye doctor, only there wasn't an eye doctor, all they had to do was stop squinting their eyes shut when they got mad at each other.

There just didn't need to be all the drama.

She sighed. A life with no drama?

Maybe just not all the drama. Up with the fun drama and down with the soul-killing, depressing drama!

She wandered through the fridge until she found a homebrew that Harry had wanted her to try but she couldn't remember what it was and the ink had smeared on the cap. She popped off the top and drank it. Ginger and orange and cloves and she didn't know what else, in a wheat.

She knocked it back, drinking it until it was gone, burped, and went to bed, even though it was still daylight in January. She was so tired, all of a sudden, like she'd been shoveling snow all day.

She slept like a baby, woke up the next morning, and dumped three different wines from glass to glass by hand for an hour, content.

∙∙∙∙∙∙∙∙∙

She put up the contest to try to trap her Horrible Internet Troll.

It's a sloooow January, and I'm bored here at FoodSlutOnli ne.com, so it's time for a contest! Tell me all about the weirdest (or sexiest) thing you've ever eaten, and I'll select from among the entrants for the grand prize...a printed collection of the recipes we'll be using at January's cooking class, APHRODESIACS FOR A COLD WINTER'S NIGHT. I'll also include a box of the truffles that Sweet Granadilla Catering tested out at the chocolate festival...I'm not promising that I'll give you the recipes, but I miiiiiight...

She left the contest open for two weeks and got some killer entries:

- Steamed duck tongues that totally looked like the creatures from Aliens, only skin-colored instead of black (there was a picture).

- Live shrimp in lobster sauce. This included a link to a short clip of the shrimp thrashing around in a bowl, trying to escape, and the eater picking them up with chopsticks and shoving them into his mouth, still twitching.

- Honeycomb tripe in curry sauce. Sam mentally filed the recipe to try later. She'd never really had tripe, except in menudo once, and it had made her sick, so she'd never tried it again. But the way the woman rhapsodized about eating it with a childhood friend she hadn't seen for years, then having an affair with, and finally marrying twenty years ago, well, she had to give it another shot.

- Panna cotta with dragonfruit and pomegranate topping, served from molds that the cook had molded from her own breasts.

- And, finally, a simple recipe for crepes with jambon de Bayonne, asparagus, Emmentaler, an egg, and mornay sauce, which had been passed on from lover to lover as a morning-after breakfast, all the way back from Paris in 1887.

She didn't want to give any of them up, and she hoped and hoped that the Horrible Internet Troll wouldn't come along and give some lame example, which she would then have to pick in order to get the Horrible Internet Troll's address.

But the Horrible Internet Troll stayed lurking, and she awarded the grand prize to the woman with the panna cotta breasts, but also got contact information for the rest of them, and sent them everything but the chocolates; she'd had the recipes printed up by a digital printer in a cute little cookbook with photos and everything. It was fun; she was thinking about selling them from her website.

But of course she hadn't seen the last of the Horrible Internet Troll.

· · · · ● · ● · · ·

CHAPTER 18

She was actually writing a blog entry for FoodSlutOnline.com when the comment came in.

SNOOTY AND THE FEAST YOUR LAST JOB LOL.

She stopped typing in the middle of the word *ambrosia* and looked at it.

She saved the comment to the same folder as the others, then went back downstairs and called Harry.

"It's him," she said.

"Who?"

"The Horrible Internet Troll. He sent another message just now. "Snooty and the Feast, your last job, LOL.""

"I'm coming," he said.

"Please do," she said. "I want to be able to have Ralph sit out, if his leg bothers him. He insisted on coming, but I don't know if he's really going to be up for it. I'm going to send you his list."

"His list?"

"Harry, this is a huge project, with lots of timing issues. There's a list."

"Okay. Right. A list. No problem."

"Thank you, Harry. I'll feel a lot better if you're there."

He laughed nervously. "I'll feel a lot better if I catch this jerk."

"Yeah. Do you want to ride up with me, or do you think you can make it up there Thursday by five a.m.?"

"What?" he said. "Seriously?"

"Seriously. It's going to take two full days and most of a third to get this all done, even with all the prep we've been doing over the last two weeks. Plus, I'm planning a half-day's extra time, just in case the Horrible Internet Troll strikes again."

"You're hard-core," he said. "I'm going to call Jack and see if I can spend the night up there. If I have to be functional at five, I don't want to have to try to drive two hours first."

"Hm...good idea. Let me call him, and I'll see if they have room for all of us."

Harry didn't say anything.

"What?"

"Nothing," he said. "Sorry, just thinking about something I don't want to talk about."

Sam smiled out of the corner of her mouth. She wondered if he was thinking the same thing she had been, that they could double-up space for the two of them and save a room. Maybe. But it had been an idle thought.

"Fair enough," she said.

"You're just going to let it go?" he asked.

"You already told me you don't want to tell me. Consider it an open invitation to tell me if you change your mind."

"...Right," he said. "Okay. Well, call me back and let me know what he says."

"Okay."

• • •• • •• • •

Wednesday night before the feast, they ascended to the chalet in a convoy of SUVs: Sam, Kaley, Harry, Dale, Ralph, and Donia. Danielle had promised to come up on Friday afternoon with anything they needed. They weren't the only guests there; the set-builders were finishing up, and the costumers were buzzing around, trying to pick someone to head down into town and pick up some replacement fabric for the queen's dress. Nobody wanted to go; nobody wanted to miss anything.

Sam couldn't blame them.

Cheryl seemed about ready to bite someone's head off and was showing clear signs of trying to make sure everything happened smoothly for her son while two dozen people ran around, perfectly capable of running things smoothly on their own.

There hadn't been a lick of extra space in the vehicles for extra food, but Sam and Kaley raided the existing supplies and magicked up a supper for everyone, dragging Cheryl into the fray.

Sam, who had spent many a time hiding out in the kitchen while her parents had gotten divorced, smelled the roast pork for Cuban sandwiches wafting around the kitchen and smiled. Food made everything better. Not all better, but better.

The bread wasn't authentic, but she had no intention of trying to make Cuban bread using five-year-old yeast, so it was hamburger buns fried in butter and squished with the bottom of a skillet. And it was delicious. They set up a table across the kitchen door and had Harry load up plates: one beer, pile of chips, Cuban sandwich (either pork or marinated pressed tofu, because Jack had had five pounds of the stuff in his fridge), out you go thank you very much.

One woman had gluten problems, but it turned out to be fine as long as they just gave her just the meat and a tequila sunrise instead of the beer.

"You guys should come out to LA and cater," more than one person told her, which was flattering. "You made enough for leftovers, didn't you?" from Jack was even better, though.

Eventually they were done and went out into the living room.

It was amazing. Even more amazing, because she'd seen it before the crew had changed it. It looked just like the movie, the weird, rippling walls that seemed like a cross between cement and chewed up paper. The vines. The grooves for the fountains in the walls, with the streams that wound through the room. The couches—she put her hand on one, and it was soft.

"Go on," one of the builders said. "Climb up."

She already had her shoes off, so she slid up onto the couch, which kind of melded into the "stone" around it, and made an odalisque's pose, with one hand behind her head and looking airily up toward the ceiling. It was comfy.

A flash went off, and she spotted Jack taking a cell phone snapshot of her. "Too bad we don't have the camera crew in yet," he said. "Still life, with caterer."

She grinned and climbed back down.

The crew put on a quick show of where everyone was going to be during the feast: the guests, the actors. Where the fight was going to take place, where Jack was going to be at the end.

"There." She pointed to a place that would be by Jack's left hip. "We need to move the bee larvae right there, with the acid bath."

"The what?" Cheryl said.

Jack said, "Oh, *Mother*, didn't I tell you? We're serving bee larvae."

"He put you up to this, didn't he?" Cheryl said.

"Um, no," Sam said. "I had to talk him into it. And several other people as well."

"Nobody's going to eat them," Cheryl announced.

"I'll eat them," Jack said. "And all the guests will be disgusted. And that's what's important."

"How...?" one of the crew asked.

"Bland and squishy," Sam said. "They taste like milk. They're better if you dip them in the sauce. The acid bath isn't really acid; it's a coconut-banana-lime sauce. The bubbling just comes from the citric acid in the sauce plus some baking soda we're dusting the larvae with. Like Alka-Seltzer ."

"No," Jack said. "Don't listen to her. They're terribly disgusting, and I'm going through a great ordeal that shouldn't be replicated by someone without my impressive acting skills."

"Who made the beer?" someone asked, and another conversation spun off. Some of the set builders made homebrew; the conversation could go on for hours.

It had all the makings of a superlative party. Sam knew she should head off to bed, but she just couldn't rip herself away. But Kaley went to bed only an hour late, with Donia and Ralph after her, doubling up, Sam noticed. Lord, she could be dense some times; they'd probably been seeing each other for quite a while, with as blasé as they seemed about it.

Dale stood in the living room and rubbed his hand across one of the stone benches, looking lost in thought. Sam walked over to him.

"Headed to bed?" she asked.

He glanced at her, then took a second look.

"What, do I have something on my face?" she asked, brushing her skin.

"You're a good woman," he said.

She rolled her eyes. "What brought that on?"

"Look at you. Nothing shakes you. You just walked into a Hollywood party, took one look at the people around you, and started talking like you owned the place."

"This is not a Hollywood party," she said. "How many movie stars do you see? One."

He shrugged. "I'm just saying you're the most adaptable person I know."

She smiled up at him. "Thanks."

He looked like he was about to say something else, something that made him uncomfortable—it could have been anything from a protestation of eternal love to asking her when they were going to get around to making their flaming chocolate cake—but he shook his head, grinned, and headed toward the stairs. "I'm out. So tired I don't know what I'm saying. Have to get up early."

"Watch out for the Princess room," she said.

He waved absentmindedly and headed upstairs.

Sam went into the thick of the beer discussion, which was still going on, and pulled Harry out of it. "Come on. Bed."

The crew whistled at them, but she shook her finger at them and went upstairs. They had the Kitsch Room, of course, with a cot set up. A compromise between Jack's romanticism and his mother's practicality, probably. Sleep together or not sleep together: up to them.

Harry sighed. "I'm not tired yet."

"Some of us don't normally stay up until two a.m."

"Some of us do." He yawned. "Is the alarm set?"

"Yep."

"I can't sleep. You take the bed. I'm going to stay up for a while."

"You just want to sneak back downstairs and talk beer."

"I do. But I'm just going to relax for a while. Watch some TV in the bathroom."

"There's a TV in the bathroom?"

He showed her: in a cabinet across from the tub, with a stack of old favorites like *The Court Jester* and *The Adventures of Robin Hood* beside an old DVD player.

She brushed her teeth and got into bed while Harry ran the bath. It was both like and unlike being married. More like being on a road trip with a girlfriend than like being with Harry, in the old days. She couldn't really put her finger on it.

········•·••··

The alarm went off with a gentle hiss, the sound between radio stations. Slowly, a voice started to speak to her.

"Wake up, it's time to wake up. Right now, I'm being gentle about it, but in about ten minutes or so, I'm going to start getting angry. You wouldn't like me when I'm angry. Meanwhile, I'm going to start, ahem, declaiming a few scenes from *A Midsummer Night's Dream...*"

It was Jack's voice, coming from the alarm clock. She listened to the two sets of young lovers arguing, two of them in falsetto, for a few minutes, then flailed around on the nightstand until she hit the top of the alarm.

Instead of stopping, the alarm said, "Do you hereby swear to get up?"

She grunted.

"Swear," the alarm insisted.

She said something nasty but not especially creative.

"See?" the alarm clock said. "That wasn't so hard, was it?" and switched off. Sam laughed to herself, blinked her eyes clear, and sat up.

Dawn had not yet arrived, but it would, eventually. Like a threat rather than a promise. Harry was asleep on the cot: his face turned to the side, one arm dangling over the side, the blanket on the floor. He was wearing shorts and a gray t-shirt with the name of a German beer company on it. She thought it was German. It had umlauts, anyway.

She should just let him sleep.

No! He had lists of things she needed him to do, and they weren't married, so she didn't have to be nice to him. He was working for her now.

She looked down at him. Flip him off the cot? Get a glass of water and stick his hand in it? Get busy with a permanent marker—that was always good, but she didn't have one handy, was the problem.

As though smelling mischief on the air, like smoke, Harry's eyes popped open, and he scrambled off the cot. "I'm awake. I'm ready."

Sam grinned. "Brush your teeth. I don't want your breath ruining the food."

They were downstairs in a few minutes: Kaley, Ralph, and Donia were all awake, but Dale was nowhere to be found.

"Which room did he end up in?" Sam slurped her coffee, which was good but not great. Hard to get fresh beans up in the mountains unless you roasted them yourself.

"Maybe he bugged out," Donia said. "He kept saying that he wasn't sure he belonged here last night."

Sam frowned at her, then peeked out the foyer windows at the rows of cars. A dusting of snow was over everything, but not enough to worry about. Dale's big truck, which had parked next to Harry's SUV last night, was gone.

"Shit," she announced. "He is gone. I thought he was just sleeping in or he'd found someone to shack up with."

Kaley gripped the sides of her coffee mug. "I don't believe it. No. I do believe it. Of all the unreliable jerks. He's always like this. It's all fun and games until you really need him. And then he's not there. He's never there."

The last thing that Sam needed was drama. She drank the last of her coffee and put the mug in the sink. "You don't have to worry about it."

"It's all my fault."

"No." She took the mug out of Kaley's hands before she crushed the heavy stoneware in her bare palms. "Dale is the way he is. You're his sister, not his mom. Not that this is your mom's fault, either. You don't have to...Kaley, he's out. He's just out. We won't use him for jobs anymore. Go ahead and be angry about it, but it's not your fault. He's your brother, but I'm the one who asked him to do this with us. Maybe it's for the best that he's gone."

Maybe he'd just driven back down the mountain for something and would be back later, but she'd deal with that then. In a fight, Sam would back Kaley, and that's all there was to it. Fair didn't have anything to do with it: if Kaley couldn't work with Dale, then Dale was out.

Kaley was standing perfectly still, staring at her, and yet shaking at the same time she was so upset. Sam gave her a hug.

"He just won't let it go," Kaley whispered in her ear. "That stupid garage. He's the son. He's older. It should be his. Over and over and over, whenever we're alone. What does he even care? He refused to help in the shop when we were growing up. He'd just sit in the corner and sulk and read books about space. He was going to be an astronaut. And now he's just a stupid engineer."

"It doesn't matter right now," Sam whispered back. "Don't talk about him, don't think about him, don't check your phone, nothing. We're putting on a party, and that's what we're going to think about."

On the one hand, it was a totally selfish thing to say; on the other hand, Kaley had done the same thing to her, while she and Harry were going through the divorce. Focus. Focus on something else. Anything else. Until the horrible storms inside you went away. You'd still be angry, but at least you wouldn't be chewing the walls.

"We have a lot of people who are just going to be delighted," Sam reminded her. "Or disappointed. We have a lot of people who need you. People that are actually worth caring about. If Dale isn't worth caring about, then we won't care about him."

"He's my brother!"

"You can't make him be a person worth having as a brother. If he's going to be a shit, that's not your fault, and you can't fix it. Work with me. I'll give you the noodle dough for the egg casings. You know how good it is to knead dough when you're angry."

Sam felt Kaley nod against her cheek and stepped back, leaving her hands on Kaley's shoulders. "Call Robert," she said.

"What?"

"He'll be up here in a flash. We could use the help, even if it takes him until tomorrow to get here. If Dale changes his mind and tries to come back, well, it'd help us tell him 'no' if we knew we had someone else here to help out."

"Robert has to work."

Sam snorted. "That man doesn't do a lick of work that he doesn't feel like doing. You should see him during service whenever someone famous comes through. Fawning all over them while the plates stack up. No. He trains his staff to cover for him. He works his ass off. But he knows when to jump on a chance, too. I think...after the way he's been acting lately, I think he'll jump at the chance."

"I don't think we're—"

"He doesn't have to be the love of your life, Kaley. He's a good cook, and he's good company. And he had to learn how to follow directions at some point in his life, didn't he? Or else he would have never learned to cook. Chefs aren't born, you know. They have to study."

Kaley turned, pulled a paper towel off a nearby roll, and wiped her face, then blew her nose.

"Use the house phone," Sam advised. "Cell phone coverage sucks up here."

"I know that." Kaley rolled her eyes as she left the room.

Sam smiled. "Right. Now, the lists—"

"What if he's not awake?" Kaley called. "Or in bed with someone else?"

"Would you get out of bed for this? Yes. Call him," Sam yelled out at her. She hoped, for the crew's sake, that the rooms were muffled from the main part of the house. Probably they were; she couldn't remember hearing the tail end of the party up in the Kitsch Room last night.

··· • • • • • ···

It was a three-hour drive up the mountain.

Robert was there in two and a half. No sign of Dale, even though Sam had sneaked off a few times to call his phone. She hoped he was all right. Despite what she'd said to Kaley, she'd miss him if he disappeared out of her life; there was nobody else she knew who was quite as insane about trying to make things work.

She just wished he'd used some of his aptitude for making apparently crazy, impossible things happen with his sister. With people in general, really. People weren't machines, but they still had buttons, and engineers were supposed to like to play with buttons, right? Why couldn't he have played with the buttons that made people happy, instead of crying out for his blood?

By the time Robert got there, they'd already moved all the cars out of the garage and set up the gigantic double sous vide system that Dale had helped rig up for her. The first cooler was full of meat ziggurat layers; the second, with the alien they were going to spit-roast. They'd debated whether to wire the bone structure that Ralph had designed together before or after the meat was cooked through and had decided that they should wire the meat together after they arrived at the house so they could transfer the meat in a smaller container, but that they would cook it altogether in one piece, so the structure would look more like a creature and less like a construct. It might end up looking a bit different than it had in the movie, but they could just claim to have tortured the thing before they cooked it or something.

The crew that had set up the set were sent down the mountain to get them out of Cheryl's hair, but the costumers were still working furiously in their rooms.

"I'm not saying that you can't cook, Robert," Sam said. "It's just that we need to get those people fed, and I don't have time to do it. None of us do."

"Why didn't you plan for this?" he said.

"I did," Sam lied. "But Dale went missing."

"It's not on his list." Robert waved it at her.

Sam said, "Robert! Who is the chef here? Who?"

He laughed at her. "All right, all right. I'll make lunch."

Sam pushed an imaginary hair out of her face. It was worse than sounding like her mother. She sounded like her old boss. "When you're done with that, you may begin working on the jellied wormlets. As a reward."

He raised his eyebrows at her. Kaley bent over a mound of dragonfruit, scooping out the centers in preparation for turning them into ices, and smirked.

"They're in the movie," Sam snapped.

"I haven't seen it yet."

"Have Jack play you the clip after lunch."

And she was off to check the temperature on the sous vides. They had pasta for lunch, perfect homemade ribbon noodles with some variation of pasta puttanesca. Robert was humming as he served it at the table by the kitchen door. Harry allowed as people were allowed to drink wine with pasta, but left a few bottles of amber beer out for the cognoscenti.

The day flew by. As fast as the pace was, Sam knew that the next day would be worse, even if they managed to complete everything on their lists for the night.

The set crew returned with cold pizzas, which they reheated in the oven or sacrificed up to the hunger gods and ate cold with beer and glazed looks on their faces. The costumers looked about as drained as her team did, snippy and unaware of strange hairdos or misbuttoned clothing.

The set crew wanted to party again, as did Jack. Sam begged them to leave, and they headed out into a light snowfall to a neighbor's house, only five miles away, to see if they'd let the crew use their hot tub. The set crew had stocked up on Coors and were ready to go.

As the clock crept toward midnight, moving slowly enough as she looked at it but zooming along whenever she looked away, Sam gave in to one-more-thing-itis. She knew she should be sleeping, but she also knew that she wouldn't be sleeping, anyway. She was too excited. One by one, the others drifted off, until it was her, Robert, and Kaley, rolling out the silvery skin to put on the giant jellied worm. She wanted the worm woven through the holes on its trellis and in the fridge before she went up to the room to try to sleep or take a bath or something.

"Do you think it's going to work?" Kaley asked.

"There's always something," Robert said. "This is just salmon skin, isn't it?"

Sam yawned. "Silver spray goes on afterwards."

"I still don't see how anyone is supposed to eat this."

"Make sure the cord is inside the worm," Kaley said.

Robert grunted, pulling back the skin and rewrapping it with the insulated electric cord and row of tiny LED bulbs inside.

"It was in the movie," Sam said. She didn't want to hear about it. "It's going to taste delicious."

"Nobody's going to eat it."

"Don't care," she said.

"Go to bed," Kaley said. "We'll finish this up."

"You doing all right?" Sam asked.

Kaley shrugged. "I feel a lot more philosophical about it."

"Good enough." Sam stepped back from the counter, swayed, and washed her hands and arms in the sink. She scratched her nose and felt something slimy sticking to it, so she bent over the sink and scrubbed her face, too. There was no point in looking dignified when you were this far into a catering job. The guests weren't there yet, and that was good enough for her.

She yawned again and went out of the kitchen, Kaley and Robert sniping good-naturedly at each other. She'd been worried that here would be problems between the two of them, because a) they'd never worked together before and b) Robert might start acting like Kaley didn't know what she was doing and try to "retrain" her. But there hadn't seemed to be any problems.

She stumbled up the stairs to the kitsch room and tried to find her way to the bed without turning on the light, but it didn't seem to be doing her any good. She closed her eyes to try to let them adjust to the darkness for a moment. When she opened them again, she wasn't as tired as she had been just a minute before, and she found herself at the window, staring outside at the slightly-less-dark of the snowy world outside.

The catering crew seemed to be trickling in, with three cars coming up the road. They all parked together, with two of SUVs spilling passengers onto the gravel and unsteadily up the stairs to the porch. The third, a big truck, merely turned off its lights. Sam hoped the driver hadn't fallen asleep out there, to freeze to death. She should go out there—

She yawned. Probably just a couple sitting in the car, making out. She had to stop worrying herself awake sometime.

Harry was in the bed, but she didn't feel like sleeping on the cot, so she stripped down to her underwear and crawled into bed beside him. He could yell at her in the morning.

· · · ● · ● · · ·

The first thing on her list was to start working on the mucus for the noodle-shelled egg, but she couldn't help it: she had to see how the worm had come out. She was up before anyone else, and slipped out of bed, with Harry apparently not ever knowing that she'd been there, which was probably for the best.

However, she wasn't the first one up: coffee had been brewed. Maybe Kaley had made it before she went to bed (with or without Robert). Sam poured herself a cup, dosed it with cream, and went on her rounds of the fridges.

The worm looked good, twined around and through a trellis. The plug was wrapped in cellophane to try to help keep out any damp.

When Sam checked the sous-vide with the ziggurat layers in it, the temperature was up too high, and somehow, the packages were all on their sides, so a corner of each was sticking out of the water.

Sam groaned. Checking the sous vides was on Kaley's list, but Sam knew that Kaley would never do such a stupid thing. Leaving the meat out of the water meant that it wouldn't cook at the same rate as the rest...it was probably one of the crew who had been working on the set, looking for a beer in one of the coolers or fridges. She should be thankful, really, that no further damage had been done...

Sam stopped with her hand in mid-air.

Something smelled wrong, just wrong. She wasn't sure what it was, but it was wrong. She closed her eyes and tried to identify the scent. Burnt? Ozone? Burnt ozone? It wasn't a food smell. Something else. Soap?

She opened her eyes again and looked around. As she did, she noticed something sticking in the water of the sous-vide cooler. A wire.

Her stomach went cold and stiff, and she felt acid creeping up her throat.

She walked around the cooler to the back. A bare wire near the sous vide heaters led to the outlet.

She felt tired. So very, very tired.

She looked at the wire, then closed the lid of the cooler. She stepped back and looked around the garage, looking—she didn't know for what. But looking.

The cement floor next to the cooler was wet. She hadn't noticed it, but her socks were soaking.—Her shoes, like everyone else's, were by the front door.

More than that, the cooler had been turned.

They had left the two coolers along the wall next to the house, where the outlets were. The ziggurat cooler was closest to the outside wall, which was lined with shelves. Now, instead of the two coolers being parallel to the wall, the ziggurat cooler had been turned about forty-five degrees.

She looked up at the shelves. She hadn't really noticed what had been on them before, but she was almost certain that the heavier things had been on or near the floor, rather than the top shelves.

She put her hand on the shelves, which swayed. After a few seconds, she found the cuts in the supports, shimmed with slivers of wood.

She knew she should leave, locking the garage door behind her, and find Jack, but she took a second to bend over and check the floor.

The coolers had tiny plastic feet. There was no way she could move either of them, the way they were loaded, but she pushed her hand underneath the ziggurat cooler until she felt something cold. Ice. It was cold in the garage, but not that cold. She rubbed her fingers together. They felt slimy. She sniffed them.

Someone had put a thin wedge of frozen dish soap under the cooler. A mostly empty bottle of the stuff lay on the floor, but without a trail between the container and the puddle near the cooler.

She stepped back, wiped her hands on her pants, and left the garage, locking the door behind her. She hunted around until she found a sticky note, wrote "K, stay out. S," on it and stuck it to the door.

She didn't go looking for Jack. She went looking for Harry.

He was still asleep. She changed her mind about waking him up and looked out the window instead. She couldn't be sure, but she thought the two SUVs and the truck that had come in last night were all still there.

She grabbed her purse and went outside, sitting on the porch railing as her feet complained about being too cold. She pulled out her phone and checked it for messages. Her breath steamed in the air. The sky to the east hadn't crossed the line from "night" to "day," but would any second.

"Hi," Dale said. His voice crackled over the message; she was lucky to have had any reception at all. "I'm sure you've noticed that I'm gone by now. Look, I don't belong up there. I'm at the

Hangnail Bar downtown, drinking. Don't worry, I'll take a cab home. I'm fine. I just can't do this anymore. I can't be around Kaley anymore, I mean. It has nothing to do with you."

She dialed him back—wonder of all wonders, the call went through. She went to voicemail right away.

"Um, Dale?" she said. "I had a long talk with Kaley last night, and, look. She says she wants her brother back. She's willing to give up her part of the garage to make peace, as long as she can have the house. I think she's just been fighting with you for so long that it's hard for her to see the sense of something. If you want something, she has to fight you for it. That's the way it gets somehow. But she's just worn out, and she's worried that she's totally going to lose touch with you. Nobody wants things to go further than they already have, Dale. Come back up here. Finish the job with us. You know how important this is to her...and to me. I don't want to lose you as a friend. You've been a real inspiration to some of the weirder things that I do." She didn't know what else to say that could convince him to come back up the mountain. "I will make this work, Dale. I promise."

She hung up and blinked.

She wasn't sure how she'd convince Kaley to go along with it, but she would.

The door opened behind her. Harry.

"Hi," he said. "Ready for yet another punishing day."

She slid off the railing and went inside, pulling Harry to the side and shutting the door. "Come on. I have to show you something."

She led him back toward the garage, unlocked the door, went in.

He said, "Who moved the cooler? And how?"

She held a finger up to her lips and pointed to the back of the cooler.

Harry swallowed, kept swallowing. Probably trying to get the bad taste out of his mouth.

"Checking the cooler is on Kaley's list," Sam said. "I just happened to wake up early and restless and came out to check on the worm that Kaley and Robert were working on last night, and...what?"

"He wasn't here," Harry said.

It could have been apropos of nothing...except that Sam knew that Harry was thinking the same thing she was...and already trying to deny it.

He walked closer to the cooler.

"Careful," Sam said. "Soap on the floor, and the shelves are rigged to drop those paint cans and that big metal thing."

"I see footprints," Harry said.

"Mine. I opened the cooler before I figured it out."

He looked at her, down at her dirty socks. She shrugged. "It just wasn't my turn to die," she said.

"You can't prove it."

She shook her head. "It was on Kaley's list, Harry. Once I stopped thinking about it being all about me—ha ha, don't point out that I always think it's about me, thank you—it all snapped into place. I don't need to prove anything."

"What are you going to do? Call the cops?"

She sighed. "Well, for that. Yeah, I *would* have to have proof before I called the cops. And I don't know that I want it to go that far. I just want him...out of here. Out of Kaley's life. Out of her hair."

"You don't even know it's him!" Harry shouted.

"He called my phone to leave an alibi last night. He said he was at the Hangnail."

"He was there!"

"So?"

"When did you last check the cooler?"

"I didn't. Kaley checked it last night about ten."

"What if she's trying to set him up?"

Sam pointed up at the shelf. "If that fell on her, it might have killed her, Harry. Kaley isn't suicidal. She isn't setting anybody up."

Harry kicked the other cooler, hard. It didn't even move. "How could anyone have moved that cooler?"

Sam sighed. "Harry, this is a garage. How do you move a cooler full of water and meat? The same way you move a car with a flat tire. With a jack and a couple of furniture casters. Why are you being so stubborn about this? Do you just want me to be wrong?"

He stopped.

"No," he said. "I just don't think you're right."

"Why?"

"You don't have proof."

"You *do* think I'm right. That's why you want proof. You looked at what I looked at, and even before I said anything, you were thinking the same thing. Dale did this. All of this. To get at Kaley. It has nothing to do with my desserts, other than to make me look clumsy or irresponsible enough to get someone else hurt."

"How exactly did he do it? If he did do it?" Harry asked.

"I don't know," Sam said. "Isn't that kind of immaterial? Especially if we're not going to the cops? There are all kinds of ways he could have done it. Shit, Harry. When the oven screwed up my soufflés, you know who was the first person to really look back there? Dale. He could have had anything back there that could make a really loud sound or a heavy thump…hm. It was probably some kind of noise, because I didn't see him pull anything big out from behind there. But he could have hidden something in his hand when he was looking behind there, and put it in his toolbox without me noticing.

"And the ship? He had a hundred chances to screw around with things. You want proof? All I have to do is go to the cops and say, 'I have reason to suspect that Dale is out to kill his sister,' and the cops get a warrant to look around. And they either find something or they don't.

"Do you really want that? I mean, that's what you do in all the crime dramas. The good guys figure out who the bad guy is, and they turn him over to the cops. Whether he's guilty or innocent."

Harry paced back and forth. "What do you suggest we do, then?"

"Get him to confess if he's guilty," she said. "I want to hear it from his own mouth. And then get him as far away from Kaley as possible."

"How are you going to do that, ask him?"

"I'm thinking about it," she said. "I...left him a message earlier, trying to convince him to come up here. I told him that I'd talked Kaley into giving up the garage in exchange for the house, when their parents pass on. I told him we needed him up here."

"He wouldn't believe that coming from anybody but you," Kaley said, from the garage door. She was wearing her lucky jersey.

Sam spun around and looked at her. "Oh, Kaley. I'm so sorry."

"Let me see it." She walked closer to the coolers. The closer she got, the more panicked Sam felt: like the coolers were going to jump up and attack her, like Rottweilers off their leashes. But Kaley stayed a safe distance back as Sam showed her the puddle, explained about the thawing soap and the mostly-empty container, opened the cooler and showed her the meat, turned on its side, and the wire. She didn't risk touching the shelves again, though.

Kaley nodded. Every word that Sam had said made her get paler and paler.

"Are you okay?" Sam asked.

"No. But we have too much to do to think about it right now."

You know that you're doing the right thing with your life when it's all you want to do when it hurts too much to do anything else, Sam thought. She opened her arms to give Kaley a hug, but Kaley stepped back.

"Don't. Don't say anything about it until this is over. Don't feel bad for me. Don't hug me. Or I'll break down, and I can't do that yet."

Sam put her chin up. Kaley copied her without seeming to notice what she did. "All right," Sam said. "Let's do this." She scanned the shelves quickly, spotted some caster wheels and a pair of handles next to them on a lower shelf, toward the garage door.

The handles were bent at the ends, like crowbars, but with a flat plate at the end instead of a nail-puller. She handed one to Harry and the other to Kaley. "Okay, lift," she said."

"What are we doing?" Harry asked.

"Just follow directions, please," she said. She unplugged the cord with the bare wire and kicked it under a shelf, then carefully left the cords for the sous vide heaters on the cooler lid. As the other two put the furniture lifters under the cooler, she slipped the wheels underneath, then had them lift the other side and added the other wheels.

Harry's shoe skidded in the puddle as they slowly moved the cooler away from the shelves, and Sam almost had a heart attack. She had them park the cooler on the other side of the garage door, in front of a giant freezer chest, then plugged it in there.

"All right, let's lock the wheels and turn the meat. I really hope that that side won't be undercooked."

· · • • · • • · ·

When that was done, she called a quick huddle in the kitchen.

"Donia, Ralph. Robert. I have some bad news."

They all looked at her, except Kaley. A hundred different smells filled the room; the place was a mess. Sam promised herself she'd take a few minutes to clean up before the guests arrived and knew she'd break that promise in a heartbeat.

"Dale…" How was she going to say it? How could she say it?

Well, it wasn't like saying it was going to make it worse. He'd done it.

"We, I mean, I, think Dale, um."

Knowing that it was true wasn't making it any easier.

"Spit it out," Donia said. "What's he done this time?"

"Tried to kill Kaley."

Whatever it was that they were expecting her to say, it wasn't that.

"No," Ralph said, shaking his head.

Sam interrupted him before he could get started with whatever he was going to say. "I know, Ralph. It's not something you want to believe. He's my friend. I don't want to believe it. But..." She quickly explained what she'd found in the garage that morning. "And before you tell me that we don't have enough proof—"

Donia was staring at Ralph. She was already covered with flour for some reason, Sam noticed, all over her sweats and apron. She tried to remember what she'd been wearing yesterday. "Ralph. You know he had to be the one who screwed up your truck. Nothing's changed. It wasn't about you. It was about Kaley. He's the only one who fits."

"All right!" Ralph snapped. "Just because I had him install those speakers right before I had problems doesn't mean he cut the brakes. It doesn't. But I'll concede that it doesn't look good."

Sam eyed Harry. His head sank lower and lower on his chest, the corners of his mouth going with it. The muscles on his arms were like roped tied across the front of his chest as he leaned against the counter.

Robert, on the other hand, had his lips pursed and was looking right through her, through the wall, through the trees, down the mountains, and right at wherever Dale was, right at that moment. The only real experience he'd had with Dale was having the man crash his truffles. To find out that he was trying to kill the woman he was having a fling or flirtation or whatever with as well as perfectly innocent desserts...Sam knew how he felt. She was going to have to persuade him not to interfere with her plan and just pound Dale into the floor tile.

Kaley said, "He's my brother."

Ralph said, "That's right. How can we just assume that he's trying to do this, to kill his own sister—"

Without looking up, Kaley said, "She's right. He's trying to kill me. We've been at each other's throats for years. You know that. You know how...he is. Last year I told him that he'd take over my parents' garage over my dead body. Since then." She shrugged, and the overhead lights sparkled on her cheeks.

Robert walked across the room to stand next to her. He didn't try to hug her or comfort her. He bent over and whispered something in her ear, though, and Kaley's face turned to pudding, trying not to laugh and cry at the same time. She threw her arms around him, sucking tears back through her nose, and said, "I've never liked Rocky Mountain oysters, but in this case I'll make an exception."

"He's never used them, so I'm sure they'll be tender."

Kaley wound her fingers into his hair, pulled his head down, and kissed him on the cheek, then grabbed a paper towel and wiped her face. Threw the towel in the trash. "All right. Enough discussion. I need to get to work."

"I have more bad news," Sam said.

They all groaned. "What, worse than this?"

"I have to give you more work. I need to take some time to figure out what I'm going to do with Dale."

"What? You call us in here, waste our time, and then want to give us more work?" Robert picked up an empty sauce pan and slammed it on the counter.

"Knock it off," Sam said. "Ha ha, you're not the chef, so you can whine now. I know that trick. Get to work. Unless you want to be the one to tell Jack about this…and figure out how we're going to make Dale confess."

She waited a few minutes. Nope. They were quite content to take a few things off her list rather than take responsibility for that.

But that was being the chef for you: doing the dirtiest of the dirty work.

· · · • · • · · · ·

Jack listened carefully to what she had to say, squatting on the floor, looking at the stripped cord, tentatively touching the shelves and dancing back out of the way as they swayed.

"Same bloke who sabotaged the chocolate ship," he said. He'd slipped into his space-pirate accent, probably without knowing. The expression on his face looked particularly Miklos-ish, too. Sam wondered what it was like being inside the head of an actor.

"I think so, yes," she said.

"I hate being collateral damage," he said. "No, I think you're right. Go ahead with your plan, my dear. I will play my part to perfection." He blinked and switched back to his own voice. "One thing. We are not telling my mother."

Sam shook her head. "Or anybody else, if we can help it. But I'm not even sure he'll be here."

"You did your best, my dear," he said. "I would have bought it."

"Do you think it'll work?"

Jack smirked. "Sometimes with improv, you have to take a few chances. If he shows up, I don't think you'll have to worry about it being a bomb, though."

He started whistling, stuck his hands in his pockets, and sauntered out of the garage. He was going to have to have a couple of the costumers and set people make a few minor changes…

· · · · · ● · ● · · ·

Sam worked feverishly. If she ate anything other than a few nibbles from various dishes, she wasn't aware of it. She had no idea whether the costumers (who had finished up mid-morning, according to Jack, but were fussing around with a few things here and there, because they couldn't help themselves) had anything to eat.

She had just finished slathering the sausages for the alien eggs with slime and was getting ready to start filling the ziggurat with barbecue sauce when the doorbell rang.

The crew (some of whom were going to be cast members) had been in and out of the house all day, but none of them had used the doorbell. And the guests were all coming up in a chartered bus, so they could arrive at exactly the right moment. So it must be Dale.

She looked over at Kaley, who was stirring the coagulated "blood" for the sabered champagne drink. "Don't puke in the blood," Sam said.

"If you puke in those eggs nobody will know," Kaley grinned. Her face was covered with sweat.

"Remember—"

"I remember."

Sam wiped her hands on her apron and went to the door. Opened it.

"Hi," she said. "I didn't know if you'd be coming." Once she opened her mouth, her stomach relaxed. This wasn't going to be as hard as she thought. Impossible, sure, but not worse than that.

"Sorry," he said. He had a plastic sleeve of roses with him, which he thrust at her.

"What are these for?" she asked.

"I looked it up. This is what you're supposed to do when you apologize to a woman."

"But Kaley—"

"We both know that I'm not here because I give a shit about Kaley," he said.

She couldn't say anything for a moment.

"Don't worry. I'm not...all romantic about it. I won't get between you and Harry. I never have, and I never will. But you're the only person that's a woman who even remotely gets what's going on inside my head."

Sam put the flowers on the table beside the door, her head racing: what would she have done, if everything was what it seemed to be? How should she act?

What would Jack do? In this situation?

No. What would Sam do?

She hugged him. She couldn't help it. She was a hugger. Anything else wouldn't have looked natural.

"I don't want to get you in trouble," she said into his chest. "I just want this to be over. For good."

"Okay," he said.

She was tempted to believe him, and call it all off. What if he really meant it? Kaley had told her that she really would agree to what Sam had said; that was part of the deal to get rid of Dale. When the time came, he had to sell the garage, though. He couldn't stay in town.

She gave him an extra hug. He felt really skinny, like all the mass had been sucked out of him.

Then she thought of Danielle, of Jack, even of herself. Dale was someone who had decided, on the whole, that it was okay to risk other people's lives, reputations, and desserts for the greater good of Dale getting what he wanted.

No.

He could crawl and beg, but he could never be forgiven. It was over for him, here, and that was all. Their friendship was over, no matter what he wanted or didn't want. No matter how much he changed. It was too late.

"Come in," she said. "Take off your shoes. We're running behind, and I...honestly, Dale, I can't cope with any more drama today. Uh..." she ran into the kitchen, gave Kaley a thumb's up, grabbed the extra apron, and ran back out with it. "Here's your apron. You know we called Chef Robert to come up and help us, right? I had to have a very...um...firm talk with him. He's still mad about the truffles that you knocked over. But we're running far enough behind that...Dale. I'm so glad you came back."

She smiled at him. What a little faker she was turning out to be.

Dale loosened his shoes and left them beside the pile of shoes next to the door, then slipped out of his coat, looking around. Sam grabbed it and shoved it in the closet, which was so packed full of coats that no hanger was needed.

"This is going to be a bitch to sort out when it's time to go," she said. "Come on. Let's get the hard part over with."

She walked through the kitchen doorway, looked over her shoulder, and saw him put his apron on over his head. He was wearing jeans and a t-shirt; he smelled bad, like boozy sour sweat. The smell of fear, she supposed.

He crossed the threshold of the kitchen and took a deep breath, then looked around at all the chaos. "What—"

He saw Kaley, who was carefully arranging sea beans under and around the trellis with the jellied worm. The set crew had created a monstrous mouth that fit inside the thing, the same one they'd used during the actual production, so Sam had had to redesign the head. She plugged in the cord, and the jelly glowed from inside the mouth.

"Dale," Kaley said. She was pale and shaky, even worse than she had been a minute before. Sam wondered if she'd upchucked somewhere, but she couldn't smell any traces of it, so probably not.

"Sorry I ran off," he said.

Kaley's jaw moved back and forth. "Let everyone else do the work while you get the glory."

"What are you talking about?" he asked.

"Um," Sam said. "I kind of made an executive decision." She twisted up the end of her apron. "They said that one of us could be in the mock-battle that goes with the meal. And I volunteered you."

His eyebrows went up. "You really want me here, don't you?" he asked. "But...why didn't *you* want to do it?"

She glared at him and put her hands on her hips. "I'm not tall enough."

Dale started laughing. "That's the real reason, isn't it? You want to say that one of your crew was on stage during all this. And you're too short."

"Shut up. None of us except Robert are tall enough for that costume, and I'm not about to let my ex-boss have all the fun." She could feel herself shaking, and her stomach was doing flip-flops through what felt like barbed wire. She hoped it looked like her normal case of nerves to Dale. To her, it felt like she was screaming, *Something suspicious is going on here*. But Dale wasn't all that observant...about people.

"All right," he said.

Fair enough.

Oh, if things went wrong, this was going to be bad. Really bad. Her career would be over.

But Jack had thought it would work. It would work.

"Now," Sam said. "I modified your list. Here's what's left to do..."

In a minute, she had him carefully cutting the centers out of spiny chayotes, dicing the centers, getting them ready to sauté in sugar, salt, lime juice, and red pepper, then add back to their shells...

· · · · • · • · · · ·

Without Dale's help, she really didn't have time to clean up the kitchen. Fortunately, the entire kitchen had to be almost pitch dark, with only red darkroom lights to help them see, so the light from the kitchen didn't spill out into the living room and destroy the ambiance.

The guests arrived in a long row, filling up the foyer. Danielle winked broadly at them and kept talking to a familiar-looking man with a grizzled beard that Sam would later find out was the producer. Ralph and Donia stood at the kitchen doorway, passing out hot mugs of Brandy Almond Mocha, mulled cider, and Trappist Monk Cocktails. The coffee wasn't the best, but they made do.

The main part of the living room was blocked off with a curtain, and a couple of the bigger crew members guarded the corners with their arms crossed over their chests, shooing the guests away, when necessary.

Other crew members went around, collecting coats as people stamped their snowy feet on the ground.

"All right," Jack announced the door had been closed and all the guests were inside—about fifty people, as she saw when she peeked out the kitchen door. "It's time to be seated!"

He made a grand gesture, and the crew members swept the curtain aside on its clothesline near the ceiling.

Everyone gasped. Sam stretched halfway out the door, trying to see their faces. They chattered and gasped and cooed. Sam spotted directors and actors—but it was mostly people she didn't know. Normal-looking people.

They walked forward with their mouths open, not quite shoving each other to get into the room.

Sam sighed. She wanted to get a quick look of everyone sitting in the room, but she didn't have the time. She ducked back inside as Ralph and Donia abandoned their posts to take up their last-minute tasks. She stood in front of the stuffed creatures that Ralph had rigged up: half realistic-looking lemur, half shimmering lizard scales. The set guys had been very admiring of them. Their chests were spread open with binder clips, and the red-coated wires with the buzzer on the end was pulled out and waiting.

She pulled the tuna out of the fridge as she heard Donia with the hand-held beater making the wasabi foam. She grabbed a tuna "heart," inserted the buzzer into a tiny slash in the meat, and shoved it inside the creature. Down the line she went, then washed and dried her hands, removed the binder clips, then ruffled their fur until the fronts were smooth.

"We good?" she called.

"We're good," Donia called back.

A line of aliens was waiting at the other door, ready to pick up trays. The wine and modified pickle juice fountains should be trickling down the walls by now, and the edible webs were already strung around the room. Kaley was handing the aliens (how on earth had the costume designers gotten so close with the outfits that clearly had to have been CGI in the movie, Sam would never know) trays of odd fruit (dragonfruit, horned melons, a few Buddha's hands, noni fruit looking like bug vomit, lychee, cherimoya) that had been spooned out and turned into ices and bowls of delicately-flavored but grotesquely-colored "blood" globules.

Dish after dish was going out, with Kaley coordinating. Robert bent over the stove, rubbed his forehead on his shoulder to keep a drip of sweat from falling into the sauce for the alien roast. Harry dabbed gold paint into the carvings at the ends of the bones for the roast, the lamb's skull looking eerie with its bright teeth (she'd brushed the ash off them with a spare toothbrush and one of the tiny tubes of toothpaste, an ironic use of mint on lamb if she'd ever heard of one), relatively massive veal legs, and six wings.

"Don't forget to hang the silk off the wings," she reminded Harry.

"I'm on it, I'm on it."

Dale was one of the aliens, a two-headed one that towered over the others with a large black crest that jiggled suggestively. Only one of his eyes was visible; the other was hidden behind and insect-eye lens. Tentacles covered his face in a pattern that was open to the skin on one side and an impermeable mass of twisting plastic on the other.

The ziggurat was already in the room, hidden under a panel that would split in the middle when the time came.

"Oh, God!" Sam squeaked. "I almost forgot about the bee larvae!"

She pulled them out of the cupboard where she'd been trying to give them some quiet before the inevitable shock of being brought into the light and noise and terror of the main room.

Most of them probably wouldn't be eaten, either. They'd die in vain.

She wished she hadn't tracked them down, but...ah, well. Too late now. Kaley had the fake acid dish ready to go and was waving her arm at her. "Come on, come on..."

"Send out the lemurs!" Sam hissed. She half-wanted to apologize, but she didn't have time.

Kaley waved the aliens at the row of cages with the lemur-lizard-sushi creatures. As the aliens picked up the cages, Sam realized that they weren't going to turn them on. "Wait!" she shouted.

They froze, and she ran over: "Turn on the switch on the bottom of the cage." She was pretty sure they'd heard her out in the dining room, but it was too important to miss.

Kaley smacked herself in the head, and Sam shrugged at her. The aliens groped around under their cages. Within seconds, the critters were cheeping and writhing around, looking cute, pitiful, and horribly mutated.

"Go, go!" Kaley jerked her arm toward the door, and the line of aliens went out.

Sam heard about a dozen voices go, "Awww," as the lemur things came out of the room.

Sam clapped her hand over her mouth and froze. She had to get the bees ready. Had to. But she knew she was going to squeal with laughter as soon as she heard the reaction of the people in the room.

Jack said something in his Miklos voice. A split second later, the audience gasped, groaned, shouted with dismay, and, in one glorious case, screamed with horror as Jack reached into the cage, shoved his hand into the lemur's chest, and pulled out its still-beating heart on strings of red gunk (the wire).

Everyone in the kitchen had frozen, ecstatically mischievous looks on their faces. Kaley was looking out the door. Her face was clutched in a horrible grimace. It was so hard for her to keep herself from laughing that she was about to give herself a stroke.

Kaley swallowed and went through the door to the garage, closing the door behind her. They could hear her losing it out there, but Sam thought the sound wouldn't carry into the main hall, not with all the noise they were making out there.

Sam rushed to get the bees ready, breaking up the combs and putting the bees on a platter, surrounded by the combs to keep them from wriggling their way off the platter. She carried the bees over to the returning Kaley. Apparently, Jack hadn't warned the aliens: the woman, wearing a golden headdress that made her head look like it was a) expensive and b) about to explode from all the wires indented into the excessively soft flesh, like ropes across a balloon, with a strange, segmented nose, stopped, looked down at the squirming bee larvae, and obviously had to swallow back vomit.

"You don't have to eat any," Kaley snapped. "Just carry it out to Jack and let him gross everyone out."

The alien woman swallowed again.

That was the benefit of working with show business, Sam supposed. The woman picked up the platter, stood up a little straighter, got what Sam considered a real maitre d' look on her face, and went out.

The reaction wasn't as strong as it was with the lemurs, but that was all right. It was the thing was that was going to stick with people after they went home.

Harry had the roast alien ready to go, and Robert rushed the sauce over, poured most of it into the small dishes underneath the frame and chains holding the creature up. When Dale and the other alien pushing the cart were ready, Robert poured some of the thick, jewel-green sauce (chimchurri) over it, allowing it to drip and glop down the belly of the beast. Out it went, teeth grinning brightly.

After the creature went out, it was time for the ziggurat. Sam sent up a quick prayer that the video would record them using the flamethrower all right and brushed a few more streaks onto the alien eggs and sent them out, steaming with sausage and slime.

· · · • · · • · · · ·

Dish after dish passed her by. With each concoction that went out the door, Sam was impressed by the sense that yes, this was something that would only happen once in a lifetime, and she was proud to be there, doing it, making it, getting her hands dirty. As one of the guests, she'd have had more time to relax and enjoy it...but she knew she'd also have been too distracted by jealousy to be able to really get into the mood.

Finally, all the main dishes had gone out, followed by more freaky-fruit sorbets, and it was time for the show.

Sam took a deep breath and listened. The final dessert was ready, pushed back to the far end of the kitchen, under a delicate piece of silk, waiting.

"Miklos. You say I have been betrayed?" the woman playing the queen called.

A pause.

"My lady. You are in direst danger. I swear it. Your brother means to see you dead by nightfall, in seven hours."

Something went clank.

"Perhaps I wish to die," the queen said.

"But—" A pause. "What about your people, my lady?"

Another pause. "If I am crushed, then they will be crushed, too. I tire of this life, Miklos. Even you could never bring back my joy of it. I am ready to die, and my people are ready to die with me."

The aliens around the room, who were supposed to be mingled among the guests at this point, pounded on the floor. It wasn't as loud as it had been in the movie, but that was all right.

"My lady," Jack shouted over them. "Do I no longer please you? Does my lovemaking no longer give you life?"

"You come to me in chains to ask that? No, Miklos! Life has lost its savor and I wish to *die*!"

A pause. "You can take my ship. You can take my freedom. But you can never insult my lovemaking, my lady!"

Sam couldn't help it. None of them could.

They turned off all but a few of the red darkroom lamps, edged past the line of masking tape on the floor where the set crew had told them not to go beyond, lest they be seen by the audience, and slowly opened the kitchen door inward.

Fortunately, none of the guests seemed to notice. All their eyes were on the drama at the center of the room.

The scene continued as it had in the clip that Jack had shown Sam at her first visit to his house. The scene they were acting out was pretty close to the movie, actually, considering that they couldn't use digital special effects in real life.

Miklos, Jack's character, threw off his chains and started attacking aliens, cutting them down left and right. Trays of fake food set up by the crew went flying with a crash, a bang, and a boom! The aliens shrieked as they died and they died and they died.

The queen finally rose from her cushions, enraged, and pointed her fancy, impractical-looking sword at Miklos.

"Kill him!"

The fight continued. Finally the aliens had to dogpile Miklos to subdue him.

"Stop!" The queen snapped her fingers. "Bring him to me."

The aliens slowly reversed their dogpile and brought Jack out, his space suit now comically in tatters.

Underneath the tatters…Sam could have sworn she saw a peek of blue underwear.

Blue-balled the pirate strikes again.

Jack was lifted to his feet.

The queen snarled, "What are you doing?"

"Testing your will to live," he said. "And the will of your people."

The queen embraced Miklos with a passionate kiss that somehow managed not to smear any makeup, the actors spoke their lines, the alien court celebrated despite the piles of their dead.

Miklos concluded, with a roar: "And tomorrow, we fight your son!"

Another cheer rose up—a cheer that was interrupted by the boom of doors opening.

Every head in the room turned toward the entrance of the alien throne room (that was, toward the blacked-out foyer).

A tall, gangly alien entered, holding impractical alien swords in either hand.

The queen's traitorous brother.

Dale.

Dressed in a costume that made him look like a half-naked, green, mutated spider, aggressive-looking where the queen was seductive. One eye was crusted over with a multifaceted bug eye.

If Dale felt the slightest bit self-conscious about the parallels between his situation and the fictional one, he didn't show it. He didn't have any hesitation acting out his role, either; if Sam

hadn't known better, she would have sworn he was a professional actor.

*Maybe I'm wrong. Maybe I'm wrong about the whole thing. I
should call it off.*

It's not too late, is it?

No, it's definitely too late.

Jack yelled at the top of his lungs, in comic fashion. "Kill the
bastard!"

The aliens lifted their weapons...and then turned toward Jack.

Jack pulled back in horror, holding up both hands palm-out.
"Wait, no, not me! The *other* bastard!"

The aliens hesitated.

"Kill my brother!" the queen yelled. "He's the traitor!"

The aliens remained frozen in place, unable to bring themselves to attack the brother of the queen.

Only Miklos could save them now.

Jack spun, leapt, and kicked Dale.

Dale, coached, stumbled backward, landing on a soft mat dis-
guised among the weird plaster that formed most of the room.
He shuddered, his arms flying out, then lay still.

Jack put a boot on his chest and stabbed downward with his
sword, which only bent a *little* as it slid between Dale's arm and
his chest.

A fatal wound.

The rest of the scene played out as it was supposed to, with
Dale lying flat out on the mat, seemingly dead.

Jack pranced around a bit longer. Sam's fists were clenched. When she glanced back, she saw Kaley biting a fingernail.

Finally, Jack yelled Miklos's final lines, and somehow the audience all knew to yell them along with him:

"Feast and drink and wench and, er, whatever it is *you* do," they shouted with him, as he pointed toward a slime-alien. "*Live on! And you do you!*"

The audience went insane, laughing and cheering and clapping. The aliens dragged Dale back into the kitchen, then wheeled out the grand finale cart out behind them on linen ropes decorated with strange silk flowers, provided by the costume department.

The kitchen door swung closed as the lights rose in the cavernous living room.

Finally, it was just them, and Dale.

Donia knelt next to him and checked his pulse. "He's fine," she said. "Hup!"

Donia and Robert took his arms, and Harry and Sam took his legs, and they carried him out into the garage while Kaley kicked a wedge under the door.

They laid him out on the garage floor. Sam tucked a coat under his head, then opened up the bottle of smelling salts she'd raided from Cheryl earlier with a comment about "just in case somcone gets really upset about the bee you-know-whats."

She broke open the capsule and held both halves under Dale's nose, her heart shaking in her chest. Even at arm's length, the smell was making her eyes water and her nose run.

After what seemed like a year and a day, Dale gasped and shuddered. Sam gratefully put the capsules back in the bottle and sealed it, stuck it in her pocket.

"What?" he said.

Kaley stood over him, holding the cord with the bare wire. She dropped it onto his chest. "I know you tried to kill me," she said.

Dale sat up, but Donia and Robert pushed him back down again, held him down.

"It wasn't just me you hurt," Kaley continued. "You hurt Sam. You could have ruined her reputation or got her put in jail. You could have killed Danielle at the chocolate festival. Or Jack Malpeque."

"I don't know what you're talking about," Dale said, convincingly agonized.

Sam broke out in a sweat.

What if she had been wrong?

Or...what if she was right, but he wasn't going to confess?

No. She was right. And this was going to work.

"You shocked me," Dale said. "You *shocked* me. During the feast. I'll have the cops on you for that." He sounded utterly pleased with himself. He even started giggling, in the dim garage light, with oil stains around his head.

Sam squatted down next to him. She murmured, "Dale... I know what you did. You started with sabotaging the oven and had it rigged to set off something loud—like a bass speaker—whenever the oven rose to three seventy five, then dropped to three sixty. You knew my recipe.

"When Kaley didn't freak out and turn into a melting puddle of goo, you escalated.

"Next you sawed through the supports for the ship, rigged the cannons, and wired the metal ship frame to get so hot that it cooked the chocolate. That's why you were so desperate to get access to the ship the night before, and why you were messing around the ship during the truffle judging.

"At that point, it wasn't just embarrassment and it wasn't just making my and Kaley's business fail. You *knew* people could get hurt. And you went ahead with it anyway, thinking that the cops would be too busy to take a second look and that we would be blamed. And *Ralph*."

"I don't know what you're talking about," Dale said, still sounding puzzled and hurt.

Sam stood up. "We can do this the easy way or the hard way, Dale."

"I don't know what you're talking about."

His tone still sounded good but his face was getting red.

It wasn't just the end of a friendship, it was the end of an illusion. Dale wasn't just a smart guy with no social skills. He wasn't just awkward. He wasn't just arrogant because of his intelligence.

He was an asshole who had pretended to be her friend.

He'd probably been laughing at all of them this whole time, thinking about how he'd pulled one over on Sam and how she'd put so much faith in him that she'd listened to *him* instead of her own so-called best friend, Kaley.

Being mad at herself didn't make Sam feel any less ruthless.

She shrugged. "Okay. The hard way it is. Drag him over by the shelves."

Donia and Robert grabbed his arms and started dragging. Dale struggled.

"Just leave him close, all right?" Sam said. She picked up the pair of furniture lifters that she'd left by the door, handed one to Kaley, and kept the other for herself. "Count of three."

Dale yelped and twisted, but there was no getting away from a former Army Captain or a chef.

"One...two..." Sam called, cocking her arm back.

Donia and Robert let Dale go and scurried out of the way. He curled up in a ball and put his arms over his head, looking like a spider.

"Stop!" Dale yelled.

Sam lowered her lifter. "Yeah? What are you worried about? That we're going to hit you with these things?"

"Yes..."

She lifted hers again. Kaley had never put hers down.

Sam said, "Oops, my hand's gonna slip in about two seconds."

"No, I mean, no. I'm worried that the whole set of shelves is going to come down on me."

"Why are you worried about that?" Sam asked.

"Because. Because I sneaked back up here last night and rigged them to fall if anyone hit them. And moved things around so there was enough weight to crush a skull."

"Whose skull, Dale?"

"Kaley's."

"Why, Dale? What were you trying to do, kill her?"

He slid his legs out in front of him, sighing with relief. "You aren't going to call the cops, are you? That's what this means. You're not going to call the cops."

"Good call."

"But you're recording every word I say," he said.

"Another good call," Sam admitted.

"Then...yes. I did it. I sabotaged your oven with a trick miniature subwoofer that shook your oven and made your soufflés fall. I cut through the supports on the pirate ship."

"You cut my brakes," Ralph said.

Dale's one human eye flashed white as he looked over at Ralph. "Yeah. So you wouldn't be there to notice the ship."

"You're a fucking bastard."

Dale shrugged. "And this. I set it up so that Kaley would get shocked when she checked the meat this morning, slip in the soap, fall into the shelves, and get hit. If that didn't work, I meant to keep trying until something did. Or she gave up the garage. I'm the son. It's mine."

"I don't care," Sam said. She waited a few seconds, looking at him. Fixing the image of him in her mind, cringing on the floor in an alien suit. Making it the last she would ever see of him, making sure that she wouldn't be tempted to speak to him ever again.

Then: "Here's the deal. Leave. If I ever see you in this town again, for any reason, the recording goes to the cops. Never contact any of us again. Never act against any of us. If any serious injury ever happens to any of us, or if any major financial setback ever happens, and there's any mystery as to where it came from, the recording goes to the cops."

"Understood," he said.

"Say your name," Sam said.

"Dale Lugano."

"And the date, including the year."

He said it. "You know you'll be in a shitload of trouble too, if this ever comes out," he said.

Sam squatted next to him again and said, "Look in my eyes and tell me if you think I care."

He stared at her. She had no trouble, no qualms, no problems staring back. "You tried to hurt Kaley," she explained. "To me, you're not even human anymore. Going to jail would be worth it. But finding a way to cut your balls off would be even more worth it."

He nodded.

He seemed to believe her.

She leaned back, stood up, and brushed off her apron. She turned her back on him. "Disappear, Dale. It's time for our curtain call. I'm going to go to your apartment the day after tomorrow. If you're still there, well. That's what cell phones are for, isn't it? Calling the cops in case of emergencies."

The others followed her out of the garage. Kaley locked the door.

"Thanks for doing the talking," she gasped out. She rushed over, gave Sam a quick hug, and ran for the bathroom in the foyer, wiping her face.

Robert stood next to the garage door.

Sam said, "You aren't going to make this harder than it has to be, are you?"

Robert shook his head. "He's not coming back in here. That's all."

"Remind me not to piss you off anymore," Harry said. She looked at him: it was exactly the kind of hostile thing he would have said when they were married. But his tone was wrong. He was grinning, his arms spread.

She grinned back at him. He shook his hands impatiently at her, and she gave him a hug: it was what she did, when she wasn't trying to threaten to murder people.

He squeezed her so tight that she felt the air whoosh out of her. "Harry!"

"I'm so proud of you," he said. Then he let go, let her inhale, and planted a kiss on her cheek. "You didn't listen to a word I said."

"That's not true," she said, but he wasn't listening, just staring at her, smiling. She untangled herself from him and peeked out of the door into the main room. The guests were making contented noises, so she took a chance to step closer, to get just a glimpse.

The dessert hadn't been in the movie; she'd come up with it all on her own. No, scratch that. The core idea, that of a crystalline forest made out of sheets of flavored sugar glass, had been her idea. But they had all worked on it, all contributed inspiration.

Donia had ordered her to include the blueberry-white chocolate dip from the pirate ship in several of the pools under the panes of sugar; Kaley had come up with the cute little ma rzipan...things, whatever they were, like some kind of weird cross between guinea pigs and octopi; Dale, heartbreakingly, had designed the tiny, tinkling sugar leaves wired throughout. Harry had painstakingly sugared all the flower petals and attached them to the lattices of gingerbread cookies that she'd interspersed among the forest. The smooth purple cream-cheese frosting covering the ground and the tiny candy pebbles they'd sprinkled at the bases of the trees—well, she couldn't remember where that had come from. Ralph. Duh.

When they'd made it, it was beautiful, all layers and angles and sparkle from the spray-on silver and gold that they'd added at the last minute. The leaves swayed, making tiny, sugary noises against each other.

They'd bent over it, and Kaley had blown a breath right into the middle of it, making the sugared flower petals sway. One of them fell down, and Kaley had tried to pick it up again, but Sam had stopped her.

"It's perfect that way," she said.

Now, of course, it looked a *little* different, with drippy trails of blueberry leading from the pool to the edges, plates of sugar glass snapped off, cookies crumbled, leaves plucked and wires in a pile by the side of the base. More flowers were scattered on the ground, and frosting had been scraped away to reveal the layers of cake underneath, supporting the sugar glass: red velvet, lemon, and mocha, with a layer of blackberry cream between each layer.

Sam's eyes filled with tears.

This.

The room was filled with people laughing and talking and drinking. One woman was scooping "blood" goblets out of her champagne with a spoon, sucking them as gingerly as though they were hot soup. Jack was still wearing his shredded space suit, waving his arms and thrusting his hips forward sugges-tively: telling some story, she was sure. Cheryl was talking to Danielle and a woman with blue hair. Suddenly the blue-haired woman burst out in laughter, squealing, and Danielle looked shocked for a second, then smirked.

Jack looked over at them. "Ladies and gentlemen, you have met the cast and crew...now, for the chefs!"

The room was filled with cheers.

"Wait!" she shouted. Sam ran back into the kitchen, to the foyer, and pounded on the door of the bathroom. "We're on, Kaley! We're on!"

A few seconds later, the door opened, and the red-faced, weeping Kaley came out. Sam took one hand and held it. It was ice cold. She squeezed it; Kaley squeezed back. Sam led her by the hand out to the former living room.

Jack said, "May I present Sam and Kaley of Sweet Granadilla Catering, who have put together this magnificent feast for us!"

And then they were enveloped by the party, talking and laughing, and even Dale couldn't take that away from Sam, or even from Kaley.

CHAPTER 19

Dale was gone, really gone.

. . . . . **.** . . . .

After Sam checked out Dale's apartment, she found herself at the brewery, pulling to a stop. She watched herself getting out of her SUV like she was watching a movie. She walked up to the front door, went in, smiled at Brady.

"Is Harry in?"

He pursed his lips. "I'll check."

But before he'd moved, Harry was there, beside her. The night of the party, they'd slept like the dead, cleaned up, and gone home. She hadn't called him; he hadn't called her.

So she wasn't really sure what she was doing here. She only knew...scratch that. She didn't know anything.

He grinned at her. She took a step closer to him. He grinned at her some more, and she took another step toward him. He was within arm's reach now.

Another half step, and he grabbed her and kissed her.

All things considered, it wasn't as good as the first time he'd kissed her, but her lips burned anyway.

Brady moaned, "Oh man, not again," as various regulars laughed or cheered.

"I'm going to claim that favor you owe me," Harry told one of them, and the man reached into his pants pocket and pulled out a key.

"Been keeping it on me, just in case," the man said.

"All stocked up?"

"Checked it yesterday, and the bears still ain't got into it yet," the man said.

Brady put his head on the bar, over his crossed arms, shaking his head back and forth.

"Excellent," Harry said. He kissed her again, then pulled her along by one hand. Sam looked around the bar, trying to guess from the faces around her what was going on, but they only grinned at her. Except the bartender.

Harry led her to his SUV through the snow in the parking lot.

"Where are we going?" she asked.

He stopped and smiled at her. "It's a surprise," he said.

"Will I need to bring...um...clothes or anything?"

"Nope. I had Kaley pack a bag for you."

Sam frowned. When had Kaley...? Ah. Sam had gone out with Danielle last night to recount the whole story, and Kaley had said she wasn't up for seeing people. The little liar had been raiding her closet, which was why she couldn't find her favorite pair of underwear this morning and had ended up wondering if she'd thrown away her negligee after all.

She blushed. "Does this mean you still love me?" she squeaked.

He laughed. "Don't get all bashful on me now. Let's say…we're going to try it out for a weekend and see if we like it. If you can manage not to be a complete fruit loop for a whole weekend, I'll consider it."

Sam laughed. She could remember times when a comment like that would have been insulting: someone pointing out the blatantly obvious, that she couldn't keep it together. She would have felt like Harry was just rubbing it in her face, being cruel.

Now?

She reached over, grabbed a handful of snow, and threw it at him. He ducked and ran.

"It's not me being a fruit loop you have to worry about," she shouted. "It's not having snow shoved down your pants!"

A snowball hit her shoulder and exploded, sliding down her neck and inside her jacket. She chased him, grabbed him, kissed him. Tried to shove snow down his pants as he danced out of the way. He grabbed her and kissed her, and she melted against him, knowing that she had to get away from the bar before she tried anything else: there was no such thing as privacy, at the brewery.

Harry cleared his throat, opened the SUV door for her, and closed it after she got in. She was still blushing; he was still grinning like a fool. He whistled under his breath as he got in, started the SUV, and put it into reverse.

He backed up, shifted into drive, and said, "Don't worry. It's not that far. And there's heat, electricity, and running water."

"And food."

"Yep," he said.

"Bacon?"

"Yep," he said.

She closed her eyes.

"What are you thinking?" he asked.

"Just imagining what I want to make you for breakfast," she said.

Hi all!

So this book, YOUR SOUFFLÉ MUST DIE, was first written in [checks notes] 2011. I *thought* I'd written it in 2015, but then I found another archive folder inside another archive folder inside another archive folder, and yeah, there it is: 2011.

I've been sitting on this novel since then, thinking, "Oh, whatever, nobody will want to read a cozy mystery written by a horror author. I'm not a chef, I only have minimal experience in a professional kitchen (I worked at a Panera for a while), I'm a foodie but so is everyone else, etc., etc."

It's now 2023.

When I initially finished this, I sent it out to a bunch of New York publishing editors, some of whom said, "Meh, cooking cozies." One of them said, "I like your book! Would you think about throwing this one out and rewriting it as a brewery cozy?!?"

The response hurt worse, got under my skin worse, than any insult could have.

Why don't you just throw this whole novel out and start over with the part that doesn't thrill you?

I get it, that I was trying to shove yet another cooking cozy mystery through New York publishing at a time when a) I still had some vague notion of wanting to be published by them, and b) they were flooded with enough cooking cozies, thank you very much.

Since then, the publishing landscape has changed.

The Big New York Publishers are collapsing in on themselves, self-cannibalizing, falling under the control of bigger and bigger conglomerates who are more interested in books-as-real-estate-investments than as books-to-read-and-love. Most of the editors I submitted to have left the industry, either being laid off or just plain escaping before their love of reading and editing got irrevocably broken.

Since then, I've written a *lot* of books, mostly for ghostwriting clients on the indie side, and watched the clients and my books rise and fall, never taking over the Amazon charts but still somehow generating sales and gathering reviews.

And since then, I've given up on the idea of having a bunch of different pen names, and keeping horror away from mystery away from romance away from the big "what if" dreams of sci fi.

I think that's just how it is with me. I'm the kind of author you read if you secretly like it when the food touches on your plate.

I'm publishing this book because I needed to give something to a potential editor, Alicia Cay, that I wouldn't be upset about if we didn't work out well together. "Oh hey, I still have that soufflé book somewhere…I'll just give her that one and see how she does, before I go completely nuts on her."

She did a great job—although of course any remaining errors are mine—and managed not to mess with my style, to let my flawed self shine through, while still asking some hard questions.

I kicked the project down the road, time passed in the blink of an eye, and it's…September now.

Over half a year after I sent her the project.

Sheesh.

Wait, I thought. *I could actually publish this. Under my own name, not a mystery pen name. It's not…awful.*

Okay, it actually made me laugh in parts.

And cry.

So here we are, from 2011 to 2023.

What's been going on with me lately? I'm in Tampa, Florida, surviving hurricane season, living with my daughter Ray and doing some freelancing but mostly working on my own fiction.

I've been learning how to live with myself after my own divorce.

Some of the parts of the story feel ironic here, although the characters were based off a couple I knew and not off my ex and myself. (Although I definitely see parts of him in Dale.) I feel like even back then that part of me was trying to tell me to get out! But that's probably hindsight.

It feels like I have a lifetime of work on myself to catch up on, answering questions of "who am I?" that I didn't really ever get to answer, because of how I was raised—I was punished every time I trusted my gut or put my needs above other people's wants—or how my marriage went—pretty much the same.

Who am I?

It's an ongoing question; it turns out after you figure out one part of yourself and learn how to cope with it, then ten other parts try to push their way out and go, "Pay attention to me, too!" It's like fighting a hydra, only you're trying to love all over it instead of chop its heads off.

Learning how to be me has been rewarding so far, an exercise in both embarrassment and genuine gratitude. The more I care for myself, the more people feel safe in letting themselves open up to me, be their weird selves around me, and ask for (and receive) support.

It's been a bootstrapping operation, to be sure; it's not like I just woke up one morning and said, "I'm gonna love myself today!!!11!!!" But (after over a year of making it a conscious purpose), I can safely say that I don't *hate* myself constantly. Which is a big stinking deal.

It's really hard to accept the people you love if you can't accept yourself.

If you're struggling to care for yourself, I hope you find a way to give your inner hydras a little breathing room today.

Love, De

Tampa, Florida,
September 2, 2023

Acknowledgements

Many thanks to Ann Griner, Larry Fish, Steph Fischer, Christina Tarvin, Margie Hill-Kleerup, Richard Bamburg, and many others who helped with inspiration, writer feedback, and foodie feedback through early drafts of the book, way back in the day. I miss having cooking parties with all of you!

I've been looking through my cooking inspirations and trying to put together a list, but there are too many to mention them all! But I'd like tip my hat to Heston Blumenthal TV series *Heston's Feasts* for being a major inpiration for the weirder parts.

Many thanks to my editor, Alicia Cay, who managed to restrain her excellent editorial skills enough to let my weirdness shine through. Thank you <3

Thanks to Kris Rusch and Dean Smith for continuing to raise a generation of writers who are increasingly unhesitatant to let their madness shine through; thanks to Pikes Peak Writers for helping me get the early information I needed to become a writer at all—and who helped me become more confident in my expertise. Thanks to all the writers I've met through both of those groups, too, for being a great support network and a constant source of inspiration.

Thanks particularly on this novel to my friend and fellow writer Jamie Ferguson, without whose support I would not have made it from 2011 to 2023 as well as I have, and who has always believed in me—sometimes to the point of wanting to shake me silly.

As always, for Ray.

MORE TO READ!

A DARK AND COZY NIGHT

If you enjoyed this story, please consider checking out *A Dark and Cozy Night.*

Nobody surprises—or unsettles—readers quite like DeAnna Knippling, veteran author of over 80 books.

Sharp-eyed mystery writer Liz Hicks seethes in the wreckage of her Colorado mountain home—books and knickknacks scattered everywhere, thunder shaking the tarped-up windows, the house heavy with the smell of spilled cleaning supplies and the lingering ghost of a leather motorcycle jacket nobody wears anymore.

The burglars only took one thing from the chaos: her dead husband's carved longhorn skull. And to Liz's grief-poisoned, plot-twisty instincts, the "accident" that killed him still reeks of something stronger.

Murder.

A cunning, wicked cozy mystery about the dark side of nice people.

—This one is about playing with the cozy mystery trope: the detective is an amateur with an interesting job in a vaction-able location, nothing bad ever happens in direct view, and it's more about the satisfaction of solving mysteries than anything else. After ghostwriting a number of cozies for clients (and getting kind of bored with them), I asked myself, "How far can I take those boundaries?"

A Dark and Cozy Night is a cozy-ish mystery that sticks to the main cozy mystery rules...but goes a little nerdier and a little darker, more in the vein of a Ruth Ware or an Agatha Christie than a mystery about a dead body, a bookshop and/or pet store, and a cheeky cat. (Not that there's anything wrong with that.)

A Dark And Cozy Night

It was seven p.m. on one of those June summer evenings in the Rocky Mountains that could go either way. Either the clear blue snippets of sky could join together into a clear, star-spangled night—or the clouds could squeeze tight and turn into a hailstorm banging off the hood of my 4Runner.

I didn't much care which.

My husband, Jack, had been dead just over a year. He had died on a dark and stormy evening, riding his motorcycle during a sudden rain squall. The cops had told me, from the line of rubber that he had laid down on the road, that he must have swerved out of his lane and into oncoming traffic.

Had he swerved to miss a car impatiently passing someone on the twisty mountain highway? Had he swerved to miss a deer?

I looked. There was only one skid mark on the road. Whatever he had swerved to miss hadn't even slowed down.

Afterwards, I researched how to cut brake lines and how to identify slippery, fishy-smelling brake fluid as it leaked out of an automobile. I learned the place to press on someone's neck to make them pass out—at the carotid sinus baroreceptor—and where the weakest place on someone's skull is—at the pterion. I studied poisons, sniper rifles, drug overdoses, and, even more importantly, how to get away with all of it.

I had an excuse, though: I was, and am, a writer.

Before Jack died, I was at least hypothetically on schedule with the seventh novel in my mystery series, about a cabal of British historians who dug up the truth on historical cold cases. The seventh book was about a possible serial killer in the time of The Three Musketeers, crossed with an apparent modern-day copycat killer who had killed one of the historians. It wasn't the kind of book I could personally resist writing. I had been researching rapiers for months.

But then there was Jack, his motorcycle, and the side of a mountain, and I couldn't seem to do anything but research how a hypothetical wife of a hypothetical dead man might go about her hypothetical revenge.

My deadline came and went.

That June, I was over six months past deadline and I didn't feel any closer to putting words into my manuscript file. I was still going to conferences, though. I drank burnt-yet-under-brewed coffee and told newbie writers two correspondingly weak and bitter truths.

The first was that no matter how bad a writer was, writing wasn't a waste of time. Writing was an enrichment activity, like giving the elephants tractor tires to play with at a zoo. Creative types who don't create are at risk of going nuts. *You need to write*, I told them. *Unused gifts turn to poison.*

I didn't tell them that I was currently experiencing that poison myself.

...

You can find *A Dark and Cozy Night* via my website (wonderlandpress.com)

About the Author

DeAnna Knippling is a versatile author celebrated for her imaginative storytelling across multiple genres, including gothic horror, steampunk, puzzle mystery, psychological suspense, and dark fantasy. Her works, such as *The House Without a Summer* and *The Clockwork Alice*, have garnered praise for their inventive narratives and unique twists on classic tales. Readers commend her ability to blend the macabre with the whimsical, creating immersive worlds that captivate and intrigue. Whether exploring twisted fairytales or unraveling crime, DeAnna's stories linger long after the final page. Find her at WonderlandPress.com.